Horseplay

Horseplay

A NOVEL

Judy Reene Singer

RANDOM HOUSE
LARGE PRINT

Published in the United States of America
by Random House Large Print in association
with Random House, New York.

Library of Congress Cataloging-in-Publication Data

Singer, Judy Reene.
Horseplay / Judy Reene Singer.
p. cm.
0-375-43416-X
1. Women—North Carolina—Fiction. 2. Female
friendship—Fiction. 3. Riding schools—Fiction. 4. North
Carolina—Fiction. 5. Runaway wives—Fiction.
6. Horsemanship—Fiction. 7. Horse farms—Fiction.
8. Horses—Fiction. 9. Large type books. I. Title.

PS3619.I5724H54 2004
813'.6—dc22
2004048520

www.randomlargeprint.com

FIRST LARGE PRINT EDITION

10 9 8 7 6 5 4 3 2 1

This Large Print edition published in accord with the
standards of the N.A.V.H.

To my dear husband, Alex, who was always there, believing in me and cheering me on: There aren't enough words to say how happy I am to have you in my life.

Acknowledgments

To my wonderful and elegant agent, Jane Gelfman, for opening the door to the magic kingdom of publishing and to my gracious and witty editor, Deb Futter, for guiding me through it: I will be forever grateful to you both. Thank you.

Thank you too, Britt Carlson and Anne Merrow, for your supportive and ever-helpful e-mails.

And to the Silk Purse gang: Laura Pelner McCarthy, Maria Gil, Laura Liller, Linda Gould, Lynn Hoines, Marlene Jones, and Debra Scacciaferro, thank you for laughing in the right places and groaning when things went awry.

Horseplay

Chapter One

When you're running away from a bad marriage, Willie Nelson is the music of choice. His voice has just the right nasal, reedy, twangy quality, which encourages singing along, as well as making it okay for an occasional self-indulgent splash of tears to roll down your cheeks. I was driving to North Carolina and listening to "Blue Eyes Crying in the Rain," and although my eyes are green, it did actually pour the day I left my blue-eyed husband, Marshall.

Marshall and I had been together eight years. He had had three affairs. I had forgiven him twice. And it was about four months after his last fling that the realization struck me: I had been far more gracious than any woman had a reason to be. I was tapped out. Not only did I no longer love him, but the way he walked annoyed me, the color of his hair annoyed me, his ears annoyed me, the fillings in his teeth, the air he exhaled—all had become intolerable. I had begun to hate him, and found myself spending alarmingly more frequent moments planning his dramatic and imminent demise. There was choking, electrocution, car accidents, hanging, knifing, head wounds, poisoning . . . well, it wasn't a good omen for our relationship, and I made my decision.

The first one I told was Ruth, my older sister. Saint Ruth of the Perfect Life, as I had always thought of her, was horrified. We were having our weekly ritual of coffee and fabulous scones from a secret-source bakery whose location she was reluctant to share, since Ruth always likes to have the best of everything, as well as exclusive rights to it. I dropped my news.

"I am leaving Marshall," I casually mentioned. She choked on a mouthful of fabulous scone.

"What did you say?" She wheezed crumbs at me from across the table, trying to compose her lungs.

"I said, 'I am leaving Marshall.' "

She looked alternately alarmed and sympathetic, but I could see in her eyes that she was secretly pleased with my news. Now she would have the best marriage. She recovered quickly.

"Are you sure you want to do that?"

"Yes."

"Why don't you let Henry prescribe something for you? You're probably just going through . . . something."

Henry, her husband, was a psychiatrist, and like many psychiatrists, he was more of a pharmacist than a therapeutic patch maker of holes in the psyche.

"Jesus, I finally come to my senses, and you want to drug me out of them again?"

"Not drug—just to calm you down a little, restore some tranquillity, so you can think clearly. Just view it merely as a misdirected discharge of his sex glands. All he did was fuck some woman!"

"Three women—that I know about. There could be a line around the block where his office is."

Ruth tapped her manicured fingers on the gleaming granite countertop.

"They all fuck around. Live with it, darling. He was a great catch."

"I can't live with it."

"It would break Mother's heart."

She was not above firing off her ultimate weapon. Citing our mother was the one thing she could always count on to sweep me back into line. She always used it, whether it was the time I wanted to get engaged to a handsome illiterate named Bolt, or when I ran off to try my hand at Clown College before Real College. Ruth knew my weak spot: I was on an eternal quest to find the ultimate mother figure. One who would guide and comfort me and share some of the burden of my having been put on earth without consultation. And the fact that Ruth was older than I and had spent more time with our mother bestowed upon her, she felt, a certain cachet and authority, which I always acquiesced to.

Except this time, it wasn't working.

"Mother's been dead for ten years," I said. "She doesn't care anymore."

"Mother liked Marshall."

"Mother needed better taste in men."

Ruth rolled her eyes heavenward, as though looking for a conciliatory vision from Mother.

"How can you end a marriage so casually?" She poured us more coffee.

"I'm not being casual at all."

"And how were you planning to tell him?" she continued. "Marshall's so . . ." She trailed off vaguely.

She could have finished with any number of descriptive adjectives: **nasty, controlling, selfish, lying, cheating . . .**

"Vulnerable" was what she finally said. I never would have thought of **vulnerable.**

"Vulnerable?"

"I think it's his blue eyes."

"I am going to leave him a note pinned to my pillow," I said. "He's going to find it after I'm gone. Now promise me you'll keep your mouth shut."

She sighed and blinked twice. I took it for a yes, finished the last of my fabulous scone, and left her fabulous house.

And that's how I left him. Of course, after waiting a few weeks.

First and most important, I needed a

place to go. Second, I would have to quit my job of rendering high school students comatose by trying to instill the wonders of the English language. And last, I needed to take stock of my worldly possessions and then cull them down to a box or two that would fit neatly into the back of my little Mazda.

That first one was going to be a bit tricky.

I was thirty-three. And a tad overweight. Okay, chunky. With no devouring passions in life except cheeseburgers, chocolate, and my weekly horseback-riding lessons, a holdover from childhood and college. There were no promising adventures looming on the horizon, no ambitious plans. I just wanted somewhere else.

It was at my riding lesson that lightning struck and gave me the rest of my plan.

I was grooming Sunny, the old Palomino that I usually rode. Like me, he was a dirty blonde, overweight, and given to brief naps and wobbly knees. I loved pushing the brush across his faded yellow hair, rubbing in slow, round circles, grooming his cellulite-covered body. Now his eyes fluttered closed, his breathing grew deep and sonorous, and he buckled to the ground.

"Come on, Judy, don't let him do that," Mickey, my instructor, chided as Sunny leapt once again to his feet and gave an embarrassed snort. "You know enough to smack him when he gets sleepy."

While resuming my grooming routine, which now included brushing and smacking, shouting Sunny's name into his ear so he would stay alert enough to remain vertical, I looked around and took a deep breath. It was wonderful to stand in the aisle of the old barn. The ritual grooming of horses while birds chirped at us from up in the rafters was almost hypnotic. It occurred to me that I was happiest here. Happy to help Mickey muck the horse shit out of the stalls, happy to carry the backbreaking sixty-five-pound bales of hay and fifty-pound bags of grain, happy to scrub the slime from the water buckets and fill them back up again with fresh water. There was a peace and a sense of timelessness, a feeling of being insulated from the outside world. I took a deep breath. I loved the scent of horses, that warm, peculiar smell that only horses possess. And there was the horse equipment—the hard brush, the soft brush, the curry comb, the hoof pick—the way all of it lined up in plastic shoe-shine boxes, the sour leather smell, the comforting weight when I carried the bridle and saddle.

Most of all, I loved sitting on a horse.

That an animal weighing over a thousand pounds could be controlled with the touch of a leg or the movement of a hand was an amazing thing. Mickey was a good instructor and had made sure that the basics of riding were constantly emphasized: sitting correctly and quietly and in balance. I mounted Sunny and took him out back to the ring, where we picked up a slow, contemplative trot, with me doing the contemplating.

I was being too quiet.

"What the hell is going on?" Mickey finally asked me after my third excursion around the muddy ring. "You're usually chewing my ear off."

I told her.

"So, are you getting an apartment near your school?"

I hadn't planned to.

"Too bad you're not a kid." She shrugged. "I know an Olympic trainer who takes a few working students every year—they work their asses off, but she teaches them to ride to the top levels."

I stopped Sunny short for more information.

Mickey obliged, but she warned me that I was not a twenty-year-old kid. The work was hard, and besides, what was I going to do with all that training? It's not like there is a riding center in every strip mall, where I could earn a living teaching little girls to sit properly on ponies. It was an impractical thought, Mickey apologized, she had just thrown it out there. "You have to be crazy," she said, "to even think of interrupting your life at thirty-three to pursue something this outlandish."

Of course I wanted to hear more.

Katarina Rheinboldt was the trainer, Mickey explained, and her farm, Sankt Mai, was in North Carolina.

The whole thing was a preposterous, ridiculous notion, and I wrote Katarina as soon as I got home. Her answer came three weeks later in the form of a personal note tucked inside a brochure filled with photos of lithe young women on gleaming horses. She was willing to take a chance on me. There was also a page with a carefully drawn map. I was hooked.

I withdrew all the money Mother had left me, mentally reassuring her that it was for a good purpose, turned my resignation in at school, and started composing a note to Marshall. It was going to be brief and unsentimental. Something along the lines of "Buh-bye, and make sure you use condoms."

Another week was spent struggling to cram a lifetime's accumulation of clothes, books, and all my music tapes surreptitiously into two cartons and a suitcase. What didn't fit, including the old fox-fur coat that Marshall, never an animal lover, had given me, was taken over to Ruth to store in her basement.

She followed me down the stairs.

"You've gone crazy," she said more than once. "You're going to learn how to be a jockey? You're five foot eight, for chrissake, and I can't imagine what you weigh."

"It's only the freshman fifteen," I said defensively.

"You haven't been a college freshman for what? Fourteen years? And to think you always were the **pretty** one!"

"Are you trying to say that now I'm not the pretty one **or** the smart one?" I said. "Just because I fill out a B cup doesn't make me a family aberration."

"That wasn't my point. Why on earth would you want to take up riding? I mean, what comes next? Rock-and-roll camp?"

"I'm just going for the experience." I decided to stuff the fox coat into an old trunk next to her oil burner. "I don't know what I'll do after this. I can always teach high school again."

"And don't you have to be like three years old to begin this kind of training? Like ice-skaters?"

I stacked some books neatly in a corner.

"And there's the matter of money. What will you do for money?"

Apparently, she hadn't heard from Mother yet.

I kissed her good-bye and promised to call.

● ● ●

I put Willie into the tape deck and got ready to drive to North Carolina. It was twelve hours from Long Island, New York. I had a map, two hard-boiled eggs, and a couple of tuna sandwiches.

Me and Willie, we were ready.

Chapter Two

It was pouring. Heart-wrenching, sky-depleting buckets. Raindrops big as lemons rolled across my windshield while I peered through it like a mad scientist through a microscope in order to locate the washed-out yellow line that divided the road. Interstate 95 was on the verge of becoming a major body of water. By now, I had driven through most of New Jersey, a slice of Pennsylvania, and half of Delaware. Willie wailed and I wailed, but there was no heading back. It was on to North Carolina, and I would get there if I had to sit on top of the Mazda and paddle.

Three hours into my drive, the tuna sandwiches were gone. So were the eggs, an apple, two wilted celery stalks cleaned out of the vegetable bin at the last minute, a bag of chips, a banana, and a box of stale Oreo cookies rescued from the back of my desk.

It was all nerves. I always get hungry when I'm nervous, and this was proving to be the granddaddy of nervous occasions. In deference to not arriving at Sankt Mai Farm grossly overweight, I decided to drive at least another hour before eating again. I wanted to stop and take a hamburger break. Never an inspired cook, I love eating out. One of the things that attracted me to Marshall was that he loved to eat in restaurants, too, following restaurant reviews with the fervor of a groupie. It had been part of his charm, the enthusiasm with which he pursued things. The enthusiasm with which he had pursued me left me dazzled. The enthusiasm with which he pursued other women left me frazzled.

McDonald's loomed over the horizon. Marshall had always discouraged the consumption of fast food, declaring it unworthy of his sensitive palate, and I had always meekly followed suit, because somehow during the course of our marriage, Marshall had become my mother figure of sorts. Before we married, I mistook Marshall's imperious attitude for maternal supremacy, his rare good moods for maternal affection, his constant need to be in control a perfect fit for what mothers stood for. It had taken me those few years with him to realize that Marshall hadn't been so much of a mother figure as a motherfucker.

I pulled into McDonald's without one pang of guilt. I was going to have a hamburger. After all, Marshall, Keeper of Family Nutritional Standards, had very high cholesterol and still allowed himself to tuck into a cheese omelette every morning. He justified it the way he justified his sexual indulgences: It was available and he wanted it. Now I would allow myself an indulgence of my own. A hamburger. A double cheeseburger even. With fries.

While savoring the dripping composite of burger, pickle, and the who-knows-what-they-put-in-that sauce, I looked at my map and calculated how many cheeseburgers it would be to North Carolina. At the rate of one every three hours, I had about three and half more to go.

That gave me courage.

I've never been one for road trips. People

who actually plan their vacations around navigating endless strips of asphalt puzzle me. Pick a spot, I've always thought, go to it quickly, then sit around in the sun, eating good things. **That's** a vacation. But this wasn't a vacation, I quickly reminded myself; this was my flight from marriage and, for all I knew, maybe men forever. Instead of relationships or sex, the rest of my life would be spent in pursuit of frequent and meaningful cheeseburgers. With chocolate for the afterglow.

Back on the road, Willie was wearing thin by now. The false bravado he had provided at the beginning of my trip was gone, the rain pounded the car, and the traffic had slowed to a cautious crawl across the slippery roads. I couldn't help but wonder if God might be male after all, casting some Good Ole Boy Sympathy with Marshall.

For the first time that day, I allowed myself to wonder how Marshall would take the news. I was feeling a little bit sorry by then, too; after all, I had once loved him. I had thought he was funny and strong and sexy. His ambitious, restless nature, the way he always wanted something more, excited me. Until it included more women.

Well, his note would be waiting for him, pinned to his pillow. It was 4:30 P.M. by now—I had gotten a late start, having had to wait until Marshall left for his office—and I hadn't a clue as to when he would be getting home that evening. It all depended, I guessed, on how fast he could wine, dine, and bed his latest conquest, the real estate woman who had, in fact, rented his new office to him.

Grace.

Miss Grace Cairo.

She was the overwrought pseudoglamorous type usually found in small Long Island real estate offices: big blond hair, frosted blue fifteen-years-out-of-date eye shadow, fluorescent pink-and-white monogrammed fingernails that were long enough to slice cheese, and big dangling earrings. I remember the earrings because they were big gold cages, obviously designed to accommodate parakeets, and they kept swinging forward when she tilted her head sideways in that subtle, adorably flirty gesture meant to captivate my husband. I had originally viewed her head tilting and eyelid batting with smug amusement, feeling safe, because Marshall had never been the big-hair type. But then, I hadn't thought Marshall would go for the petite bucktoothed redhead who was his dyslexic secretary or the lisping brunette loan officer who handled all his business loans. Actually, any woman that was athletic enough to lie down on a bed was Marshall's type.

Except me.

For some reason, Marshall was always too tired, too rushed, too thirsty, too hungry, or too full to make love to me. It was always too early, too late, too hot, too cold, too Sunday night, too Monday morning. Too near his mother's birthday, Labor Day, or Boxing Day. Sometimes it was because he needed a haircut.

Eventually, our sex life came to a limp halt. A man whose idea of foreplay was turning the volume down on the television was hardly worth the angst. In those rare times we had sex, he reminded me of a gazelle—those fleet-footed animals on the

Discovery Channel that copulate in sixty seconds of hit-and-run romance while dashing over the African plains.

The big-haired blonde could have him. The burger I was eating was lasting a lot longer and was lots more satisfying.

By 10:30, I was tired. Tired of driving, tired of harmonizing with Willie, tired of trying to be upbeat and cheerful. I had also gotten tired of cheeseburgers somewhere south of Virginia and had treated myself to an entire bucket of fried chicken, ditching my table manners and driving with the window down so the gnawed bones could be tossed onto the highway. Like Gretel, I was leaving a trail of detritus, but I doubted Marshall would be following. Now I needed to get some sleep. My late start meant a much too late arrival at Sankt Mai Farm. I doubted if anyone would be awake past midnight. Arriving tomorrow was a better strategy.

The next motel met my critical standards—it had a vacancy. I signed in and threw myself across the musty-smelling bed.

I spent a restless few minutes wondering

if Marshall had read my note yet, wondering if he was on the phone with Ruth, screaming with rage, if he was feeling betrayed or worried sick, when I realized that the rain had stopped. The night outside grew quiet and expectant. I got up, retrieved my toothbrush from my luggage, brushed the chicken out of my teeth, went back to bed, and threw a musty blanket over my clothes.

Then I slept like a baby.

Chapter Three

North Carolina is green. It's a darker, richer green than Long Island, which is also green, but more tenuous and timid about it. I was impressed with the lush look until I noticed that a lot of the green I was admiring was courtesy of obscenely huge kudzu vines, which enveloped almost everything that hadn't moved out of their way. There were green-shrouded silhouettes of trees, bushes, signposts, traffic lights, abandoned shacks, mailboxes, barns, and something that might have resembled a dog. Kudzu was consuming most of the state.

It was disgusting. I drove on, averting my eyes.

Sankt Mai Farm, according to Katarina's directions, was accessible from a major highway and "three good roads." By mid-morning, I was finished with the major highway and calculating that this was the last of the three good roads. Though the first two turned out to be winding, twisting, and obscure, at least they had been paved. This last one, really a wide dirt path dotted with holes, gullies, and axle-busting ruts, was presenting more of a challenge.

While driving out of the upside of a rut so large that, had it been covered, could have passed for a tunnel, I noticed a sign ahead. SANKT MAI FARM, LEADING BREEDER OF HANOVERIANS AND WESTPHALIANS, HOME TO FRUHMAUS, THE WORLD-RENOWNED OLYMPIC STALLION. ONLY THREE MILES AWAY. FOLLOW THE ARROWS.

Suddenly, I became overwhelmed with shyness and nausea. Maybe it was nerves, or maybe it was gas from yesterday's uncontrolled feasting, but I needed to pull over. My hands quivered at the wheel, and my stomach beneath it.

Katarina Rheinboldt had mentioned a riding audition where she would evaluate my skills. In a panic, I now realized that any such skills just didn't exist. The lessons on Sunny, the trail riding on Brownie, the fat pony of my childhood—what was that compared to an Olympian? She would laugh at me. Worse, she would reject me and I would have to drive back to Long Island and stay with Ruth, in disgrace. I had visions of Katarina: a Teutonic dominatrix à la **Cabaret,** taking a quick puff on the cigarette in her black cigarette holder, throwing her head back and laughing raucously at my attempt to ride, then dismissing me in a heavy accent, sneering as my limp body got tossed onto the back of a waiting horse, to be sent galloping home. This was going to be a watershed moment, and I was scared.

I pulled over, wondering if my nervous stomach was planning to revolt, or to hold things in abeyance until my actual arrival at the farm. I hate leaving decisions like that to a brainless organ, and so I sat by the side of the road, sucking on a mint and wondering if I should just stick two fingers down my throat and preempt my stomach from making a decision at the wrong time—like when I would be shaking Katarina's hand, or, worse, mounted on a horse, auditioning.

"Do you need help?"

There was a face at my window.

He was gorgeous.

Late thirties, tall, dark hair and dark eyes, jeans, leather jacket opened to reveal a red plaid shirt, and driving a new green pickup truck that was pulling a horse trailer. And a cowboy hat that he had taken off as a polite gesture. A dark gray cowboy hat. I took a deep breath and swallowed the mint. This man had just stepped out of every sex fantasy I'd ever had, and he was waiting for me to respond. He apparently had quietly pulled behind me while I was contemplating the condition of my digestion.

"I'm fine, thank you." My voice took on a breathy quality that was threatening to transform itself into a burp.

"Are you looking for Kat Rheinboldt?"

"How did you know?"

He smiled. Damn the stomach, I thought as I started mentally pulling off the red plaid shirt. No! What was I—out of practice? First the jeans . . .

"Almost no one comes down this road unless they're looking for her farm. No one except the mail truck, and you're too pretty to be hauling mail."

I flapped my mouth open, waiting for it to come up with something witty, articulate, smart, and intriguing.

The burp rose ominously. I flapped it shut.

He poked his hand through the open window.

"Speed Easton."

I shook it. **Speed**? My cowboy fantasy shriveled up. Speed is a bad name for a fantasy lover. I was suddenly picturing gazelles.

"Speed?"

"Yes, ma'am. It's a surname. My momma's family. Good Kentucky stock. I'm really Lawrence Speed Easton, but everyone's always called me Speed—since I was a boy."

The gazelles disappeared. "I'm Judy."

"Well, hello, Judy." His voice was deep and southern and slow. I kept thinking, Deep and slow. Deep . . .

He walked back to his truck and gestured for me to follow him. I stared at his leather-jacketed back and started my car.

I would have followed him to the end of the world.

Chapter Four

The first thing I learned about Katarina Rheinboldt was that she had that German obsession with perfection and order. The entrance of the farm was announced by another large sign that read FARM, with an arrow and a prancing horse. Behind the sign stood freshly painted white iron gates and a neat gravel driveway flanked by an arcade of groomed trees. It looked like the entrance to a luxury resort. I followed Speed's truck up the driveway and into a parking lot.

He jumped out of his truck and waited until I pulled in next to a new maroon Jeep, which was parked in front of a little white cat sign, with KAT printed across its chest. I wondered if the horses were labeled, too.

I unwound from the car and looked around. The effect was stunning. Everything was gray and white, with maroon trim, including a large horse van that stood at the ready on the other side of the Jeep. I had trouble matching two socks together, and this woman had color-coordinated four barns, a horse van, a Jeep, and three thousand acres.

"Kat should be in the indoor arena." Speed gestured in the direction of a wide domed gray structure. "She usually rides about now."

I nodded, trying to think of something I could do to keep him with me. Throwing myself down and grabbing his ankles might have done it, but that was tacky.

"Thank you."

He gave a little nod of his head, extended his hand, and gave me a lopsided smile. "It was a pleasure to make your acquaintance, Judy."

I watched him disappear in the direction of one of the barns, where he was immediately swallowed up by a contingent of young women. Workers, I surmised, since they appeared to be in various stages of employment. Some were leading horses; some were holding pitchforks. All were laughing flirtatiously, giving off auras of nubile availability. Built-in competition, and they'd already had a jump start. I sighed. So much for my vows of chastity and cheeseburgers.

A cream white Jaguar pulled in and settled next to my car. Its matching driver, slim, beige, elegant, and blond, slithered out. She wore tan riding britches and a tailored brown tweed jacket, opened at the collar just enough to reveal an expensive thin necklace of tiny gold horses galloping carefully through a trail of diamonds.

"Hello," she said, sizing me up with a bemused look. Then she glanced at my dusty Mazda groaning under the luggage, the cardboard boxes, and the bag of leftover chicken next to the driver's seat.

I extended my hand. "Judy Van Brunt."

"Candace Valesco." But her hands remained at her side. Flustered, I dropped my own. I knew right away she hated me.

"I suppose you're looking for Katarina?"

I nodded dumbly.

"She's probably in the indoor. Does she know you were coming?"

"Yes, she wrote me a let—."

"What level do you ride?"

"Level?"

"Oh." She paused significantly. "Well, I suppose we can use another groom." She hardly bothered to look at me after that. "There's the indoor." She waved vaguely in the direction of the gray dome and walked away.

"Nice to meet you, too," I mumbled to the perfumed air.

• • •

I crunched along the path to the indoor arena, trying to assess my surroundings without appearing too much like Alice lost in Ridingland.

The farm was bigger than I'd imagined. Mostly flat green pastures with gently rolling hills dotting the edges. Sitting on top of a hill at a distance behind the arena was a huge Tudor-style house—probably Katarina's. To my right were two large riding rings. Behind the rings were the barns. Here and there were women leading horses. I looked at the animals with awe. The brochure hadn't done them justice. The morning light outlined their rippling muscles and magnificent conformation as they arched their long necks and glided along next to their grooms. Nothing like Sunny; it was hard to believe they were the same species. Their playful nickering carried across the farm as they passed one another, commenting on the day.

Ahead was the arena, glowing inside from fluorescent lights. As I approached, I could hear a voice giving instructions. I gave my stomach a final warning and entered.

Inside, a woman was riding a dark brown horse. He was large and well muscled, his coiled neck glistening with sweat. He snorted with every stride, cantering with slow, rhythmic motions, like a merry-go-round horse come alive. His mouth dripped with white saliva and his rider sat like a figurine on his back, unmoving and regal.

"Zo, are you happy with thees canter?" asked the woman in the center of the arena, her clipped German accent overlaid with British. She was short and wiry, with close-cropped curly brown hair that framed a friendly looking, but weathered face, and she was puffing on a pipe. Next to her sat two Jack Russell terriers, watching the horse with avid interest.

The rider answered her with a tenuous "No?"

"No! Zat's right. Vee don't like thees lazy canter!" She took an emphatic puff on her pipe. "Tap him mit der vip, pliz. Get him to zhump under himself more. Such a lazy boy!"

Katarina Rheinboldt! I tried not to swoon. An Olympic champion standing only a few feet away. Then she noticed me.

"Zo? Vee seem to haff here an audience."

I introduced myself.

"Ja, ja." She flapped her hand at me. "Zo, Zhoody, vat you tink of dis horse?"

I thought he was perfect. "He's so beautiful, and I just love his color! Is he a Thoroughbred?" I blurted out. But I immediately saw that she wasn't interested in an evaluation of his attractiveness, and I couldn't offer any more. As soon as the words left my mouth, I realized that I hadn't guessed his breed correctly, either.

"A Thoroughbred, with dis much bone? Hah! He's Dutch Varmblood!"

She turned away from me and focused again on the rider. I felt like a jerk. I should have known from the horse magazines I devoured monthly that a horse with that much build couldn't have been the more refined breed of Thoroughbred. I had never heard of a Dutch Warmblood. I didn't know that the Dutch would have anything other than warm blood flowing in their veins, let alone name a breed after their sanguinary condition. I couldn't see anything wrong with his canter, either.

"Tap him again."

The rider tapped him lightly once more with her whip.

The horse arched his neck in an even greater curve, bringing his hind legs deeper under his body. His canter transformed from that of a soft rocking horse to a vigorous thrust, making him brilliant and animated. I was transfixed by the change.

Katarina was satisfied. "Zo! Better," she pronounced, and took a satisfied puff. "Go large, around der school, dann giff him a break. Now he can haff his lunch."

She walked over to me, the terriers following in tandem. "Zo, you come from New York, ja?"

I nodded, afraid to say more.

"Lonk Kisland?"

Close enough.

"Veer are your britches?"

I hadn't thought to drive from New York to North Carolina in britches and boots.

"First, you put on britches und vee audition! You can share apartment over der main barn if you stay here. Ja?"

Before I could answer, she strode over to an intercom on the side of the arena and pressed a button. A voice squawked hello.

"Hallo! Hallo! You haff here new person!" Katarina shouted into the intercom at the top of her lungs. "Come get her."

"Lenni comes for you. I see you later. You come beck at vun in britches."

She left, the terriers tumbling behind her. The horse and rider had exited somewhere out of the back of the arena, and I was left standing alone. It occurred to me that I could dash to my car right then to avoid embarrassing myself any further, when a figure came toward me. It was a tall, thin woman wearing a faded blue fleece jacket. Her straggly dark blond hair was pulled back in a ponytail. Late thirties, I decided. I was surprised that she was that old, since Mickey had told me everyone would be much younger.

"It's too late to escape," the woman called out.

She pulled off a leather work glove and extended her hand, giving me a broad smile. Her name was Lenora Griffin, Lenni. She looked kind and friendly. And tired. I remembered Mickey's admonitions about the hard work. Now I was worried if I would hold up if Katarina did accept me. Lenni beckoned me to follow her.

"Too late to escape?" I asked.

"We say that to all the new people. They always walk in here so intimidated. And Kat knows it, too." She laughed. Ha, ha, ha. I tried to join her.

She led the way to the main barn, questioning me all the way: where had I come from, how long had it taken me, what level did I ride. I didn't know riding had levels.

"Uh-oh" was all she said to that, then continued talking. She had already handled six young horses that day, teaching them ground manners, had ridden three others, groomed them, too, and it was only 11:30. She explained that she did the saddle breaking and was the one who helped Katarina, who preferred to be called Kat, select which young horses would be put up for sale and which would receive further training. She ended by saying, "And this is the boarders' barn. We live right upstairs."

I had just enough time to glimpse a barn full of expensively blanketed horses, all munching on hay and staring back at me, wondering what level I rode, before she led me up a staircase just inside. She bounded up, two steps at a time. Her energy was intimidating. At the top of the steps hung a small handmade sign. ABANDON HOPE, ALL YE WHO ENTER HERE. The warning was too late. I had abandoned it when I'd come up the driveway.

To my surprise, the apartment was big, bright, and pleasant. It covered the barn below in its entirety and was Laura Ashley at her finest—all country plaids and florals on overstuffed furniture. A television stood in the corner. To the left was the large eat-in kitchen, with an enormous fern sitting in a brass pot in the middle of the table. The pot had another small sign taped to it that read EDNA.

"Edna?" I pointed.

"That's the fern," Lenni said, and continued to show me around.

On the other side of the living room was an alcove with five doors. Lenni pointed out two doors, one that led to an unoccupied bedroom, and one that led to the bathroom. I needed them both. Then she recited the names of the occupants who had bedrooms behind the other doors. I immediately forgot every name.

The empty bedroom was small and had a single bed, a few pieces of maple furniture, and a closet. Simple and clean, and I liked it. I hoped it would be mine.

"The other gals probably won't be coming back until dinner, so you'll have some privacy."

She grabbed a yogurt from the refrigerator and left, then popped her head in again.

"Oh, and take some yogurt if you're hungry. We all chip in for the food—so don't worry about it."

I started to feel at ease and took a yogurt and sat down at the table, where Edna sat in leafy repose. My plan was simple. I would put on my britches and boots before meeting Kat at one o'clock. I would beg and plead to stay. Maybe even offer bratwurst. If I passed my audition, I'd have the rest of the day to lug my stuff up into the apartment and unpack.

Back at my car, I found my britches after digging to the bottom of one of the cartons. My boots were more accessible, lounging across the backseat. I carried them under my arm back to the apartment. While going up the stairs again, a young woman with pink-and-purple rainbow curls that sprang out around a freckled face impatiently squeezed past me.

"Oh, Jesus," she commented, racing up the stairs. "Not another one!"

I followed her up. Like the white rabbit,

she was nowhere in sight by the time I got into the apartment. I guessed that she was in one of the other bedrooms. Well, I had other things to worry about. I pulled on my riding clothes and hurried back to the arena. It was already one o'clock.

Chapter Five

Kat was waiting for me in the indoor, standing next to a sturdy-looking six-foot-two Alp with blond pigtails who was holding a chestnut horse, already saddled and bridled.

"You're late," said Kat.

She gestured to a large clock on the back wall with the horse whip she held in her hand. It read thirty seconds past one o'clock.

"I'm sorry."

"Hmm," she replied. I waited, wondering if she was planning to crack me with the whip for this first transgression.

"Gertrude," she finally said.

"Eevon," said the Alp.

I wondered if my audition was for language comprehension. Then I figured out that Gertrude was the blond and Ivan was the horse.

"I giff leck op," Gertrude announced. I stood in momentary confusion, but she cupped her two hands together next to the stirrup. I understood that. It was the traditional leg up that horse people give each other. I was to step up into her hands with my left foot and leap while she pushed. It would boost me into the saddle.

I stepped; Gertrude boosted. It worked. I was astride Ivan.

Kat said something in German and Gertrude produced a helmet for me.

"Einstellen Sie den Steigbügel," Gertrude said. I smiled. She repeated herself. I smiled again, trying to look pleasantly conversational, but she shook the stirrup impatiently against my leg. She wanted me to adjust the stirrup leather for the length of my leg.

"I'm sorry. I don't understand German."

Kat apologized, too. "Gertrude doesn't spik too good der English. I am tiching her." She puffed on her pipe. "Zo, vat level do you rite?"

There was that level thing again.

"I'm not sure," I answered truthfully.

"Vee find out. Left rein." Kat gestured for me to walk, left side in, in a circle around her. I touched the horse with my leg.

His walk was rapid, as though he were in a great hurry to get it over with and was anticipating a signal to trot at any moment. I held him lightly in my hands, afraid I was going to break him. He arched his neck and pranced a little. I tried hard to sit softly, hoping to settle him.

"Too much arch in beck," Kat pronounced. "Soft."

I tried to soften even more without melting into a spineless puddle. Kat studied me, taking small puffs on her pipe. Her terriers sat next to her, evaluating me with serious expressions on their faces.

"Ah zo, trot."

Ivan glided forward into a strong trot. Faster than old Sunny could ever have mustered.

"Too busy. **Langsam, bitte.** Slow."

I gently pulled on the reins, but Ivan only trotted faster, compounding the problem by throwing his head straight up in the air. Now we were eyeball-to-eyeball.

"Use your seat," Kat commanded. The terriers jumped to their feet and barked. They knew all along what I should have been doing.

I had learned to use my seat in a rudimentary way from Mickey, but I'd only touched upon it, as any strong pressure on Sunny's back would have made him crumble. I tried pushing my seat down into the saddle. Ivan slowed and lowered his head in response, his eyeballs disappearing over the horizon of his ears. I wanted to kiss him.

"Gut," Kat puffed. The terriers sat down again, satisfied.

She ordered me to change direction, to do figure eights and serpentines and leg yields. Basic equitation that I had learned from Mickey. Ivan's trot became animated; each stride drew me more deeply against him, until I felt we were joined through the saddle, his legs becoming my legs. We had fused together into one being, and I loved the feeling.

"Canter, left lead, pliz."

I asked for the canter. Ivan took great offense and bucked out. I landed on the dirt floor of the arena. The terriers bounced around me, barking with delight.

"Pliz, do not leaf the settle," Kat said.

She helped me to my feet as Gertrude ran after the now joyously free Ivan. "You need verk mit canter!"

I agreed and brushed myself off.

"Don't vorry." Kat smiled. "Ivan is ferry fussy. He's olt and he tinks he chust knows everyting."

Gertrude returned with a smug-looking Ivan and gave me another leg up. We cantered some more, moving at a dizzying pace around the arena. My face burned with embarrassment at my lack of control, and my legs burned with effort. Just when I anticipated sliding off Ivan's back from exhaustion, Kat called for me to halt. I was afraid to look at her.

"Gut," she pronounced. "You are soft and you haff gut basics. I tich you the rest. You go mit Gertrude now."

I dismounted and stood limply as Gertrude threw a cooler over Ivan. The terriers ran over and licked my boots in welcome. The audition was over.

• • •

Gertrude marched Ivan from the indoor arena, and I wobbled behind her, my legs shaking with fatigue.

"He's spunky," I commented to Gertrude. "How old is he?"

She calculated in German. "Tventy und eight."

"Glad I got to ride him when he's old and mellow."

We crossed a gravel path into another barn and Gertrude led me to an indoor spa for horses. It had hot water, heat lamps, ceramic tile, and big terry-cloth towels hanging from heated towel racks.

Ivan was untacked and bathed with herbal shampoo and warm water from the pulsating showerhead, then rinsed and slicked off with a squeegee before getting wrapped in a prewarmed terry-cloth cooler and allowed to stand under the heat lamp. I watched, dripping with perspiration and envy.

When he was dried enough to meet Gertrude's approval, she walked him to a large airy box stall filled with fresh hay. I couldn't wait to get back to the apartment and do the same for myself, sans hay. Gertrude had other plans.

"Now vee verk. I show you." She led me to a barn across the path, where she pointed to an aisle of empty stalls mounded with horse shit, pointed to a wheelbarrow, and handed me a pitchfork. Then she motioned me to follow her outside, where she pointed to a ramp that led up to a Dumpster. I got the picture.

"**Vier Uhr,** four," she held up four fingers.

"Four stalls?" I asked hopefully.

"**Nein,**" she shook her head. "**Acht.** Eight." Then she left.

She wanted me to do all eight stalls by four o'clock. It made me wonder if I had been mistaken about Lenni. Maybe she was really only twenty and just overworked. I grabbed the pitchfork. There was no time to lose.

Chapter Six

There are really only a few things that one needs to know about horses in order to care for them properly. They eat, they drink, they shit. Little else occupies them, save for an occasional gallop around their paddocks so that they can work up an appetite to eat and drink and thus shit some more. And conversely, little else occupies their groom except to make sure they are fed, fluffed up, and that the shit is cleaned from the stalls on a daily basis. It's all very simple; the rest, as they say, is commentary.

Lenni came for me at four o'clock. I had just finished dumping my last load of manure.

"Congratulations." She gave me a quick hug.

"Yep, I'm pretty surprised myself, but I got it all done."

"No, that you passed the audition!"

"Well, thank you."

"It's time to quit," she added. "They're bringing the horses in for dinner."

Two grooms appeared at the barn door, each one leading two horses.

"Stalls look good," Lenni commented. "Let's go home." I crawled after her.

"You should probably get your luggage," she said as we reached the boarder's barn. "Grab a wheelbarrow from behind the barn and put your stuff in it. It'll be easier that way."

She pointed to a long row of wheelbarrows that were stored behind the barn, handles up in a salute to neatness.

"Do you need help getting your things? I don't mind helping you," she continued. "Where's your car?"

"In the parking lot, but thanks, I can manage."

"I don't mind helping."

"Thanks, I can manage," I repeated, and thought for a moment that she looked disappointed. She truly wanted to be of some assistance. I couldn't help but like her. She was a human cocker spaniel.

I grabbed a wheelbarrow, while Lenni disappeared into the barn and up the stairs.

Suitcases and cartons carefully balanced, I pushed the wheelbarrow back to the barn. A fresh start on a new life, I thought, and it begins in a wheelbarrow. I hoped it wasn't symbolic.

I lifted out my suitcases, carefully re-aligned the wheelbarrow with its compatriots, then made my way upstairs, suitcases banging against my knees on every step.

The other housemates, including Lenni, were in the apartment by now and greeted me with unabashed curiosity. Though the Technicolor girl was nowhere to be seen, two other women introduced themselves.

Patty Crumensko was short and chubby and had a mop of curly silver-blond hair. I was surprised at her age, which I guessed to be mid-fifties. She shook my hand with a firm grip.

"You can fill us in on your life story over dinner," she said in a pleasantly husky voice. "We're dying to know everything."

"Hello." Diana Selinger rose from her chair like a spring slowly uncoiling and crossed the room with a leonine grace to shake my hand. "Ignore Patty. She's making us sound so nosy." She was a cool and elegant foil to Patty's exuberance, tall, with a slim but muscular build and silky dark blond hair that she wore in a single braid.

"What level do you ride?" she asked.

I hung my head in shame. "I don't have a level."

Her eyebrows shot into her hairline. The question seemed to be the standard greeting, and I realized I'd better figure out an answer to it pretty soon.

Before long, we were all seated around the table. Edna Fern was pushed aside to accommodate a large platter of spaghetti and meatballs. I asked why a houseplant had a name.

"Shh," said Patty. "She isn't just a houseplant." She put her hands over the fronds as if to cover its ears.

"Edna gets the phone bill in her name," said Lenni.

"And the horse magazines," added Patty.

"She was bequeathed to us," explained Diana, "from the apartment's previous occupants. We keep the phone in her name because everyone here is transient. Same thing with the magazines. If we used a real person's name, things would get messed up if she moved and put in a change of address."

"Edna even gets junk mail," said Patty. "And once, a jury summons."

"Where's Jillian?" Lenni asked suddenly.

"In her lair," said Diana.

Lenni left the table.

"You haven't met Jillian yet, have you?" Diana asked me. "She's Lenni's fourteen-year-old daughter and she lives in the bath-room."

"C'mon, Diana, it's hard on her here," admonished Patty.

"She's a snot and she looks like Raggedy Ann on acid. If she were my kid, I'd shave her head and paddle her ass," said Diana.

"That's why God gave her to Lenni and not to you." Patty took a plate of food.

"What makes you think she's from God?" Diana retorted.

Lenni returned alone, her face fallen into sad lines that looked habitual.

"She'll probably eat later; she's kind of in a bad mood right now."

Diana opened her mouth to say something, but closed it when Patty raised her eyebrows at her. So the pink-and-purple curls belonged to Jillian.

The women were eager to learn about me, and I was curious about them, as well.

"I thought that Kat only took working students in their twenties," I commented.

"What's wrong with you?" asked Patty. "We **are** in our twenties."

"We're not working students. I'm the farm manager," explained Diana. "I work here full-time. And train with Kat. And teach."

"I'm a full-timer, too," volunteered Lenni.

"I'm Patty," said Patty, and added nothing more.

"Well, I'm here to be a working student," I said. "And it looks like I've got a lot to learn, starting with German."

"Oh, you'll understand it pretty quickly," said Patty.

"Yeah," agreed Diana. "Before you know it, we'll be the ones sounding abnormal."

Conversation rippled around the table

until Jillian appeared, arms folded across her chest, her mouth set in a firm line.

"It's fucking slave work," said Jillian. "Kat runs a slave camp for women who are too stupid to do anything else." She plopped some spaghetti on a plate and stalked back to her bedroom, carrying the plate with her.

"I'm sorry," said Lenni softly. "She really just wants to go home."

"That's okay," said Diana. "We really want her to go home, too."

"Diana!" Patty rasped, then leaned over to pat Lenni's arm. "She's just teasing. You're doing the best for the both of you. We know that."

Lenni sighed. I sighed and looked happily at Patty.

I had a new mother figure.

After a restorative hot shower, I unpacked. I planned to call Ruth in a few days. We would have more to tell each other; maybe by then she and Mother would have come to a resigned acceptance of my life.

I fell into bed and went to sleep right away. An hour later, I bolted upright, thinking I heard Marshall calling me. There were angry voices coming from the other room. It wasn't Marshall, I realized; it was Lenni and Jillian. I pulled the pillow over my head. The sound of anger was universal, and apparently so was the relationship of mothers and daughters.

Chapter Seven

Morning starts practically in the middle of the previous night on a horse farm. It seemed like only a few minutes had passed since I had buried my head under the pillow, when there was a knock at the door. It was Patty.

"Don't you have an alarm?" she asked when I sleepily opened the bedroom door. "Life here begins around six-thirty A.M."

"What time is it?"

"Seven-fifteen. I let you sleep out of pity, but Lenni and Diana have already gone."

I hurriedly dressed, gulped down coffee, and left Patty humming to herself while mopping up the remains of her eggs with an English muffin.

There was a misty quality to the spring air as I walked across the gravel paths. Feed buckets banged, workers carried bales of hay in overloaded wheelbarrows, a barn cat meowed as I passed, and Kat's terriers trotted to and fro on important business. I figured I'd head for the little building labeled OFFICE. I wondered if Kat's house was labeled HOUSE.

I opened the office door and the terriers barged ahead, announcing my presence. Kat was sitting behind a large polished cherry-wood desk strewn with papers.

"Aach ja, Setzen Sie sich, bitte. I am calling Germany and this is der beste time. They are haffing lonch now."

She pointed to a chair and the terriers jumped right into it. I stood.

There were pictures all over the walls of Kat competing, dressed in the formal black cutaway jacket, white britches, white gloves, and top hat worn at the highest level of dressage. There were several pictures of her standing on a platform with medals hanging from ribbons around her neck. I was properly intimidated.

She was speaking rapid German now to a Herr Rauchmann. They spoke for some time, and Kat seemed pleased with the conversation. When it ended, she commented,

"My sorries, but I am negotiating for a von-derful stallion to buy, and this vas gut time to reach der breeder. Zo."

She pushed a sheaf of papers at me and handed me a pen. They were insurance forms, workmen's comp, liability forms, and possibly a burial plot. I signed and read and signed and read and signed. She explained that Gertrude or Gail Brace, manager of the broodmares, would assign me my duties. I would work five to six days a week, which would entitle me to a small stipend and five lessons with her. In addition, I would have one lesson a day from Diana, time permitting. My room was free, but I would share phone and food expenses with my housemates. It seemed pretty fair, and we shook hands. Then she pressed one of the buttons on the intercom next to her desk. It squawked back. I recognized Gertrude's voice.

Kat shouted something in top-decibel German, then directed me to wait for Gertrude outside. The terriers showed me out. A moment later, Gertrude clamped a large hand on my shoulder and steered me

toward the barn I had worked in the day
before.

"You make shtalls clean **von gestern, und
denn ich habe andere Arbeit.**"

Either she was speaking better or I was
beginning to get the hang of her heavily ac-
cented speech. I grabbed the pitchfork.

When the stalls were done, Gertrude
came by again. After a bout of pantomime
and mock English, I learned I was to be totally responsible for six pregnant mares,
which included grooming them, keeping
their water buckets scrubbed and filled,
dishing out their breakfasts and dinners,
turning them out into their field in the
morning, and bringing them back in at
night. I was relieved that I hadn't also been
assigned to scrubbing the barn walls down
with a toothbrush.

I finished the bulk of my work before
lunchtime. The afternoon would be re-
served for bringing the mares in and grooming them before they had dinner. I decided
to break for lunch. Patty was at the apartment, eating a sandwich.

"How's it going?" she asked.

I had just made the fatal mistake of sitting down and could only drop my head onto my arms, which were outstretched across the table. I was moaning softly.

"Yeah. Well, it's your first day," she consoled me. "You'll get stronger."

She fixed me a sandwich and poured some coffee. "Stop breaking my heart. Here, eat something." She put the sandwich down in front of me.

I stared at it helplessly, too tired to pick it up.

"You have about half an hour left," Patty said.

I ate. The food revived me.

"I'm curious: How long has Kat been in the States?" I asked, wondering about her command of English.

"About nine years. She was in Canada before that. For about four years."

I guessed that she was a slow learner in language arts.

"She just spent all her time training," Patty added, as if reading my thoughts. "Was first on the German and then the Canadian Olympic teams."

I whistled. "Why did she leave Canada?"

"Divorce," said Patty. "Why did you leave New York?"

"Divorce," I said. "I mean, soon. And you?"

"I'm a widow, dear. I needed a place to pull myself together. Someplace I hadn't shared with **him.** I closed up my house and packed my clothes—and Kat had this empty apartment. Although it's filled up pretty fast."

I counted. "I guess I make five of us." Does Lenni share a bedroom with her daughter?"

"Yeah, guess you heard the discussion."

I nodded.

Patty made a face. "Jillian isn't happy about anything right now. You'd think she'd be grateful that Lenni is safe and working at something she loves."

I caught the word **safe.**

"Lenni's husband used her for a punching bag. She came here to get away and straighten her life out. Brought Jillian with her."

I pictured Lenni's sad, thin face, followed,

for some reason, by Marshall's blue eyes crying in the rain. I sat pensively for a moment.

Patty got up to peer into the refrigerator. "Honey, don't look so guilty," she said. "Men are like horses. If they're even-tempered and sweet, you stay on for the ride. If they buck and run around, you get off before you get hurt." She slammed the refrigerator door. "Damn, we're out of cake."

I was back in the barn when Diana walked in with Gail Brace, the manager of the broodmares, and another link in the hierarchy of horse management. Gail had several workers under her, Diana mentioned, including me now. I was beginning to understand how big Kat's business really was.

Gail was a ponderously obese woman somewhere in her thirties, with a loud braying laugh and bad complexion. She wore dusty oversized jeans and a soiled maroon jacket that had SANKT MAI FARM over one breast and GAIL unraveling over the other. Every time she spoke, she would unconsciously tug at the dirty red bandanna that hung askew over her tangled, greasy brown hair.

Most of the mares were gentle, Gail assured me while leading me to the field where they were turned out. But like any pregnant lady, they got moody. She warned me to be very careful when I walked among them. We reached a herd of about twenty mares. They trotted over to the fence, pushing and nipping at one another's flanks to be the first in line to check me out. Occasionally, one kicked out in protest at being squeezed by the others. I had no intention of ever walking out there among them; it would have been suicide.

I held out my hand and they sniffed it with approval. Then Gail held out the bucket she carried and they quickly abandoned me for the carrots it contained.

"Hello, ladies. Be patient. There's enough here for everybody." She dispensed the carrots, grabbed one for herself, taking big bites out of it, then held the bucket out to me.

"Want one?" she asked through carrot-filled teeth.

I declined. We watched the mares for a few minutes more as they sorted themselves back into little groups.

"So you're living over the boarders' barn." Gail snorted between bites of carrot. "Lucky you! You get to meet all the snotty boarders."

"I think I met one." I was thinking of Candace Valesco.

"There are about twenty of them. They pay a ton of money to board here, but don't get too friendly with them. Just keep your place."

"My place?"

"You're just the hired help, dearie." Gail hooted loudly. "Most of them are okay, but there are one or two I would like to run through with a pitchfork."

The picture of Candace Valesco squirming at the end of a pitchfork gave me a small measure of satisfaction.

"Do you live on the farm?" I asked.

"No, I just work here during the day. Kat keeps the apartments for people who work and train with her, too. She wants me to lose weight before she'll let me ride her precious horses, so I figure, To hell with her. At least I get to go home to a real house at the end of the day."

It was time to bring in the mares. Gail opened the gate and summoned me into the field with her. I tried not to scream as the mares galloped to within inches of where we were standing, leaving a small but respectful space around us. Gail introduced my charges to me: Rio, Natasha, Coco, Kara, Fanny, and Celebrity. She had ten others to care for, she said, then introduced me to Anna-Helga, young, blond, and Swedish, who came for the remaining four. She pointed out that Anna-Helga lived over the stallion barn with two other Swedes, Anna-Sofie and Anna-Helen. My head swirled with more names I knew I wouldn't remember.

"Let's go," Gail said.

I picked up a lead line, thankful that at least I knew how to lead a horse. That was the first thing anyone learned at a barn. Horses 101, basic kindergarten stuff.

Gail watched as I started with Natasha, who immediately objected to being led. She reared up and pulled back against my lead line, nearly removing my shoulder from its socket while giving me a good view of her stomach as she flailed her hooves over my head. Searing pain shot down my arm. Gail grabbed the lead from me, snapped it hard, and growled in a booming voice, "BAD GIRL, KNOCK IT OFF!" The mare's feet returned to earth. Tossing her head indignantly as Gail led her, she pranced all the way back to the barn. I rubbed my arm and tried to wiggle feeling back into my fingers.

The rest were gentle. Their bellies hung low and they swayed like small ships floating on a lake as they slowly walked next to me. Each mare had a little brass nameplate attached to her halter and, in continuation of Kat's penchant for labeling, a larger brass nameplate on her stall door. All I had to do was match them all up. After they were settled into their stalls with hay, I went from mare to mare, brushing each one down and picking out her hooves. Even the petulant Natasha. I was reflecting on the interesting phenomenon of six muddy horses and one clean human and how we had all quickly exchanged states of hygiene, when Diana poked her head in the barn and called down the aisle.

"Judy! Kat says get your britches on! She'll give you your first lesson."

I thought I caught a scowl from Gail as I left to change.

Chapter Eight

This time, Ivan didn't wait for the canter signal to throw me. Kat was putting me through some basic figures when Ivan thought he saw a ghost. There was no one in the ring except the three of us, me, Ivan, and Kat, the terriers having gone on a reconnaissance mission, but suddenly Ivan raised his head and bugged his eyes out as though something were stalking him.

"Oh, poo." Kat laughed. "He is chust playink a game."

It was a game of toss and I was it. I brushed myself off and caught a bemused Candace Valesco peeking into the ring as she walked by.

I scowled at Ivan and remounted. He didn't care. He saw dead people. He bucked and bolted. I came off again.

"You **must** stay in settle. You are makink him nervose mit all dis fallink," Kat admonished me several times. We worked for close to an hour. I spent most of it re-mounting. Kat took a last puff on her pipe and finally told me the lesson was over. As I stood caked in dust, she pointed out how sweaty the poor horse was, and even a tad dusty from all my remounting. She asked me to give Ivan a bath, said nothing more, and left the ring. I wondered if there was a level low enough to describe me.

My butt and my ego were in equal pain as I led the grinning Ivan to the wash stall. I was trying not to hate him.

Candace was already there, buffing dry a pretty chestnut horse with a white blaze and four white socks.

"Heard you purchased some real estate." She smirked.

"I **what?**"

"Got thrown. It's a horseman's term."

"Oh yah," I answered, running the pulsating shower over Ivan's back and lathering him up. "I guess I bought the whole state of North Carolina in one lesson."

"Well, they say it takes three falls to make a good rider." Candace threw a heated sheet over her horse's back. "Maybe more in your case."

She led her horse away. Gertrude came for Ivan.

"She's not very nice." I nodded toward Candace's disappearing figure.

"Ach ja," agreed Gertrude. "She rite only her horse. She is wury afrait fur rite Ivan."

• • •

There was a line waiting to use the bathroom when I got back to the apartment. Water noises from inside told us that Jillian was in a marathon shower.

"This may be a record," said Diana, first in line. "Two hours and sixteen minutes."

Ten minutes later, Lenni finally broke rank to start dinner. I was moved up to behind Patty.

"I'm making meat loaf," Lenni called to me from the kitchen. "Do you eat meat loaf?"

"Love it," I answered. "Although I never got to eat it much. Marshall and I always ate out, and he liked to order for me."

"So who's Marshall?"

"My husband."

"Well," Lenni mused, "I had a dog named Marshall when I was a kid. My husband's name is Bill."

"I had a dog named Bill when I was kid," Patty chimed in. "My husband's name was Ben."

We looked at Diana.

"I 'ben waiting too long to use the bathroom," she announced, speaking loudly into the bathroom door, "and I'm going into kidney failure. She has a minute left before I kick the door in."

The door opened and Jillian appeared. "How'm I suppose to know anyone wanted to get in?" she announced, her voice rising with indignation. "I was hardly in there."

When my turn came, I tried hard not to fall asleep under the warm water. My muscles were so tight, the only way to relieve the pain was to curl up in fetal position, a tricky way to shower. The bath soap felt too heavy to lift. I wondered if people could die standing up.

We ate Lenni's meat loaf and exchanged the day's "News and Bruises," apparently an apartment postprandial tradition. Diana displayed a huge purple welt forming on her ribs where she had been kicked by a feisty young show prospect she was training. Lenni had been stepped on by a youngster and was sporting a swollen ankle. My shoulder was stiff and sore, courtesy of Natasha. Patty had broken a nail getting dressed.

"Don't you work on the farm?" I asked her.

"No, honey. I shop. I lunch. I ride my horse. It's enough."

"You have a horse? I didn't know you had your own horse here!" I exclaimed.

"Why else would I live here?" she asked in surprise.

I felt stupid. I should have realized that people desiring to live over a horse barn didn't exactly constitute a huge real estate market.

"So, what's your horse's name?" I asked.

"Sam."

"My best college sweetheart was named Sam," said Diana wistfully, and we all laughed.

Patty made tea, which apparently was also

a nightly ritual. She opened a box of chocolates and passed them around. I languished in my chair and felt happy; it had been a good day.

Lenni commiserated with me on having been assigned to the mare barn.

"It's too bad you have to work with Gail Brace. She can be moody."

Patty snorted. "I'd like to throw her in a tub of hot water and scrub her with Brillo."

It was getting near eight o'clock. I eyed the time and decided to call Ruth to let her know how I was and give her my new cellphone number. I wanted to tell her how much I liked the apartment and the women who lived there. How excited I was about training with someone of Kat's caliber. I hoped she would be happy for me.

"You should have called me right away," Ruth scolded me over the phone. "How was I to get in touch with you?"

"Have you heard from Marshall?" I asked.

"Oh yeah—every night for an hour. Henry says I should be charging him for therapy sessions."

"I'm sorry, Ruth. Is he worried?"

"Worried? Nah, but **I** was positively beside myself."

I was touched. "Oh Ruth, I really—"

She interrupted me. "I'm changing the entire color scheme of my dining room. I have to decide between peach with navy or mauve and hunter green. I was absolutely desperate to talk with you—you have such a good sense of color. I mean, besides Andre, my new decorator. Don't ever do that to me again, darling. I'm drowning in color swatches. You must leave me your number so I can always reach you."

Chapter Nine

My days had taken on the quality of endless nights. I woke up before dawn and worked until almost sundown. The work was grueling. I felt like I was perpetually sleepwalking in a gray haze of weariness and fatigue, like the undead. I hated my torturous lessons with Ivan and knew it was mutual. Natasha pulled me wherever she pleased, making ugly faces at me at every opportunity, and I dreaded handling her. The only levels I was conquering were new levels of pain and exhaustion. I worked until I couldn't muster the energy to think. I fell asleep as soon as I ate dinner. I started all over again the next day. I wondered if anything was worth this kind of agony.

One morning, I heard music.

Gail and I were in the tractor, toting bales of breakfast hay to the field just before bringing out the mares, when the soft strains of Bizet wafted across the morning air. It's happened, I thought gloomily. The work load has finally killed me. I waited to be airlifted from the tractor by an angel, hopefully well hung, and ruminated on the fact that apparently God Almighty had a predilection for Spanish opera. I mentally prepared to meet Him and enjoy an eternal pass to **Carmen,** when we drove by the main outdoor riding ring. I hadn't died after all. The music was coming from a pair of speakers attached to tall posts planted next to the ring.

Kat was riding, color-coordinated as usual, with soft gray britches and a dark maroon sweater. This time, she matched her horse, as well. He was a steel gray, his body ringed with light silver dapples, mane and tail gleaming with metallic highlights, his legs wrapped in maroon work "bandages." I couldn't take my eyes off him. As Kat put him through his paces, he carried his neck in a stately arc, every fiber of his body exuding a magnificent presence. His muscles rippled as he trotted sideways across the ring with an easy grace, his legs crisscrossing underneath him. Every footfall matched the music, note for note, movement for movement, in an echoing pattern of orchestra and equine choreography.

"Oh my God," I whispered in awe. "Who is that? What's he doing?"

"That? Oh, Merkury, Kat's new horse from Germany," said Gail. "He's doing a half pass. I personally think his training is being a little rushed, but I guess there's always a temptation to push the good ones."

Merkury glided from one side of the ring to the other, back and forth, executing his dancelike movements with the greatest of precision. His head was tucked and still; his tail flared out gently behind him. He was a picture of elegance and brute strength under perfect control. Kat sat on his back with the soft relaxation of someone in an easy chair, regal and imperious, floating sideways with the horse, her face a study in concentration. The chill in the early-morning air turned the moisture from his body into plumes of white vapor, which surrounded them both in a cloud, like ethereal figures in a dream. I could only stare.

Gail brought me out of my trance by gunning the tractor.

"Let's get the hay out," she yelled into my ear.

But it didn't matter. I had discovered the hidden world. Here was a level of riding I hadn't known existed. A universe had suddenly opened up to me, allowing me a glimpse of something secret and preternatural: this fusing of horse and human into moving poetry that caught the essence of both creatures. I was transfixed. I had to be a part of this. I swore to myself that I would work as hard as I could. Whatever Kat demanded of me, I would do. I would clean stalls. I would let Natasha rip my shoulders from my body. I would lick Kat's boots. There would be nothing that would stand in my way. I would achieve this level, this excellence, this command of a horse's spirit and flesh.

The music came to an end as we drove back to the mare barn. But it didn't matter; it never left my head again.

Chapter Ten

The mares were waiting for us, nickering with impatience. Natasha gave me a sulky look over her stall door, waiting for me to open it. She had already planned her morning.

I hooked the lead line onto her halter and opened her door. She raced out, nearly running me over, then reared up, jerking the line out of my hand.

"Don't let go of her," shouted Gail. "Merkury's a stallion. If she gets loose and in the ring with him, there's going to be a mess! Kat will kill us."

I lunged for the line but was no match for the mare. She reared a second time, whipping the line over my head. I leapt forward and managed to snatch the end of it, but Natasha jerked it hard. I was sure she had severed my arm for good this time, that it was dangling in the air, still clutching the end of the lead line. In a flash, I saw myself being sent home in shame. I would never learn to ride like Kat. I would spend the rest of my life helping Ruth decorate.

"NOOOO!" I screamed at the defiant mare. "NOOO!"

I made a last leap and grabbed the dangling lead, catching it with the tips of my fingers. I snapped it hard against her nose, over and over again, thinking peach and navy. Mauve and hunter green.

"No, no, NO!"

Natasha suddenly stood still. She lowered her head in respect, an instant picture of decorum and manners.

We walked calmly to the field together.

"Good job." Gail patted me on the back. "She just wanted to see where you fit in."

"Fit in?"

"Horses are herd animals. Even humans are part of their herd. And they will try to dominate you. So you have to do it back."

We were standing at the gate now and watching the mares in the field. Natasha approached Rio and suddenly spun around backward, kicking out at her with her hind feet. Ears pinned back, head swinging up and down, Rio returned kicks of her own. But their kicks carefully missed each other. I saw that they were performing a stylized and ritualistic social dance. Rio backed away from her hay pile and allowed Natasha access. Natasha patrolled the pile for a few moments, making faces at the other mares, holding one hind leg menacingly in the air. Then she looked around triumphantly before allowing everyone to settle down and graze peacefully once more.

"I call that 'the horse dance,' " said Gail. "They do it every day. They always have to settle things among themselves—who's gonna be the dominant horse."

"Do they ever hurt each other?"

"Naw." She adjusted her red bandanna over her greasy hair. "It's part of their social graces. Who's got the power. Who's gonna be in control. Just like people."

Chapter Eleven

It was six weeks before I saw Speed Easton again. By then, I had earned Ivan's grudging respect by surviving six weeks of daily lessons on him. Even Kat was more sanguine about my riding future; she puffed less furiously on her pipe while instructing me. The terriers hardly watched me anymore. It was boring not to have me endlessly falling and screaming, so they could spend their time more productively now, supervising the rest of the farm.

We were full into spring. The buds had started opening and the trees resembled girls wearing little green bows in their hair, the birds were exchanging addresses and phone numbers, and I was, as usual, pushing the wheelbarrow up the ramp to the Dumpster. A familiar pickup truck pulled into the driveway, hauling a green-and-white horse trailer. I recognized it right away. Suddenly, the wheelbarrow got light, the manure lovely.

Three Swedish workers scurried over to the truck. Speed jumped out, his cowboy hat in place.

"Good morning, ladies. I've got a delivery." He flashed an engaging grin at the three giggling young women, then unlocked the ramp of the horse trailer and ducked inside to untie the horse and back it down.

The horse was a handsome bay with a white star. He wore a green blanket and had his legs wrapped to protect him while being shipped. There was something familiar about his looks.

"Where's Kat?" Speed looked around. "Tell her I brought this horse over for her to train. I'll leave his blanket with him, but I want his shipping wraps back."

The Swedish girls giggled some more. I knew Kat's name was the extent of their English, so I walked over to help translate with my well-honed skills in pantomime.

"Well hello, Judy," Speed drawled, and smiled at me. I was flattered that he remembered my name.

"Can I help you with your horse?" I asked.

But Diana strode over before he could answer me.

"Who's this, Speed?" She took the horse from him, looking it over.

"This is the gelding I picked up in Sweden last year. Nero, Natasha's full brother."

So that was why he looked familiar. I tried not to flinch at the sound of Natasha's name.

"How's his temperament?" Diana asked. "Is he quiet?"

"Great temperament," Speed replied.

"Really?" Diana countered. "His sister's a bitch."

"Look."

Speed took off his hat and placed it carefully on the truck fender, then laid his hands flat on top of the horse and, in a flash, was doing a handstand in the middle of the horse's back.

"Quiet enough for you?" he asked, upside down, walking around on his hands before gracefully dismounting.

I laughed, but Diana wasn't impressed.

"We don't need a circus horse," she said dryly.

"Tell Kat he's here for training," Speed said. "I want her to ride him for me. He does a weak fourth level. I want her to find out if he has the starch to go higher."

"I'm the one who'll be riding him," Diana said, leading the horse away. "I'll evaluate him if I have the time, and let you know in about a week what we can do with him."

Speed turned to me.

"What level do you ride?" he asked. "If Diana's not going to do it, maybe you can."

"Oh, I'm sure Diana's more than up to it," I replied.

"And tell the grooms I want my shipping wraps back. I don't want them disappearing. You can't trust these grooms, you know."

That hit me. After all, I was a groom, too.

"The grooms here are quite honest," I replied stiffly. "I'll personally make sure you get your wraps back."

He stopped at my tone.

"No offense meant," he said, "but I've lost a lot of equipment to grooms."

"I'll personally guarantee their safe return."

"Well thanks, Judy."

We stared at each for a moment. I suddenly felt embarrassed about my huffiness.

"Well, guess I'll be seeing you around," he said.

Then, with the confident grace of a man who was used to having the world handed to him, he put his hat back on, gave me a two-finger salute from his brow, and swung himself back into the truck.

I stood there a moment, offended by his cavalier manner, the hint of arrogance that lay just beneath his easy smile. I wanted him to see me as more than a mere groom. I wanted him to find me fascinating and sophisticated. I wanted him to like me. I . . . wanted him. It wasn't until he drove away that I realized I was still holding the wheelbarrow full of manure.

Chapter Twelve

"What do you know about Speed Easton?" I asked Patty. I had half a day off and we had earlier completed a tour of the apartment pantry in order to compile the shopping list. Now we were driving into town for supplies. It was all very **Little House on the Prairie**.

"Oh, I've known Speed his whole life," she answered, driving with one hand and using the other deftly to unwrap several mini candy bars at a time and pop them into her mouth. "His father is Podge Easton."

"Podge?"

"Peter Ogden Easton the Fourth. Better bred than some of Kat's stallions. Important lawyer around here, and Speed is a junior partner in his firm. They handle all of Kat's business; plus, they do a lot of horse breeding. Why?"

"Oh, I don't know."

"So, you met Speed. Well, stay away from him. He's always been trouble. Wild kid, wild man. And I don't like his father, either. Put him right out of your mind."

I obediently forced myself to stop thinking of him and concentrate on what I would be making for dinner that night, since it was my turn to cook, a task I was dreading.

I would prepare something speedy. And easy. Speedy. Easy.

"Why is he a wild man?" I asked Patty.

"Oh, I don't know. He did drugs as a kid, into trouble all the time. Lucky for him, his father always managed to bail him out."

"People can reform, can't they?"

"I guess. Except that I hear he's still . . . into things."

"Like what?"

"Flaky things, honey, but it may be just gossip. His family has enough influence to hush things up. They're all lawyers and quick to sue. They got the whole town intimidated, so be careful."

We finished our shopping quickly,

though I did find myself lingering over the huge carrots, the pepperoni sticks, the bananas, and the cucumbers. I tried to stay focused on the culinary challenges coming up that evening.

Plus, a tiny idea was tickling the back of my mind and I couldn't wait to get back to the barn. Once back, I did some sleuthing and found Speed's shipping wraps, rolled up neatly and put on a shelf in the tack room.

Diana came in to hang up a bridle.

"Where does Speed live?" I asked. "I want to return these wraps to him."

She narrowed her eyes. "Mighty thoughtful of you."

"Well, he made a remark about grooms stealing from him, so—"

Diana laughed. "There's always a rivalry between owners and grooms. The owners think the grooms never do enough work and steal from them; the grooms think the owners are ignorant twits and useless around the horses. Don't worry about the wraps. He'll be back in a few days to check on that horse he brought in. You can give them to him then."

After she left, I stuffed the wraps under my coat, took them back to the apartment with me, and hid them under my bed. I didn't want anyone else to be thoughtful.

Speed came to the farm two days later, driving a BMW. Somehow the picture of a cowboy in a BMW hadn't before been part of my sexual fantasies, but improvisation is always good. It might have been the sight of him behind the steering wheel, cowboy hat cocked back, or the black leather jacket left open to expose a well-fitted black shirt, but I had enough fodder for the next fourteen nights.

"How're you doing?" he called to me as he pulled into a parking space. I had just given Ivan a bath and was wet and dirty. And limping, as my last dismount from Ivan hadn't been mutually agreed upon. Plus, I had a black eye from a brief encounter with Natasha's muzzle the day before.

"You're a beautiful woman, but you look beat to hell." Speed whistled. "I guess farm life is taking its toll."

"I have your shipping wraps."

"No problem. I forgot I left them here. Already replaced them. How's it going?"

A brief spark of anger flared inside me again.

"You blame grooms for stealing your equipment, but you really just forget where you leave your stuff!"

He stopped smiling. I immediately wished I could take my words back.

"You're right," he said quietly. "I apologize for the remarks I made last time. I don't have anything against grooms. I just didn't see you as a groom."

"Well, I'm a groom until I finish training here," I said.

He put a hand on my shoulder. "I didn't mean to offend you." He flashed Godiva chocolate eyes.

Yes, yes, yes, I moaned passionately, take me now!

"I'll get your wraps," I said.

"Meet me in the indoor arena," he said, dropping his hand to his side and leaving a warm print on my shoulder. "Diana is riding Nero—that horse I brought in? I want to watch him go."

Diana was mounted and talking to both Kat and Speed when I came back with the wraps.

"He's stiff to the right when we do lateral work," she was saying to Speed, who was nodding.

"Yeah, he's always had a problem there. I tried loosening him up with right shoulders-in, but he still resists," Speed answered.

I sighed, frustrated with my ignorance, although I knew their conversation had everything to do with levels.

"Vell, let's see him go," said Kat.

Diana was a lovely rider; she had Kat's trademark elegance and strength. Her position was flawless, her hands unmoving as Nero trotted around happily. They ran through a number of movements. I thought Nero looked perfect.

"Ja, ja," said Kat. "He iss tight. He neets more loosening to come through."

"Better than he was, though," said Speed.

Kat and Speed discussed some more training options, and Kat left to ride another horse.

Speed turned to me.

"You should take a spin on him some-time. Tell me what you think."

"Oh yeah, thank you," I said. **Spin** was just the word to keep me off his back.

I handed him his wraps.

"Sensitive, aren't you?" He took the wraps, then called to Diana. "Keep up the good work. You, too," he said to me. "I hope to see you soon."

That was my hope exactly.

Diana continued to ride Nero. She can-tered and asked for a flying change, a move-ment where the horse changes his leading canter leg in midair to his other front leg. Nero suddenly bolted sideways, momentar-ily unseating Diana.

"Damn!" she yelled. "It's the Evil Twins. Get them out of here!"

Sure enough, Kat's terriers were sniffing behind the boards of the indoor arena.

"Damn them," said Diana, repositioning herself in the saddle. "When Kat rides, she locks them up. When anyone else rides, she lets them run loose. Scares the shit out of the horses when they hear those little beasts back there but can't see them."

In a flash, I realized why Ivan was so un-predictably spooky. It had been the terriers all along.

"I'll get them," I said, and called them to me. They scampered out from behind the arena wall. I plucked them up, carried them to Kat's office, and locked them inside.

As I walked away from the office, I caught Speed and Gail talking in earnest outside the mare barn. They finished their conversation just as I approached, and then Gail disappeared inside.

Speed noticed me right away.

"Gail tells me that Natasha's been beating up on you." He reached over and touched my black eye gently with his thumb.

I nodded.

"I own that mare, you know. I bred her to Kat's stallion and left her here to foal, so I feel kind of responsible."

"She can be difficult."

"I'm real sorry she did this. Let me make it up to you. Maybe dinner?"

"That would be nice," my mouth said calmly while my brain cheered with delight.

"I'll pick you up Saturday, after you finish

work. I know a great place that'll make you forget your pain."

He walked back to his car. I was overwhelmed with feelings of gratitude for my wonderful, beautiful Natasha.

Chapter Thirteen

It took several years for Saturday night to come. I tried on everything I owned and some things I didn't own. I had lost weight, and my skirts were hanging like blankets now.

Patty was in the kitchen, stirring heavy cream into a pot. She had just started the Atkins diet and everything she cooked had cheese and cream and bacon and steak. Sometimes all on the same night. "I wish you would reconsider this date, dear," she said as I passed through.

"Because I'm still married?" I asked. I eyed the pot, glad I had a dinner date. "It's just dinner. We're not eloping."

"He's not your type," she said. "That boy is trouble. I'm just trying to look out for you a little bit."

The trouble with mother figures is that sometimes they act like mothers. Patty was full blast in maternal mode and I was feeling a bit of teen rebellion perking within me.

"You don't know me well enough to know my type," I protested.

"Well, I know you well enough now to know what isn't."

I tried on several skirts from Lenni's closet, and they were way too tight. Though I had lost weight, Lenni was a stick and I was nowhere near her tiny size. Then I raided Diana's wardrobe. She was taller than I by two or three inches, but to my surprise, I found a respectable skirt and sweater combination that met everyone's approval.

"You clean up good," Diana said. The ultimate in compliments.

"I'm so glad you don't mind me borrowing this." I thanked her for the fourth time.

"Not at all," Diana said. "I haven't worn a skirt since grad school. I don't know why I still keep that stuff."

"You were in grad school?" I was surprised. "For what?"

"Reproductive biochemistry. I have my Ph.D."

"Diana!" I blurted. "You should be doing smart things! Why are you wasting your time here?"

She smiled at me. "Ever see Kat ride?"

That's when I knew she heard the music, too.

• • •

Speed was right on time. He knocked on the door and I peeked out from my bedroom as Patty let him in.

"Howdy, Mizz Crumensko," he drawled.

"Speed." She extended her arm. He kissed her hand.

I expected her to curtsy and cover her face modestly with a fan. Instead, she gestured to me and said unceremoniously as I came out of my bedroom, "Well, there she is. She even took a shower."

"Wow," he said, stepping back and looking me up and down. "I guess Natasha didn't do that much damage."

• • •

The drive to the restaurant was luxurious and fast; the BMW flew over the road.

"I'm a lawyer," Speed said, making conversation.

"I don't mind," I replied. "Some of my best friends are lawyers."

"I wasn't confessing to a sin."

"I wasn't forgiving one."

He drove the car the way a jockey eases a racehorse down the home stretch—urging it forward, hugging the curves, asking for more and more velocity. My fingernails embedded themselves into the rich leather dashboard.

"So you left it all behind to train with Kat?" he asked, turning his head to me.

"Sort of," I replied, watching the road for him. "Things just weren't working out. My marriage was getting crowded. It was time for one of us to leave."

"You may have jumped from the frying pan into the fire," he commented. "Kat's training program can be pretty brutal."

"I really want to do it. There's so much to learn from her. She has so much knowledge. She's like—"

"The queen of dressage!" he finished for me. "Just don't let her work you to death.

She forgets that horses aren't the only ones with feelings."

"She's a good teacher." I tried not to sound defensive. "That's all I came for. I want to learn everything."

"Very diplomatic." He smiled. "And what will you do when you have learned everything there is to learn?"

I didn't know. "I guess whatever one generally does after finishing with someone like Kat," I mused. "Conquer the equine universe."

"On horseback?"

"Whatever it takes."

The restaurant was upscale and French and served food bathed in heavy cream and bacon and steak, with a few oysters thrown in for good measure. Speed spoke wine well: Names like Château Oeuf à la Pouf and Charbout Shiraz Cabernet et Fils tripped off his tongue with ease as he ordered them in three or four shades. This impressed me greatly, as my knowledge of French is limited to **hors d'oeuvres** and **Perrier.**

Dinner was served. I settled into my chair, which was upholstered hip-deep in velvet, and traded backgrounds with him. He told me he was an only child, that his mother had died when he was seven, and that he worked for his father. I told him I was the less perfect of two children, that my mother died when I was twenty-two, that I had two master's degrees and a year toward a Ph.D., had dreams of being a writer, and still wound up teaching high school English.

"You do realize," he said halfway through dinner, "that all this training you're getting is pointless unless you are able to utilize it. And to do that, you need to be on the competition circuit. And then after some international riding and a good ranking, you still have to kill yourself trying to build up a following of students and clients in order to make some kind of living."

"Is that how Kat did it?"

"Hell no." He laughed. "Her family owns a chain of fancy department stores in Germany. Plus, it didn't hurt that her grandfather was on the German Olympic equestrian team back in the thirties and forties." He poured me some more wine.

"That was during World War Two, wasn't it? My grandfather was probably trying to shoot him off his horse."

"Well, I'd hate to see you get disappointed in the end. After all your work."

"I've been disappointed before," I said, thinking of Marshall. "I can survive disappointment."

"And competing is very costly," he added. "You will probably need to find a sponsor at some point."

"You mean like a commercial? Do I hang a billboard from under the saddle: 'Watch me ride, and by the way, please use Charmin toilet paper'?"

He laughed. "Something like that."

He leaned toward me and covered my hand with his. "When you're ready, maybe I can help you."

"Why would you do that?"

"I find myself very attracted to you. You're bright and fun to talk to, and you look smashing in britches." His hand was big and warm. I thought that bode well.

I watched him as he drained his wine-glass. I liked the way his dark hair fell across his forehead. "Conquering universes is a specialty of mine," he added.

"And conquering women?" I asked.

He laughed but didn't answer me.

Charles Aznavour, the Willie Nelson of France, sang softly in the background while I sipped a last glass of Sauterne and enjoyed the ministrations of an overachieving waiter. The crème brûlée and I were getting torched around the same time, but I didn't care.

Speed paid the check with a titanium credit card encrusted with diamonds. At least it looked that way to my dimming vision.

And too soon, it was time to leave.

"I'll take you home." He guided me to the parking lot with his arm around my waist. I floated next to him. He opened the car door for me and waited for me to get in. His manners were impeccable. I was hoping he would drive back to his house, but home it was. He navigated the driveway of the farm and swung into a spot in the parking lot. He got out of the car and came around to help me out. When I stood up, he put his arms around me and tilted my head back, kissing me gently on my black eye.

"Bad, bad Natasha," he said softly.

Then a deeper kiss on my lips as he pressed his body close. He was either happy to be with me or he had sneaked a baguette out of the restaurant. He whispered good night. I was too drunk to care about being disappointed, but I knew one thing: Patty was wrong. Speed had been charming and sweet and a perfect gentleman.

Chapter Fourteen

The next morning, I faced the Inquisition. Lenni, Diana, and Patty were sitting expectantly around the table when I walked into the kitchen to get myself some breakfast. They said nothing, but all eyes followed me as I poured myself some coffee and made toast. All eyes squinted at me while I buttered it. Lenni was the first one to crack.

"For God's sake," she blurted out. "Did you or didn't you?"

"No," I answered. "He was a perfect gentleman."

Suddenly bets were being paid off.

"I owe you a free lesson, Patty," said Diana.

"I owe you one dinner out," said Lenni to Diana.

"No," protested Diana. "I said by the **second** date. It's only the first."

"Oh, right."

I finished my toast and left them exchanging IOUs.

I passed Candy Valesco on my way to the mare barn. She was at the farm for an early lesson with Kat.

"Aren't you a little out of your element?" she said.

"Excuse me?"

"Speed. Heard you had dinner with him. You have to know the horse world is very small. Was it groom's night out?"

"I don't see how my personal life concerns you."

She stopped. Her blue eyes were like ice. "I have a little advice for you, honey. Stay on your side of the manure pile. Let's just say you're not up to speed, if you know what I mean."

She walked away, her expensive custom boots clipping along the path.

I spent the rest of the morning cleaning stalls and wondering what the penalty for justifiable homicide was in North Carolina. Even Gail's tacky jokes and loud braying laugh did nothing to bring me out of my funk.

It got worse.

The barn intercom suddenly squawked to life as Kat shouted into it.

"Zhoody, you haff here a phone call."

I raced to her office, mystified as to who would be calling me on Kat's office phone. Ruth and Mickey, my old riding instructor, were the only ones who knew where I was, and they had only my cell-phone number.

Kat handed me the phone without comment, never looking up from her paperwork. The terriers lay at her feet and stared at me sullenly. They had stopped speaking to me days before when I had confined them to Kat's office.

"Hello?"

"Did you think you could hide forever?" Marshall's voice, dripping with sarcasm, almost made me gasp out loud.

"Um, no, I thought I gave you the correct address," I answered, trying to make my voice light and unconcerned.

Kat shuffled some papers and continued

to read. The terriers turned their noses away.

"Are you brain-dead?" Marshall said harshly. "I know where you are."

"That's fine," I warbled. "That's absolutely fine."

"I'm coming down and dragging you back by your hair if I have to. No one walks out on me."

"Uh-huh," I said, eyeing Kat and hoping she couldn't overhear him, "I can take shipment right away."

Kat typed something on her computer, seemingly unaware.

"What are you talking about, you ass!" Marshall continued. "Your little game is over."

He went on at some length. I was embarrassed.

I finally interrupted him, "Ohhh, you only have navy? Well, they'll do fine. Thank you so much. Good-bye."

I hung up the phone and thanked Kat.

"New britches," I lied. "They were trying to locate me for delivery."

"Ja, ja." She smiled. "It's ferry nice for your husband to brink you britches."

I slunk back to the barn, my heart pounding. I spent the next hour struggling to finish cleaning stalls and fight back tears without Gail catching on.

Diana poked her head in the barn.

"I'm taking Nero for a trail ride," she announced. "Tack up Ivan and come along. Kat's orders."

I hate trail rides, but for the first time since my arrival, I couldn't wait to get on Ivan.

The farm had miles and miles of trails, and our horses were ready to take them all on. They pranced and skittered and, in general, acted like idiots. Nero gave little half rears, which Ivan thought were worth emulating.

"Trail riding is great to take your mind off things," Diana remarked as her horse produced a series of low bucks and crow hops.

"Oh yeah," I agreed. Ivan was twirling like a barber pole now, and I was hanging on tightly. "You're so busy concentrating on staying alive, you can't think of anything else."

The horses finally settled down and walked along, until something in the woods caught their attention. It was the terriers.

I should have known that the terriers, still gravely offended over their confinement, were not going to take my insult lightly. They had waited patiently for several days now, plotting retaliation. In a flash, two little brown-and-white bodies flew from the bushes and grabbed onto the horses' tails with their teeth. The horses spun and jumped, but the avenging terriers hung on.

"Gallop," yelled Diana. "Gallop!"

She leaned forward and put Nero into a gallop. I followed suit. The terriers were clamped on for a good quarter mile or so before they got tired of thumping against the back legs of our speeding horses. They opened their jaws and dropped back on the path.

We broke our horses to a walk.

"Little bastards," muttered Diana. "One of these days, I'm going to have them stuffed and put up like weather vanes over the indoor arena."

We continued to walk. I was silent.

"So, what's the matter?" Diana asked.

"My husband called. I think he's going to try to come here."

"How did he find you?"

I repeated what Marshall had told me on the phone.

It seemed that Mickey, my old instructor, was retiring to North Carolina and had put her farm up for sale. And who was handling her sale? Ms. Grace Cairo, bearer of dangling gold birdcages and Marshall's latest attentions. Although Marshall only mentioned that a real estate friend of his had discovered where I had gone, my mind filled in the rest. I just knew that Grace Cairo and Mickey had exchanged pleasantries and gossip. And Mickey, unsuspecting that Grace was the very reason I was fleeing Long Island, mentioned how one of her students had gone to this working student situation. . . . The horse world was small indeed.

"So?" Diana shrugged. "Send him away."

"He's difficult." I sighed. "He's head-strong and he has a nasty streak."

"You will deal with it," Diana said firmly. "You're strong, too."

The trail opened into a grassy knoll, and we let the horses stop and put their heads down to graze.

"Diana," I said, "did you ever date Speed? I mean, you're so pretty—I was wondering—I don't want to cut in—"

Diana shook her head. "He's asked me out, but I turned him down."

"Because of his reputation?"

"No," Diana said. "He's not my type. I'm gay."

I blinked, confused. "But you said your big college love was someone named Sam."

Diana threw her head back and laughed out loud. "Samantha, kiddo. Samantha."

Chapter Fifteen

Six-thirty A.M. the next morning, and Jillian and Lenni preempted my alarm clock.

"None of the other kids bring a bag lunch," Jillian was saying, tossing her pink-and-purple hair indignantly. "It's humiliating. They all go out and buy pizza and stuff."

"That gets expensive, Jilly. This is what I can afford."

"I'm only going to toss it once I get to school," replied Jillian. "So if you really want me to eat lunch—"

"I hate to see you waste good food," Lenni told her quietly, her thin face sagging into even sadder lines.

"We didn't have to eat like beggars when we lived with Dad." Jillian's voice was defiant.

"We're not eating like beggars. We're just—"

"We're just living like beggars!" Jillian grabbed the little brown bag and slammed out of the apartment. Lenni looked into her coffee cup as though she found some comfort there. Finally, she said, half-joking, "We're supposed to love them unconditionally, right?"

Patty was concentrating on a huge pastry, an illegal supplement to her Atkins diet.

"I don't think we have to love anyone unconditionally except babies and small dogs," she said between bites. "When everything else gets big enough to make choices on how to treat you, they have to earn the love you give them."

"Was it easy raising your daughter, Patty?" Lenni asked.

"Naw! She hated me from the time I nursed her until the day she got married." Patty shrugged. "I used to think it was something in my milk."

I gladly left them discussing the philosophy of child rearing and ducked out for the mare barn. Gail was already at work and wearing the same clothes that she had been wearing all week, the red bandanna still crooked over her hair.

We started our morning chores. Two hours into our work, the barn intercom squealed a signal. Gail ran over to answer.

"Hallo? Hallo?" Kat's voice screamed from the speaker. "Can you write for me how much hay you are usink for der mares? Giff me bale count. Der hay mann is comink."

She clicked off.

"Why does she always scream into the intercom?" I asked.

"She doesn't believe that it really carries her voice," Gail explained. "She thinks she's sitting in Germany."

We did a quick calculation of our hay usage and then I followed Gail to the hay barn, where there was an excited discussion going on in three languages.

Kat appeared. She had already taken off her riding boots and was wearing the black leather clogs that were the traditional footwear among the German and Swedish girls. Clogs were the sign that she was finished riding for the day. I had been in awe of how immaculately groomed she always looked, despite riding sometimes as many as five or six horses every day, until Lenni pointed how this was due to the fact that Kat hadn't actually groomed a horse in twelve years. Here she was again, impossibly tidy as she padded over to us, followed by the terriers. The terriers stood safely behind Kat's legs as Gail and I approached. They hadn't forgotten the trail ride. We gave Kat our numbers: The mare barn used about two tons of hay per month.

She puffed on her pipe and did some mathematics.

"Hmm." She exhaled a mouthful of smoke. "Vee use normal six tons. Sixty-pount bales. But I order eight tons of sixty-five-pount bales, but I tink dey are comink fifty-pount bales. Vee should not haff finished all der hay. **Richtig?**"

I had no idea what she was talking about, including the **richtig,** but I agreed anyway.

There was a loud rumble behind us as a tractor-trailer loaded with hay pulled up to the back of the barn. The terriers, glad for an excuse to take leave, ran up to the truck and barked it into position.

Kat strode over to it. A burly man in a blue shirt jumped out of the truck. So did his assistant, who immediately began setting up a long aluminum roller tray to roll the hay into the barn for stacking.

"Vee haff problem," Kat said curtly. "You are not brinking me all mein hay."

"Lady, Ah brought ya twelve tons," drawled the driver. "Ya'll ordered twelve tons and this here is twelve tons."

"Nein. You are sheating me." Kat was visibly angry.

"These are very heavy wire bales, lady. Mebbe seventy pounds each. They're gonna look smaller, less to the ton."

"Nein. Mein verkers say fifty pounts."

"These skinny little girls?" The truck driver looked over the group with incredulity and laughed. His helper laughed, too. "What do they know about weighing hay? It probably takes all three of them to lift one bale."

The two men guffawed loudly.

"Vee vill chust see," Kat said grimly. "We sheck dem out. If dey are not gut, you vill make better, zo." She turned and gave Gertrude an order in German. Gertrude disappeared and reappeared with a hay scale. They hung it in the entrance of the hay barn.

"**Vee** vill count," commanded Kat.

"Just a minute," said the driver. "How do Ah know that this here scale is on the level?"

That seemed like a fair protest to Kat, who turned to Gertrude and issued more orders in German. Gertrude disappeared with two of the Swedish girls, Anna-Sofie and Anna-Helga. We waited. Kat puffed on her pipe. The driver picked at his nose. One of the terriers lifted his leg on the front wheels of the truck.

A few minutes later, like slaves from the **Arabian Nights,** Gertrude and the two Swedish girls came back, each one bearing an item to be weighed.

Kat nodded to Anna-Sofie, who was carrying a new one-pound salt lick. She wrapped it up in a piece of twine and hung it from the hay scale. It weighed exactly one pound. Kat smiled. The driver grunted and wiped his fingers on his shirt.

Anna-Helga was next. She was carrying an unopened ten-pound box of sugar cubes. She and Anna-Sofie made a series of slow but neat knots out of the twine and hung it from the scale. Ten pounds.

The driver made an impatient noise. "All right, all right. This ain't necessary. We're wastin' time."

But Kat was not to be stopped. She waved Gertrude forward. Gertrude had an unopened fifty-pound bag of horse pellets. She ripped a small hole in the top and hung it from the scale. Fifty pounds exactly. The Swedish girls cheered. Gail and I gave each other a high five. The terriers ran around in happy circles.

"**Now** vee veigh hay." Kat gave Gertrude the signal.

Gertrude took a bale of hay from the truck and swung it onto the aluminum rollers. It rolled down toward the Swedish girls. Kat pointed for me to grab the bale and hand it off to Anna-Sofie.

"**Ein,**" counted Gertrude

I grabbed the bale and helped Anna-Sofie lift it onto the scale hook. The needle pointed to fifty-five pounds. Anna-Helen duly noted the weight with a pad and pencil. Anna-Helga and Gail stacked it in a pile.

"**Zwei**," counted Gertrude, swinging the second bale down the slide.

It, too, was hefted onto the scale hook. We waited until the needle settled. Sixty pounds. It was noted.

Blue Shirt caught on.

"Are you crazy?" he squealed. "Do ya'll know how long that's gonna take? Ya'll got twelve tons of hay here, at least. Are ya'll crazy? Y'all can't weigh every bale!"

His speech was making me dizzy, but the Germans and Swedes persevered.

"**Drei!**"

Third bale. I mentally calculated that there were probably forty to fifty bales to a ton. Times twelve tons.

"Jesus Christ! They'll be here all night," thundered the helper. He turned to Kat.

"Y'all can't do this to us. We have other deliveries to get to. Ah can't wait for a bunch of girls to play around in the hay."

"Vier!"

"If you vant money, I vant to count hay," said Kat. "Maybe I call owner of hay company." Her farm had the biggest account in the state and they all knew it. "Maybe I call Bureau of Veights und Majors. Maybe I tell dem you take my hay und sell to udder farms under your sleeve."

"Y'all are fuckin' kidding me," said Blue Shirt. He looked at his watch.

"Funf!"

"Ah can wait it out," he said loftily to his assistant. "They're not going to count it all. They're girls. They ain't gonna last."

"Maybe we can get us a little roll in the hay when they're all tuckered out." The helper chuckled.

"A roll with Swedish meatballs," said the driver. "Mmm, mmmm!"

The two men elbowed each other and laughed loudly. They laughed and laughed.

Blue Shirt sat down on the fender of his truck. And then, realizing that the color of his teeth hadn't yet completely reached an attractive and rich dark shade of brown, he took a large wad of chewing tobacco from his dirty pocket and stuffed it into his cheek. His assistant scratched his nether parts. But they had sadly miscalculated the precision and persistence of the German personality. And the tenacity of the Swedes.

An hour passed. We had lifted and counted out about two tons.

"Vait," said Anna-Helen. She held up her pad and said something in Swedish to Gertrude, who translated it into German for Kat.

"She made mistake."

They decided a recount was in order.

It was all too much for Blue Shirt. "All right, all right," he relented. "Maybe Ah might've made a few mistakes in the past. Ah'll throw in a few extra bales for free."

"Ein!" Somebody was counting again in the barn.

Kat stood her ground.

"Okay. One ton," said Blue Shirt.

"Zwei!"

"Three tons," he moaned. "And five tons next load. That's it, lady."

"Drei! Vier!"

"Okay, okay. Ah'll take care of y'all through the end of summer."

Kat did some fast figuring, then took a satisfied puff on her pipe and summoned her crew.

"Dis nice man is goink to finish loading hay mit his nice helper," she announced. Then like they do in foreign airports, she re-announced it in German to Gertrude, who translated it into Swedish.

"Whoa!" squealed the driver. "Are y'all crazy? Ah got eighteen tons of hay here to unload and stack. Who's gonna help us?"

Kat looked over at the girls and then back at the driver. "Vee hoff only skinny girls." She shrugged. "Dey are too veek for verking hay."

The girls melted away. One of the terriers gave the truck tires a final baptism and trotted off. The men were left alone to load eighteen full tons of hay and stack it in the barn.

It was my first lesson in international business.

Chapter Sixteen

It was only a few days later when the apartment phone rang for me.

"I've been thinking about you," Speed drawled on the other end of the line.

"You have?" I said, trying not to sound like a happy puppy, panting and licking my lips.

"How about a picnic?" he said. "You said today is your day off."

I peeked out the apartment window. It was a chilled, grizzly gray outside and though it was late spring, I wouldn't have exactly called it picnic weather. But I wasn't about to turn him down.

"Picnic sounds great."

"Good. I'll pick up a few things and you can bring the coffee," he said.

I thought I might also bring earmuffs, mittens, and thermal underwear.

"Don't worry," he reassured me. "We'll stay warm."

Patty watched as I poured coffee into the large thermos I'd borrowed from the mare barn. Gail and I had been using it for mixing medication for some of the mares. I sniffed it. Despite several washings, it still smelled a little funny.

"You think progesterone will hurt the coffee?" I asked Patty.

"Nah, and it might do Speed a world of good," she said. "Neutralize some of his testosterone."

"He's been a perfect gentleman, Patty."

"One date, Judy. Maybe he's a little slow starting his engine this time, although I don't know why. He usually goes through a lot of women very quickly."

"Maybe they just weren't right for him."

"All I know is, there's got to be a reason he's dating you."

"Isn't it possible that he just likes me?"

"Hmm." Patty thought about it, then shook her head. "No, I don't think it's that."

"So you think it's just that he's run out of women from North Carolina?"

"Don't laugh. He's very much like his father. After Speed's mother died, his father became a real ladies' man. That woman was hardly cold in her grave. Plus, there are other reasons why I don't like his father— my late husband was an oral surgeon, you know, and Podge Easton tried to cheat him once on an extraction."

"That's not fair, Patty. Blaming the son for his father's teeth."

She grabbed a box of doughnuts, settled into a kitchen chair, and pointed the box at me. "Apples don't fall far from trees, you know."

Then she put the doughnuts down. "Damn," she said, "now I want an apple."

Speed arrived an hour later, wearing jeans and a sweater, black cowboy boots, and his black leather jacket. He kissed me on the lips, looking irresistibly sexy. It made me wish Patty weren't in the kitchen, crunching loudly on the apple. We waved good-bye and left.

Speed planned for us to have a picnic lunch at his farm. Then we would go on a trail ride. The first part sounded like fun. I was dying of curiosity to see what kind of farm Speed had, but the part about the trail ride made me apprehensive. I hate trail rides. It's the element of wonder and surprise attached to them that I find disconcerting. Asking a horse to run through the woods wild and free with the wind whistling up its tail like Fury, then expecting it to graciously give it all up to bring you home again was against nature. The wonder and surprise was that the horse brought you back at all. I suggested lunch first, as I firmly believe that no one should die on an empty stomach, but Speed just said, "You'll see."

I settled back into the BMW and, knowing Speed's propensity for matching his driving skills to his name, prepared for lift off. We flew over the roads at mach velocity and landed ten minutes later in front of a huge farm with the obligatory sign outside: EASTON STUD.

"Easton Stud?" I read and turned to him. "You?"

"This farm's been in the family and under that name for generations," Speed said.

He turned in at the signpost. It seemed like miles of white fences spread out in front of me as we drove up a winding driveway. To the right stood a traditional southern mansion, big enough to house the complete cast of **Gone With the Wind,** including the extras. I looked up at the imposing architecture of white columns and gables and verandas and wondered how many generations of Eastons had been begatted there.

The car thrummed to a halt in a small paved area near a barn and we deplaned, taking the thermos and food hamper with us.

The inside of the barn was no less magnificent than the outside of the house, all done up in with cobblestone floors, polished oak walls, and gleaming brass stall fittings. Speed's horses lived in equestrian splendor.

After showing me through the barn, he walked me to the indoor arena, which was attached to the barn by a covered breezeway, constructed to protect horse and rider in inclement weather. I peeked inside. There were bleachers along one wall and, like Kat's arena, this one was fitted with overhead mercury lights and an elaborate speaker system. I whistled through my teeth. It was big enough for a cattle stampede.

"We used to have all sorts of things in here—horse shows, charity auctions," Speed explained.

"Used to?"

"My father got tired of the whole social thing."

Remembering that Patty had described him as a ladies' man, I wondered if Podge Easton hadn't just worn himself out.

A man in green coveralls appeared from nowhere.

"The horses are ready, Mr. Easton."

Speed led me back into the barn.

Two horses stood in the aisle, held by another worker in green coveralls. They were already groomed and saddled. The worker nodded to me and handed me a stout medium-size brown horse.

"Ma'am."

I am rarely ma'ammed, and I liked it. I wanted to throw my head back and do a Katharine Hepburn from **The Philadelphia Story** thank-you, but he had already walked away. I mounted by myself with my thermos in hand. Speed mounted the other horse, a brown-and-white paint. He leaned back and strapped the food hamper behind the saddle.

"I thought we were going to eat first," I said.

"There's a great picnic spot off one of the trails." Speed walked his horse out of the barn and gestured for me to follow. "We can only get there by horse; it's too far by foot."

We walked a few yards side by side.

"So, what are our horses' names?" I asked, making nervous conversation.

"Mine is Pilot," said Speed, "and yours is Co-Pilot. They're barn buddies."

Now, I am inherently suspicious of, and will not ride, horses named Hurricane, Dynamite, Dynamo, Rocket Launcher, Twister, Tornado, LadyKiller, BoneCrusher, Hold on to Your Hat, or any other intimidating descriptive designation, but these names seemed innocuous.

"Great names," I said.

My horse followed right next to his, walking at a comfortably slow pace. He reminded me of Sunny. My wish for a safe return was beginning to look promising.

We passed the indoor arena and another long barn. Behind it stood several cottages.

"For the workers," Speed explained. "It's easier for them to live right on the property."

There were green coveralls everywhere, working in the barn and surrounding fields and gardens.

"How many people work for you?" I asked in surprise.

"About twenty outside, and five or six in the house. Just the minimum really, as my father is a very private person."

I surveyed the army of workers and guessed that the extremely rich have a different definition of privacy.

When we reached the perimeter of the farm, Speed asked his horse to pick up a trot. My horse didn't need to be consulted; he trotted off, as well. I could see that he was clearly not a horse who thought for himself. We trotted for about a mile, then Speed urged his horse on to pick up a canter. My horse went along for the upgrade.

After a few minutes, the canter was kicked up a notch into a gallop. Now I got the idea behind their names. My horse was a designated lemming. I felt like I was sitting in Speed's car while he was behind the wheel. I had become a mere passenger. We galloped at a breakneck pace. I pulled on the reins a bit to rate the horse back, but he didn't respond. He was running full tilt now, totally out of control.

"I can't stop him," I yelled over to Speed.

He turned his head, giving me a puzzled look, and screamed back into the wind, "Why would you want to?"

We galloped on for another mile or two. My eyes were tearing from the wind and my hands were numb where my fingernails had embedded themselves into my palms. Finally, Speed broke his horse to a trot. To my relief, Co-Pilot also cut his engines. We walked along to give the horses a break. It took another mile for my heart to resume beating.

The trail smelled of pine needles and spring and young wildflowers. The horses blew rhythmic breaths through their nostrils as we walked along. The pale sun finally started lifting the gray cast from the sky. Birds sang, and I was still alive and mounted. It was a good thing. I looked down at the soft piney footing and thought it might be a nice place to make love.

The trail led to a lake. Speed stopped his horse and mine stopped automatically. Swans paddled across the lake, pushing past small, protesting flotillas of ducks. Several deer were drinking at the water's edge but took no notice of us.

"I love coming here," Speed said, dismounting. He stood next to his horse, looking over the lake. His face looked relaxed, like a boy's, filled with wonder and appreciation. Yet there was an aura about him, an easy air of divine right. It was apparent that the graces of life had been gifts and not grappled for, and it was very becoming. The breeze blew his hair back a little. Something inside me stirred.

He turned to me. "Great, eh?"

I nodded. "Does this lake belong to you?"

"Yeah. And this trail forks off. One part goes out near the road and the other side, if you follow it straight ahead for a few miles, goes to the back of Kat's property."

I dismounted, too. We stood hip-to-hip and watched the swans and ducks and geese.

"It's a beautiful place," I murmured. A rabbit hopped up to my horse and sniffed it. My horse blew his nose on the rabbit's head.

"Are you hungry?" Speed finally asked, taking the hamper down from his horse.

"A bit," I lied. I was hoping he had a restaurant in there.

I looked around for a good picnic spot— someplace soft, where we could make love after we ate. Speed opened the hamper and took out a thin blanket, which he spread by the edge of the lake; then he pulled out several foil-wrapped baguettes spread with avocado and brie. This was followed by grapes and chocolate biscotti. It **was** a restaurant.

"Come here," he said, and pulled me down on the blanket next to him. I was shivering. Now that I was off the horse, the small breeze that came across the lake was chilling me. He pulled me close and put his arm around me as we ate. The ducks quacked at us and we threw them the remains of our food. Then the swans paddled over with curiosity. I was hoping that Speed would notice that they were in pairs.

"So are you still determined to conquer universes?" he whispered into my ear.

"More than ever," I said.

"That's what I like about you." He kissed my neck, then turned my face and kissed me again. "You're willing to take chances on new things. You're not afraid to follow your heart."

I opened the thermos and poured coffee into the cup. We shared sips and toasted the swans.

I looked around. The lake was ringed with thick old trees and heavy underbrush. Here and there were glimpses of yellow forsythia starting to open. Purple hyacinths were bravely joining in. It was peaceful and private. It would have been a good place to make love.

"If it were warmer," Speed whispered, "this would be a good place to make love."

"I hadn't thought of that," I said.

He kissed me again, slow and deep. The ducks quacked, the rabbit was back, nibbling at the aluminum foil from the sandwiches, and the horses pawed with impatience. It was time to leave.

We walked our horses back in thoughtful silence. I wanted Speed, but I didn't want to be another contestant in what was apparently a long line of Easton Stud hopefuls. I didn't want to be the one Speed would reminisce about in years to come, saying, "Oh yeah, then there was that gal I had down by the lake." I wanted him, but I wanted him on my terms. And I wasn't sure yet what those terms were.

We came up to the barn. There were two grooms waiting for us. We dismounted and handed over the horses. It was a nice change to hand off a dirty horse to a groom and walk away à la Kat. Speed gave me hug as we headed for his car.

Well, I thought ruefully, as he opened the car door for me, sometimes a picnic is just a picnic.

Chapter Seventeen

"Do you have to get back soon?" Speed asked as soon as he settled behind the wheel.

"No," I answered. "Remember? It's my day off."

"I wondered if Kat was still giving you a whole day off."

"Well, of course. It was part of the agreement."

He laughed. "We've hired a few workers over the years who've left her farm. She tends to turn days off into half days, then no days. Of course, the foreign girls are kind of stuck there."

"She wouldn't do that to me."

"Of **course** not," he said with too much sincerity. "But since you still have a whole day off, we can spend it together. I can have Martine the Cook make dinner for us later."

I assumed that Martine the Cook was in

the house and that's where we were heading. I pictured her in a little black miniskirt and tiny white ruffled apron, like in the old French comedies. To my surprise, I felt a tiny pang of jealousy.

Speed drove up to the house.

It was not the kind of house where you make your first entrance dressed in jeans, with horse shit clumping off your shoes, but Speed marched us right through the front door and into the large front hall. My first impression was marble: marble floors and marble-topped tables and marble statues and marble columns. I almost expected to be given a token bag of marbles when I took my jacket off or, at the very least, a museum pass, but Speed just took my jacket from me and hung it in a closet. Not wanting to leave a trail of—well, trail behind me, I also kicked off my shoes.

"Let's go into the kitchen," Speed suggested. "I can use some coffee. I hate to say it, but yours tasted kind of off."

I followed him into a huge kitchen with appliances that would have had the final trump card in Ruth's game of Better Than

You. And fussing over something on the stove was Martine the Cook. She was an elderly black woman, seventy-five at least, and hunched.

"Well now, Lawrence, you look cold," she said.

"A little chilled, Martine. Could you make us some coffee?"

"Lawrence?" I repeated.

"Martine always calls me that," he explained.

"Speed ain't no name for a boy," Martine said. "It's a name for a road sign."

"Martine, this is Judy."

Martine turned and gave me a raised eyebrow. I reached out to shake her hand. She shook it firmly.

"Glad to meet you, Julie," she said.

"Judy," I said.

"Trudy," she replied, correcting herself.

Thankfully, she turned her efforts to making coffee. I felt something brush against my leg and looked down. There, sitting and staring up at me, was a Jack Russell terrier. My heart sank. Had those little beasts actually tracked me down? No, the coloring was a bit different, yet the face was disconcertingly familiar.

"That's Ripper," said Speed. "He's from the last litter of puppies from Kat's terriers."

"Is that Tippy dog in your way, Trudy?" asked Martine. "Come here, Tippy. Come have a little snack with Momma." She bent over and handed the dog a cookie from a plate. The dog shot me a raised eyebrow, then ate the cookie. I wondered if Kat's dogs could communicate telepathically.

Martine's coffee was much better than mine. Speed and I sat at the kitchen table and drank big mugfulls.

"The secret to good coffee," said Speed, "is to get all the progesterone out of the thermos."

I laughed.

"Were you trying to feminize me?" he asked.

"No," I said apologizing. "It was the only thermos I could find."

"I thought maybe Mizz Crumensko had something to do with it."

"Why do you say that?"

"Well"—he smiled—"she's had a long-running tiff with my dad. Ever since her late husband botched up an extraction and my dad refused to pay for it."

"She never said a word to me."

We drained our mugs and ate some cookies. Ripper watched us from under the table, taking secret notes, I was certain, to dispatch later to his parents.

Speed stood up. "Come on, I'll show you around." He took my hand.

The house was filled with antiques and other old things, mostly the remaining five servants that Speed had mentioned earlier. They rubbed the same pieces of furniture several times over and repolished lamps and rewiped crystal, all the while observing me discreetly. When I nodded at them, they disappeared down the halls.

There were rooms off rooms, each one spacious, with twelve-foot ceilings, carved tables and elegant chairs, and tapestries of hunt scenes with frilled gentlemen and fine ladies with cleavage. There was a solarium and a library and a music room and a small ballroom. There was even a room with walls decorated with old weaponry and satin capes.

I gestured to the capes. "Don't tell me there were Easton knights of yore."

"No. My dad collects medieval weapons and old opera capes."

In addition to Willie Nelson, I have been known to listen to more than an opera or two, and I felt an immediate wave of simpatico.

"I love opera," I said.

"I love opera, too," he replied. "I love Willie Nelson and Bizet and Rossini and Mozart."

"And do you wear the opera capes to the opera?" I asked.

"Occasionally." He gave me a sweet smile. "When the moon is full."

He led me through more rooms. The house would have provided several lifetimes of happy endeavor for Ruth: She wouldn't even have had to choose between her color combinations, as there were enough rooms to give them all a turn.

We got to Speed's bedroom.

I thought it would be done up in cowboy, since he had such a fondness for his cowboy hat and boots, but it just contained more antiques, including a plush Oriental rug. I wanted to lie down on the deep pile and spread my arms out. My legs, too, but I stood politely in the middle of the room and eyed his bed, wondering just how checkered its history had been.

Our eyes locked.

Before me stood a handsome man who rode horses and loved Willie Nelson and wore formal wear to Bizet—what more could possibly be left for me to want? He took my hand and led me to the bed. I threw my arms around him.

My terms had been met.

Chapter Eighteen

I got home late that evening, anxious to talk to someone, and found Lenni and Patty sitting at the table. Lenni looked like she had been weeping.

"What's wrong?" I stopped in my tracks.

"It's Bill," said Patty.

"My ex-husband," said Lenni. "He's making problems for me with Jillian. Every time she calls him, he tells her what a loser I am. What she's missing by living here with me."

I sat down at the table with them. This had been an ongoing problem.

"Maybe she should live with him," I said.

"That's what I told her," said Patty. "Send Jillian home to him. It would make all of us happy."

"Except me," said Lenni. "I would miss her terribly."

I reached out and held Lenni's hand. I hadn't been able to avoid overhearing the arguments she had been having almost daily with Jillian. Unfortunately, Patty and I didn't prove to be much help, as the only advice we agreed upon, which Lenni didn't take, was for her to kill Bill. It was still the only thing Patty and I could think of. Lenni finally stood up and yawned.

"I guess I'll turn in," she said. "I have an early day tomorrow. I have three colts to start breaking. Kat wants them ready for the big auction this summer."

She went to bed. Patty and I sat there together.

"I feel bad for her," said Patty. "She works so hard. And she takes a lot of risks. Saddle-breaking young horses when you're her age is not easy."

I knew it was tough, even though Lenni was a good rider. She didn't have the elegance and polish that Kat and Diana possessed, but she was a strong, patient rider, the best kind to break a bucking, playful youngster. With her long, thin legs wrapped around and knotted together somewhere under the horse's belly, she always managed to stay glued to the saddle while she installed the necessary brakes and steering.

"Jillian might be happier with her dad," I said. "Maybe we should try harder to convince Lenni to let her go."

Patty's fingers played with the fern on the table. "Do you think plants have feelings?" she asked suddenly.

"Not really. I mean, I can't picture salads getting emotional."

"I guess it's good they don't," she said. "It's so hard the other way."

"What's hard?"

"Having feelings. They get in the way of a happy life."

I blinked at this a few times. "Patty," I said gently, "a happy life has—well, feelings. **Happy?**"

She wasn't hearing me. "It's funny," she mused. "You think that when your kids grow up, they'll always stay connected to you. That it's the natural order of things. But, you know, we are the only species that thinks so. You wean dogs and cats—or even horses—and in a few months they never recognize their own parents again. Maybe that's what we're evolving toward in some way, and maybe it's better. Maybe it's just girls and their mothers, but it seems like there are more and more mothers and children who've stopped speaking to one another."

"Devolving," I said. "If we go that way, it's devolving. Alienation can't be the answer. And I don't agree—about the weaning part, I mean. I guess it's okay for a head of lettuce to forget the vegetable patch it came from, but for people, it's better if you at least remember your mother. Even if she wasn't the way you wanted her to be, you can find things to love. And I think everyone looks for some kind of mothering in their life."

I wondered if Patty knew she was my designated mother figure.

"Maybe," said Patty. "Maybe some still need mothering. Maybe you spend your whole life looking to find your mother's love in other places. And maybe some people don't need anything."

I had to think about that. "Yeah—Kat seems pretty self-contained."

"But her daughter doesn't talk to her."

"She has a daughter?"

"Bianca," said Patty, "and they barely speak. Some argument over a horse. Kat was even planning once to name this farm Demeter's Farm because of it."

"Demeter?"

"You know, the goddess who loses her daughter, Persephone, and searches everywhere for her. She can't find her and she grieves, which plunges the world into winter until her daughter returns. Then, to celebrate, Demeter allows the world to bloom into spring and summer."

"So that's why Kat is so—" I searched for the word.

"Yeah, that's why," said Patty. "I guess she's hoping for Bianca to come back."

I suddenly remembered the rest of the myth. "Wasn't the daughter from the union of Demeter and Poseidon? He transformed himself into a stallion to mate with her?"

"Wouldn't surprise me in the least." Patty laughed, getting up and stretching. "Knowing how Kat thinks, it wouldn't surprise me in the least."

Chapter Nineteen

There was a notice tacked to the bulletin board in the boarders' barn the next morning. It was on expensive cream-colored stock, embossed with a gold monogram and printed in black script. It was an invitation. I came downstairs to find Patty reading it.

"It's a brunch," she said, "to open the coming horse show season."

I read it over her shoulder. Candace Valesco was hosting a big fund-raising brunch for all the horse people in the area to come together and check out who had the deepest pockets.

"Are you going?" I asked her.

"I go every year," she said, then flushed. "I'll find out if you gals can go."

"Oh yeah," I snorted, "I can remind them of how the other half lives. Don't bother."

Diana read the invitation over my shoulder, and Lenni over hers.

"**We're** horse people," said Lenni. "We should be able to go."

"But we're not the right kind of horse people," Diana informed her. "We actually mix with the horses."

"Let me find out," said Patty. "I'm sure she means for all of us to be there."

She didn't.

"You can't possibly think that I'm inviting the hired help," Candy fumed to Patty later that day. Candy was just coming in to the wash area to hand her horse off to Anna-Helga. I was already there, bathing Ivan.

"Really, Patricia," Candy continued, "I'm surprised at you. You've been living in a barn for too long, mixing with the wrong crowd. Maybe it's time you got back to the real world."

"The real world is all over the place," Patty answered her quietly, "and if I've learned one thing from barn life, it's that money doesn't bring class."

"Not something I worry about," Candy retorted, adjusting the twin diamond bracelets sparkling around her wrist. "If you have enough money, you can stick the class." Anna-Helga brightened at this last declaration. She pointed to Candy's horse.

"You vant me stick him?" she asked Candy, then flashed me a beatific smile. I had been teaching her English.

"I hope you come," Candy continued to Patty. "It's going to be very nice. Just don't bring the flotsam."

As one of the flotsam, I felt a burning wave of resentment. "Well, Jetsam," I said to Ivan, "let's get you finished." I rubbed him dry with a towel.

Candy ignored my remark and left. Patty came over to me.

"She's a terrible snob," she said. "It's worse than being a gossip."

"You don't have to go, Patty,"

"I know. But I'm a gossip. I have to know what's going on."

I soon learned that Speed received an invitation, too. Apparently, it was an important annual social event for the horsey set.

"Go with me," he urged. "I'd like you to be my date for the afternoon."

I didn't really want to go. I knew it would be awkward for me. Maybe for him, too.

Flotsam worry about things like that. I told
him I had to think about it.

"Think about it during dinner tonight.
My father's going to be home. I'd like you to
meet him."

Now I had another thing to worry about.

"Wonderful," gushed Lenni when I mentioned it later that afternoon. "It's a good
omen when he wants you to meet the
parent."

"Great," said Diana. "Now you can check
out the true Easton breeding stock."

"Terrific," added Patty. "Martine is famous for her cooking."

I thought that would be something to
look forward to. I was tired of the fried-
chicken routine that we had all fallen into.

I dressed carefully for the occasion. Another raid on Diana's closet and I found a
nice dress. Speed picked me up after work.
A quick peck on the cheek and we were off.

Podge Easton was handsome. He was in
his early sixties and had pleasantly craggy
features and thick silver hair, which gave
him the look of a benign paterfamilias. He
shook my hand with a firm grip.

"So, you ride with Kat," he said. "You board there?"

I swallowed. Here came the rub—the distinction of class, the separation of flotsam from the wealthsam. I wanted to say that yes, I boarded my $60,000 imported equine and rode with Kat every day for $150 a pop and then, when the lesson was over, disappeared down the road in my new Jaguar to spend the rest of the day getting the strain of the lesson massaged away by my personal masseuse.

"I'm a working student," I said. "I live at the farm."

There was a disconcerting pause. Then Podge threw his back and laughed. "So you're not one of the ladies who lunch!" He shook my hand again heartily. "I like that. I like a horsewoman who understands what really goes on at a horse farm. And I guess you know Patricia Crumensko."

"I share an apartment with her."

"Feisty gal, isn't she? Like me! Send her my fondest, fondest regards." I couldn't help but get a glimpse of his gleaming white teeth as he gave me a big smile. Despite

Patty's late husband, someone had done a magnificent job.

Podge poured wine for the three of us and we talked horses.

"So what do you think of Natasha?" he asked.

I was afraid it was a trick question. If I said I hated her, he would be offended. If I said otherwise, I was afraid he would send the rest of her family to the farm. We were already coping with her brother Nero, whose seeming ambition in life was to become a rodeo star.

"She comes from a brilliant line," I said. I knew enough by now to realize that describing a horse as "brilliant" was a nice way to say it was difficult, if not downright impossible.

Podge liked that. Speed beamed.

"Good, I'm glad you like her," he said. "I have a full brother to her and Nero that I want Kat to train and get into competition. Nairobi. He's got the same great lines, a year younger."

I wanted to tell him that Nairobi was better off on a desert, but I refrained. Poor

Diana was going to have another brilliant horse to train.

"So what level is Nero doing?" Speed asked.

"Oh," I said vaguely, "he's moving up. A horse like that just goes right through the levels." I didn't add "as well as the arena ceiling."

Another hit. I was batting a thousand.

Martine invited us to eat. She led us to the dining room, which was the size of my old house. The table was set with gleaming silver and crystal and fine china. I could only wonder at the culinary pleasures that awaited me.

"Trudy, you sit here. Lawrence usually sits there. Mr. Easton, you can open the wine." Ripper sat at the head of the table, albeit one level down, underneath it.

"I made Mr. Easton's favorite dinner tonight," Martine announced.

"Yep." Podge rubbed his hands together. "Southern fried chicken."

It was disconcerting to eat southern fried chicken on Rosenthal china and wash it down with a rare vintage wine, but I was enjoying myself.

We ate dinner while Podge discussed at length Natasha's family tree. To my surprise, she wasn't sprung from a long line of inbred village idiots, but from top-notch European Olympic lines. She was due to foal very soon, and he was anxious to be notified of the blessed event right away. I promised him that much.

"You think we should put Natasha in training?" Podge asked. "She's an untapped talent."

"I think she's doing exactly what she should," I answered truthfully. "A brilliant mare making brilliant foals."

"Hear! Hear!" he said, and poured me more wine. "Great gal you got here, Speed."

Every once in a while, Martine came into the dining room.

"Don't forget to eat your vegetables, Mr. Easton," she helpfully reminded him. He gave me a helpless shrug.

"She's my boss," he said.

We shared more wine and more horse stories. I told them how Natasha used her brilliance to rule her paddock and how athletic Nero was, by mere dint of having been

able to perfect a rear, twist, and buck movement not ordinarily found in the equine
species. Podge laughed at my descriptions
and toasted my health several times. We had
a lot of wine, and I was feeling pretty
healthy by the time we finished eating.

Speed was pleased that I had passed
Podge's scrutiny. He reached over and patted my hand. Ripper squinted up at me.

At eight o'clock, Podge rose from the
table and gave me a little bow.

"I go to bed early," he said apologetically.
"I have a long day tomorrow. But please
stay on as long as you'd like."

That would have been the rest of my life,
but I demurred. He and Ripper left the
room.

Though Speed invited me, I was uncom-
fortable about spending the night. Podge's
bedroom was within the same general
mileage as Speed's, and I felt I was better off
being circumspect, my modesty inhibiting
me from being a good ole farm girl doin'
what comes naturally. Speed reluctantly
drove me home.

"It's settled, then," he said as we flew over

the road. "I am taking you to that brunch. It's a fund-raiser, too, you know. For the United States Equestrian Team. To raise money to send them to the Olympics. My father'll be there, so don't worry about not knowing anyone. And you'll get to meet judges and royalty and lots of other important horse people from all over the world."

I wondered why people who could afford $100,000 horses needed to raise funds to compete them, but I kept quiet. There are equestrian mysteries that are better left unsolved. I worried about the brunch aloud.

"Frankly, I don't know if I'll fit in, Speed," I said. "I am what I am." I realized miserably that I had just sounded like Popeye. It was not exactly sparkling repartee.

"Don't worry so much," said Speed.

We had reached the parking lot by now. The moon hung in a silver crescent and the stars made white sparkles in the sky. He turned my face to his and kissed me for a long time.

"I need you in my life, Judy," he said. "You're not phony, you ground me, and I like that you are what you are."

Chapter Twenty

Ruth was the only one I knew who had clothing grand enough for the Occasion. I called her early in the week.

"You want to borrow my what?" she squealed over the phone. "What could you possibly be doing in a barn that requires designer clothing!"

"A charity brunch, darling," I explained, switching to Ruthese. "It's going to be held at some estate. Your dress will be seen by royalty."

"Forget it!" she shouted. "What you need to do is come home and straighten your life out! You made your point, but now it's time to grow up. I don't know if you're aware, but Marshall's already found himself a lawyer."

"So have I," I said.

"And might I remind you"—she had to remind me, of course—"we're nowhere near the same size."

"I lost twenty-five pounds."

"You don't have money to give to charity."

"No, but the man I'm going to the brunch with owns half of North Carolina."

There was a FedEx package from Ruth the next morning.

Before I knew it, it was the day of the brunch. The three of us, Dolce, Gabbana, and I, were ready to go. Patty drove us. Speed and Podge were going to meet us at Candy's house. Kat would come later.

House didn't quite describe it.

If Speed owned Tara, Candy lived on the Ponderosa.

Her maid led us into an enormous house overflowing with people. Candy was a few paces behind her. She and Patty air-kissed, and our eyes met over Patty's shoulder. I waved a finger as if to say, Hi, remember me, Judy Flotsam? She scowled and took a deep breath, but Patty whisked me off to another room.

Everyone was smoking. Apparently, the jet set had outjetted all the health reports from the last twenty years about cigarette smoke and respiratory problems. We made our way through blue clouds and flocks of Balenciagas and Marc Jacobs and Yves St. Laurents to the overabundant food tables, where Patty filled two plates with canapés. She handed me one.

"Eat and mix," she commanded before disappearing into the crowd.

But Candy was right behind me.

"You do know that this is rather awkward," she began, "but I really wasn't planning on entertaining the help. I'm even surprised that you'd—"

"There you are. I've been waiting for you." Speed made his way to us through the crowd, holding two glasses of wine. He was dazzling in a custom-tailored suit and an elegant pale blue shirt opened at the neck. One glass of wine found a home in my hand.

"Speed?" Candy said, her eyes growing to the size of the wheels of Brie that adorned the food tables.

"Candace, you're such a superb hostess!" He leaned over and kissed her on the cheek. "It's a wonderful party, as usual. You always do things just right. I guess you know Judy?" He put his arm through mine and drew me close. She looked at him and then she looked at me. Then she looked at him again. I could see little cogs and gears spinning rapidly inside her head. I thought I saw a hint of smoke. She pasted a frozen smile across her face.

"Of course I know Judy," she managed to say. "I was just telling her that we really must get together and talk."

"Let's do," I said.

She looked distracted, as though the flywheel in her brain was stalled in the snob center.

"We're going to mix," Speed said to her. He gave her a quick peck on her cheek before leading me away. She stood there touching her cheek.

Speed leaned over and murmured in my ear, "You are stunning."

"Yeah, I think I stunned Candy speechless."

He laughed. "Don't worry about Candy. She'll recuperate."

Patty joined us. She was on her second

plate of food. Her eyes were scanning the room like military radar devices.

I tried to help her out. "Podge is in the corner," I said sotto voce.

"Don't be ridiculous," she said. "I'm just looking for a place to settle down and eat." She paused. "Yep, there's a nice spot in the corner."

She headed rapidly for the designated area, as though the wings of Mercury were attached to her Manolo Blahnik's.

Speed and I mixed. We passed Candy, both her eye and smile still wide and glazed. I tossed my head à la Natasha. Candy looked at my dress, her eyes sweeping it from shoulder to hem. I took another sip of wine, mentally toasted Ruth, then squared my shoulders and snuggled against Speed. Candy looked away, seemingly unconcerned. It was the horse dance at its finest.

There was a sound of yapping. A small pug ran through the living room. I was about to award Candy two points for originality, when a Jack Russell followed closely behind. It sniffed my shoe and I slipped it a canapé just to be on the safe side.

"I see why dogs like you," Speed observed.

We passed from person to person. Just about everyone knew Speed. He introduced me merely as Judy, but I was greeted as Shoody, Choody, Yoody, Julie, Yoolie, and Junie. There were more variations on my name than on themes of Mozart. And I met women with names like Muffy, and Bootsie and Topsy, Mopsie and Cottontail.

Their chatter was revealing. They had summer homes and winter homes and homes in Florida, Aspen, on the Riviera, in Tuscany, and in the villages around Gstaad. Homes for May and June, since July, August, and September were spent in Provence, and November in Innsbruck. It seemed that no one actually lived in North Carolina for more than ten minutes. The names of plastic surgeons were exchanged, nips and tucks were duly examined and admired, and personal trainers were compared. Other conversations revolved around how dreary Liechtenstein was this time of year, the hydrogen peroxide way to lose weight, the problem with getting good help, and horse grooms who were lazy and bossy. Which, of course, would have been me.

"Darlink, haff vee met?" A buxom blond with a thick German accent took my other arm.

Speed introduced us. "Judy, this is Countess Ronzerilla. She breeds Lipizzans."

"Horses for royalty," she said, taking a long drag on the cigarette in her ebony holder. "Are you royalty?"

I allowed as I wasn't exactly, although, in truth, there was more than one occasion when Marshall had referred to me as a royal pain in the ass.

"It doesn't matter." She flapped her hand. "I vill zell my Lipizzans to anyvun, but only if I like zem."

Speed wrenched me away.

"You broke up my first meeting with a real countess," I complained.

"She'll be here all afternoon, at least until the food is gone," he replied, and walked me over to an elderly but elegantly dressed gentleman who had a red sash across his afternoon jacket, weighted with huge gold medals in the shape of various Russian wildlife and shrubbery. He was smoking a thin cigar that had a six-inch ash dangling from the end.

"Prince Dmitri, this is Judy, a very good friend of mine."

Prince Dmitri bowed low, holding his cigar aloft, his eyes riveted on my chest.

"Judy rides dressage," Speed explained.

Princely but bushy white eyebrows shot up like caterpillars on a joyride. He spoke directly to my breasts.

"Achh! Dyoodi, how vondeerfyool! I myself hahv a golt metal in dressage!"

He pointed to one of the medallions on his sash with the cigar. I was afraid he was going to ignite himself, but did indeed have an Olympic gold medal. I realized at once that I was in the presence of someone, like Kat, who was on the level of a dressage deity. I was struck mute.

"You must tell her your secrets," Speed said to him.

"Da, da," he agreed, never lifting his eyes from my bosom. "I vill share **everting** I hahv."

I was sure he would. He took another puff, adding even more ash to the precarious load at the end of the cigar, and gave me a yellowed smile.

Patty came over and grabbed my arm.

"I want to Judy to meet someone special," she remarked to Speed, and took me away.

Holding court in the enormous dining room was a man with cascading black hair and a long black cape over tight black satin pants and a white ruffled shirt. He was also wearing black patent-leather ballet shoes. Patty introduced Gabriel-Rafael Valderone de la Valderone, an imported horse whisperer from Chile, or Colombia, or Argentina, who apparently had the ability to communicate psychically with horses and women with money.

He was surrounded by several surgically tailored women from my barn, who were breathing heavily en masse. He gazed fiercely at each one in turn.

"The horse must carry hees rider weeth joy," he intoned. "His soul must be freee!"

He trilled his **r**'s and rolled his eyes.

"Isn't he marvelous?" Patty breathed into my ear.

I wondered if there were such a thing as a socialite whisperer, for he had them all captivated.

Next to him was Prince Gustaf of Denmark, former vice chairman of the International Olympic Committee, conversing with great animation in German with Kat, who had arrived late. She looked beautiful in an amethyst silk suit and had amethyst and diamond chandeliers hanging from her ears. He was whispering into one of the chandeliers. Kat blushed and nudged him in the ribs and then they laughed aloud.

"They're swapping dirty jokes," Patty whispered to me.

"How do you know that?" I whispered back.

"Oh, that's all Gustaf ever has on his mind."

Podge approached us.

"Mizz Crumensko, will you join me in a drink?"

Patty dropped her eyes and blushed in true southern magnolia fashion. "Why,

Podge Easton, thank you. Ah think Ah will." She abandoned me, and I wandered off to look for Speed. As I reconnoitered the living room, I couldn't avoid making small talk with some of the population. I quickly devised a strategy for this. I first asked them what level they rode, and no matter the answer, I greeted it with a sympathetic face and appropriate noises.

"Tsk, tsk." I sighed. "Yes, it takes a long time to reach the upper levels, doesn't it!" This served the purpose of deterring them from discovering what level I rode, while simultaneously making them feel inadequate. It was a neat way to throw them off their game. Then I would toss in how Kat was just telling me the other day that improvements come in such **dreadfully** small increments.

"You know, horses must carry their riders with joy, their souls must be free," I informed them. This seemed to leave a very good impression, in addition to commanding great respect for my riding knowledge. If nothing else, I was a quick study.

The countess intercepted me again.

"I cahn't recall hahving zeen you at ozzer parties," she said, blowing smoke rings around my head. "Vat vass your name again?"

My ears caught something, but I wasn't sure. Her accent, which I would have previously sworn was German, now had a distinctive Russian flavor. I chalked it up to the wine.

"Judy Van Brunt."

"Ahnd you rite?"

"Of course," I said, and did my preempt routine. "And what level do **you** ride?"

"Grand Prix, of course," she replied. "All my Lipizzans are Grand Prix."

I was tempted to say that the souls of Lipizzans had to feel free, too, but decided to keep this riding gem to myself.

"The finest Lipizzans," the countess continued. "I import zem from zer Piber stud in Austria."

The accent again disturbed me. Parts of her sentences were slipping into French. How European, I thought, figuring it must be because she traveled so much.

"I giff you my card. You vill loff riting

zem. Pairhaps you buy vun." She opened a sparkly little handbag filled with business cards and handed me one. I slipped it into my own handbag.

Someone tapped a glass with a spoon. This was taken up by a few people.

"Ahh!" The countess clapped her gloved hands together. "It's Dominic!"

The crowd parted and a tiny, withered-looking old man in a wheelchair was brought into the room. He looked to be in his late eighties and his head and hands shook in unison.

"Who's that?" I whispered to the countess.

"Our host, of course," she said, "Dominic Valesco. You mahst meet heem. Candace's hoosband."

One again, her accent puzzled me. Now it sounded like Spanish Cockney.

A nurse wheeled Dominic into the center of the room, where he shook and quivered. She reached over and discreetly wiped a drop of spittle from his lips.

"Dominic, this is Jhoody Van Brunt of the royal Van Brunts." The countess took my hand and placed it into Dominic's, where it was thoroughly shaken. I was amused that the countess had given me a pedigree.

"Welgumtamahmm," Dominic said.

"He says welcome to his home." Apparently, the countess also spoke fluent mumble.

"Thank you," I said. "It's a lovely home."

"Duhdjouead?" he asked. "Isdefoogood?"

"Yes, darlink, der food is vunderful," the countess replied.

His questions were appropriate, and apparently he was sharply alert, despite his physical problems.

"It's a wonderful party," I said.

He nodded. Or at least I think he nodded. Maybe his whole body nodded, but I took it as an affirmative.

"Mungry," he said, "niwanchampagne."

Someone pressed a shrimp into his hand. He ate it happily and seemingly forgot all about the last part of his request. When the shrimp was gone, he lifted a quaking hand and summoned more. This amused him for several minutes, until the little group around him suddenly departed with great haste. In a minute, I knew why. He had enveloped himself in a fog of flatulence. I tried to keep just slightly ahead of the drifting air. It was clearly time to move on.

I found myself in the living room again.

"Darleeng." It was the countess again. "I muzz read you."

"Read me? What do you mean?"

"Tea leafs."

This was beyond my powers of comprehension, so I squeezed her hand and thanked her profusely before sidling away. I finally found Speed in the music room, his arm being held in a death grip by Candy. They were chatting with a group of people around an enormous grand piano, where someone was sitting and playing "Hey Jude." I thought the music was a good omen. Candy tightened her fingers and jaw muscles when she saw me approach.

Candy and Dominic Valesco, I found myself musing. Early Autumn and Late Winter. How happy could she be? I almost felt a twinge of compassion. Candy was trapped in a marriage with a physically failing and very demanding elderly mate. I guessed she was proving the old adage that when you marry for money, you earn every cent. I looked over at Dominic, who was croaking "Vhrsmywife? Vhrsmywife?" like some exotic bird while being rolled into the music room to be near his heart's desire. He held out a shaking hand to her. She reluctantly dropped away from Speed and, clasping her husband's brown-mottled hand, stood next to his chair to resume the role of devoted helpmate. I looked her right in the eye, then tilted my head and gave her my most sympathetic look before slipping my arm through Speed's and snuggling against him.

"Ah, here's my girl," Speed said, giving me a peck on the cheek. "I hope you're having a good time."

"I hope so, too, darling," Candy said through clenched teeth. "We wouldn't want her to go home unhappy."

"I'm very happy." I gave her a dazzling smile. "And thank you, I'm having a wonderful time."

Chapter Twenty-one

The piano player switched to "As Time Goes By" and there was a general drift of brunchees to the front door. The maid and another servant distributed enough furs to warm up a colony of Eskimos, chauffeured cars appeared out of nowhere, kisses flew through the air at various targets, promises were made to meet in Paris, and the party was finally over. Patty and I left the house and stood chatting together on the huge rolling front lawn while I waited for Speed to disentangle himself from the countess. It was my first breath of clean air in four and a half hours.

"Are you going to spend the rest of the day with Podge?" I asked Patty. Speed had already invited me home.

"No, of course not, dear." She shook her head, then gave me a tragic look. "A little socializing at a party is okay, but don't forget, I'm still in mourning."

I had forgotten. "I'm so sorry," I said, now embarrassed by my lack of sensitivity.

She grasped my hand and I gave her a quick hug.

Speed appeared with the countess still attached to his arm.

"You mahst promise to let me reet you," she said in a combination Australian/ Brazilian accent before air-kissing me goodbye and ducking into a waiting Lincoln Continental. "I juzz know your prefious lifes vill hahf a lot to refeal aboot you."

I looked at Speed; he stuck his tongue out behind her back.

"You can read us both," Patty said, closing the countess into her car. "I'll give you a call."

"Prima!" the countess exclaimed, waving her cigarette holder out the window as her car pulled away. "Now don't forget!"

Speed took me by the arm. "Are you ready?" he asked. Patty and I gave each other a couple of air kisses and I left.

"What kind of reading does the countess

do?" I asked Speed as we whizzed along the road to his house.

"She reads past lives. She channels them or something from tea leaves." Speed laughed at the thought.

"What happens if I don't have a past life?" I asked.

"Don't worry, the countess will arrange one for you."

"I guess you don't believe that she can do it?"

"Well, she may read people—but whether it's a message from their past, or she's picking up the satellite channels, I'm not so sure. Still, I think there's a lot to the universe that we don't know."

"Has she ever done you?" I asked.

"I like to keep my lives, present and past, private."

And to that end, we sneaked into his house, if one can discreetly sneak into a twenty-two-room mansion crawling with servants. But he wasn't totally successful. Ripper was right behind us as we went to his bedroom.

"Does he have to be with us?" I asked Speed.

"Would you rather he howl outside the bedroom door?"

Ripper shot me a triumphant half sneer as he trotted in.

I divested myself of both Dolce and Gabbana and then wrapped up in the quilt on Speed's bed. His threw his clothes on top of mine and followed me into the quilt. Ripper sat by the side of the bed with a lecherous stare.

"Can't you make him sit somewhere else?" I complained. After all, it was an enormous bedroom. "Maybe he can look out the window, like from your closet?"

"Ripper, go," Speed commanded.

Ripper disappeared under the bed. I wasn't so sure that this afforded us much more privacy.

But Speed soon made me forget about my objections. Fortified by brunch, we spent a romantic and energetic rest of the day. He was a perfect lover, gentle, considerate, and urgent. On second thought, a really perfect lover would have turned into a box of chocolates with ganache centers every time we finished, but he was close to perfect. We finally fell asleep, arms and legs entwined.

It was late in the evening when I awakened and sat up. Speed was sitting near the window.

"I didn't want to wake you," he said. "Are you hungry?"

I sat in the kitchen, wrapped in his robe, and watched him prepare scrambled eggs. He handled the combination of stove and eggs with ease; he even snipped a few chives into the egg mixture. We shared the scrambled eggs; Ripper had his two sunny-side up.

"I have something for you." Speed took a velvet box from his robe and handed it to me.

I put my fork down and opened the box. Inside was a pair of gold moon earrings with tiny diamond stars hanging from them.

"I hope they will remind you of me," he said. "They'll put the power of the universe at your beck and call."

Then he helped me put them in my ear-lobes. I looked at my reflection in my fork. They were beautiful. I had never owned celestial bodies before.

"I don't know what to say," I told him.

Speed wrapped his hands around mine. "I just want to move us to the next level."

How many times I'd wished Kat had said that! It seemed that levels were becoming a theme in my life. But the thought of going to the next level with Speed scared me.

"I do enjoy being with you," I said. "And I don't know what level we're at, but I kind of like where we are."

"Don't be afraid." He leaned toward me. "Let me into your world, Judy."

I fingered the earrings. Suddenly, it seemed like a huge responsibility to have the power of the universe hanging around my ears. I liked Speed. I loved being with him. He was considerate, he made good scrambled eggs, he had an amazing refractory time, and the fact that he owned thirty or so fabulous horses didn't hurt, either, but I wasn't sure what I wanted from our relationship. After all, I was still disentangling myself from Marshall and not above licking a wound now and then when I thought about it.

It was midnight. He stood up, took my hand, and led me back to bed. Ripper followed. I snuggled against Speed under the quilt as he wrapped his arms around me. I lay there thinking how lucky I was and that I should just enjoy what I had and forget about what was to come. Or what might never come. I touched the earrings again. I had never asked for the moon, and here someone wonderful wanted to hand it to me—in fact, had just handed me two gold ones. Was it like looking a gift horse in the mouth? Would that come next? What was wrong with me anyway?

Something awakened us early in the morning. It was Ripper, scratching at the door to go out. Speed got up while I rolled over, languid and content. He opened the door and Ripper sashayed out. Speed returned and stood next to the bed, smiling down at me.

We still had some time before I had to begin my workday. It was a great opportunity to make love again.

"I have to go," I finally said, reaching over for my clothes, Ruth's clothes, actually, and found Ripper had spent the night neatly altering the hem, the zipper, and one shoulder. Of course, I thought ruefully, a Jack named **Ripper.**

"Ruth is going to kill me," I moaned, holding the dress up.

"Don't worry, I'll replace it." Speed nibbled on my ear. "You can borrow a pair of sweats to go home."

His sweats were too long and had to be rolled up around my ankles and wrists, creating big bulky spare tires. I slipped on my strappy party shoes.

We said nothing more about the earrings, although I touched them over and over. They made me feel beautiful, but I worried about what kind of commitment Speed might expect from me. He was quiet for the whole drive back. I kissed him good-bye and raced for the apartment.

Upstairs, I found Patty standing in the

hallway in her pink chenille robe and bunny slippers.

She looked at my outfit, then at the clock at the kitchen wall, and then at me.

"You were out all night," she commented, her eyebrows wiggling up and down like semaphores.

"Yeah," I said, hurriedly slipping out of the sweats and into jeans and a sweater.

She followed me into the kitchen, where I was making myself a quick cup of coffee. Her bunny slippers made squeaky sounds when she walked.

"I worry about you," she said. "You're getting in way over your head."

Since we were on the subject of my head, I showed her the earrings.

"They're lovely," she admitted, "but you better be careful. There're things I've heard about Speed. . . ."

"Like what, Patty?" I turned and faced her. "Tell me already. You're always so vague."

She grew quiet, then took a deep breath.

"Well, like—odd things at his farm. Lights in the back fields that can be seen late at night from the road. People going there at midnight. Secret meetings. But I really shouldn't be talking about things I know nothing about."

I stopped in my tracks. "Oh Patty, you're not going to turn into Maria Ouspenskaya and hand me a garland of wolfsbane, are you?"

She pursed her lips.

"I was with him last night at midnight," I continued, a bit heated, "and he didn't grow hair on his hands. He made scrambled eggs."

She opened the refrigerator and dug around inside.

"Is that why you won't spend time with Podge?" I asked. "Because of silly rumors?"

She straightened up, an egg in each hand. "It has nothing to do with Podge. You know I'm still in mourning."

Something occurred to me.

"How long have you been a widow?" I asked.

"Twelve years."

"**Twelve** years? No one is in mourning for twelve years!"

"I am. After Ben died, I closed up our home here and went to our house in Liechtenstein. I stayed for five years. Met Kat at a party there. And then she found me Sam. But I will never get over Ben." Her eyes welled with tears at the memory.

"So you and Sam have been living here for—"

"Almost seven years. Sam and I were the first to live here."

"Jesus! Patty! Don't you think it's time you started getting on with the rest of your life?"

"It's too late for me." She cracked the eggs into a pan. I wondered why all my important conversations were being held over scrambled eggs.

"Don't be ridiculous." I said. "You're only in your fifties. Don't you want a little romance in your life again?"

"Honey, my ovaries are now producing hard-boiled eggs, my ta-tas are touching the floor. I don't know if I want the responsibility of shaving my upper legs again. I'm balding. I have more hair growing on my face than a sheepdog. And I leak when I walk."

"It can all be fixed with duct tape," I said.

"No, I still consider myself Ben's widow. I realized it at the brunch. Every time Podge smiled, I looked at his bridgework and thought of Ben."

"Maybe you could think of his teeth as little white monuments to Ben," I said.

She eyed the clock. "And maybe you should get to work," she replied.

Chapter Twenty-two

Gail made an announcement as soon as I started work. We would be doing foal watch that night. I had never heard that term before.

Apparently, mares have a predilection for foaling under the cover of night in order to protect their babies from predators. And those of us assigned to midwifery have the unique privilege of sitting up every night, watching covertly, in order not to disturb the mare's delicate emotional state. To ensure our secrecy, each mare stall was outfitted with a small camera. In addition, two security monitors were installed in Kat's office. Our other amenities included a lumpy cot that Kat had thoughtfully provided and the ubiquitous thermos of coffee. Gail and I would be on duty for three nights, swinging shifts with Gertrude and Anna-Helga. The terriers, of course, were a given.

I could hardly believe it. It was just as Speed had warned me: Kat had finally managed to turn my life into a twenty-four hour, seven-day-a-week job. After only a week on this schedule, the only universe I wanted to conquer was the one belonging to the god Morpheus.

Then foals began dropping like overripe apples. One, sometimes two per night, and Gail and I had our hands full. We dutifully sat up every night, all night, in Kat's office, nursing cups of bad coffee and watching the monitors. The terriers watched me. They had long memories and still had not forgiven me for the day I locked them in Kat's office. To ensure I would not repeat the offense, one terrier napped while the other sat up to keep an eye on me. Then they switched places. After six nights of watching them watch me, I was developing full-blown paranoia. I saw terriers everywhere: under the cot, peeping out of light fixtures, peering in through the windows. I saw their reflections in my coffee, their outlines in the patterns of the ceiling tile; I knew they were tracking me wherever I went, quickly turning invisible when I spun around. Or maybe I dreamt them. After all, I had started dozing off in the middle of most of my chores, standing upright, perfectly balanced on my pitchfork.

And no one else saw them but me.

"Are they in there?" I would make Patty check the shower stall before I showered in the morning.

"Of course not." She would give me a puzzled look. "Who were you expecting?"

But I knew they were always watching me. Somehow, they were always watching me.

"Yeah," Diana said with a sympathetic look when I complained to her about the hours I was putting in. "That's the downside of working in the mare barn during foaling season."

I asked her what the upside was. She didn't know.

I also learned that mares can hold off foaling if they feel uneasy. For that reason, too, everything was done to keep the mares' confidence level up. They were bedded knee-deep in straw and given alfalfa—the filet mignon of hay—along with honey-laced bran mashes generously dotted with chunks of apple and carrot. Tails were shampooed and wrapped out of the way, udders were washed daily, backs were massaged in scented liniments, and soft music played over the speaker system. The mare barn had turned into Canyon Ranch Spa.

All of the foal deliveries were handled by Gail and me. Even though Gertrude and one of the Swedish girls would sometimes do a rare swing shift, if there was any indication of foaling, Gail and I were immediately summoned. The foals were just too expensive to be left to language deficiencies.

Gail was the expert, having done foal deliveries for years, and to my relief, the mares were quite cooperative. They signaled their impending labor with textbook accuracy, giving us plenty of time to get to the barn and bear quiet witness to an efficient foaling. Gail's job was to wipe the newborn down with a big soft towel, put iodine on the umbilical cord, and do the few other things to ensure the delivery had gone well. My job was to hand Gail equipment and not get on anyone's nerves. If there was a problem, we had the name of Dr. Peter Bilouge, a veterinarian who was part horse obstetrician, part pediatrician. Gail had printed his name and phone number in big letters and taped it above the office monitors, as well as in the mare barn.

Dr. Bilouge always came the morning after a foaling to make sure the mare hadn't retained anything abnormal and to give the foal its first shots and a general checkup. He was a handsome man in his mid-fifties, but he never displayed much of a personality. Though he handled the mares and their babies with an ease that kept them calm, he never smiled or had much to say, except for a few medically oriented sentences. The occasional problem he had with the mares was taken care of with great dispatch but no emotion. His seemingly antisocial manner struck me when Rio's foal, born with severely defective tendons, was brusquely diagnosed right away as "PUDS."

"PUDS?" I repeated. I had spent numerous nights studying foaling books and had not run across the term.

"Pushing up daisies syndrome," he said in his flat voice. "That's what I call it, when the foal has no chance for a normal life. This one's never going to walk. Notify Kat that I will put him down later this afternoon."

Dr. Bilouge said this without a hint of emotion. He nodded a curt good morning and left me to stand weeping over the poor creature and hating the vet for his callousness.

But after watching him handle the animals with more than ample skill, I knew that he was just doing what he was paid to do: treat Kat's mares and foals with the most superior medical knowledge available. Socializing just wasn't on his list of priorities.

"Too bad you're still in mourning," I said to Patty. "He's really not a bad guy, and he's kind of attractive. Just very focused."

She snickered. "Dr. Bulge?"

"Bilouge," I corrected her.

"Bulge," she corrected me.

Next time Dr. Bilouge was at the farm, I surreptitiously eyed him over. His male accoutrements were discreetly clothed and not in any way obvious. Puzzled, I brought it up that evening at our usual News and Bruises time after dinner. Lenni had just exhibited a smashingly swollen elbow, but I was able to one-up her by displaying a neat pair of tiny purple hoofprints that were embossed on my stomach from a frisky foal.

"So," I asked after the hoofprints were duly admired by all, "what's the story with Dr. Bilouge?"

The three women looked at one another meaningfully. Jillian was sitting with us, and it was apparent she was the reason for the coded looks.

"Dr. Bulge," Lenni corrected me.

"Bilouge," I insisted.

"Bulge," said Diana.

"Bilouge."

"Bulge," they all chorused.

It will be all too obvious, they said. I only need be observant.

I tried to be. I managed to position myself several times where I had full view of the area of concern, but to no avail. There was nothing but the neat, flat line of his fly. I thought perhaps that was it: that Dr.

Bilouge might have no accoutrements at all; that maybe by some grave omission of nature, he was a eunuch.

A week passed. Mares foaled. Dr. Bilouge still remained a mystery.

Now the barn looked like a maternity ward. Dainty foal heads peered over stall doors, greeting us every morning with big soft chocolate brown eyes. High-pitched foal squeals filled the air.

Well, I decided, **that** was the upside of working in the broodmare barn during foaling season.

A few more days passed, and Natasha was the last holdout.

"She's holding out for spite," I moaned to Patty one morning. I had gone back to the apartment to change clothes and grab a quick shower with the terriers before restarting the day. "She's spiteful. She's not broke to ride Why would they even want to keep her?"

Patty laughed. "Because, unlike us, her value lies in the babies she produces. Last year's foal brought forty-five thousand dollars, which Kat split with Speed. Shit, I would have sold my daughter if I'd known she would bring that kind of money."

"Well, I don't care if Natasha's foal is the next reincarnation of the Dalai Lama," I said. "I can't take another night. I'm losing my mind."

Even Patty was starting to look suspiciously furry. I left the apartment.

Morning was the time to bring each mare and foal combination out to the field for the day. I would lead the mare, who usually spun in frantic circles if she lost sight of her baby, while Gail brought the foal. She had already taught them all to accept foal halters on their tiny faces, and she walked them with one arm around their chest and one arm around their butt. The foal usually bucked and reared under this restraint, but this was one time that Gail's enormous bulk came in handy.

And Natasha was always last.

"You know," I said to her as I led her out, "it would be a lot easier to have your baby and let it follow, rather than you schlepping it all over the place."

She only pinned her ears at me in her

usual sour way and walked very slowly. If a horse could wear curlers in her hair, a tattered robe, and pom-pom scuffs, it would have looked like Natasha.

Every evening, Gail and I and the terriers spent what was hopefully to be the last night in Kat's office. I watched the monitor, bleary-eyed, while Gail slept on the cot, her snores rumbling like a badly tuned tractor. As usual, I was hallucinating terriers and sipping bad coffee. I thought about Speed and Marshall and the small ironies in my life that had brown spots and black noses and four legs.

The snoring stopped and Gail sat up.

"What time is it?" she asked.

"Three A.M."

"Anything yet?"

I rubbed terriers from my eyes and glanced at the screen for the hundredth time that hour. Natasha was still calmly vacuuming the remains of her evening hay.

"No."

Gail poured herself some coffee.

"We really have to get another thermos for this place that we use only for coffee,"

she said. "I think we're poisoning ourselves."

We stared at the screen some more.

"So what's with Dr. Bilouge?" I asked.

"Bulge," she said.

"Bilouge."

"Bulge," she snorted. "You'll see. I don't
want to ruin the surprise."

We went back to watching the screen.
Natasha had finally decided to heed my advice. She began pawing the ground in her
stall. Before long, she had broken into a
sweat, pacing around for a few minutes before lying down. Then she got to her feet
and pawed again.

"This is it!" Gail crowed.

Even I, inexperienced as I was, recognized
the signs of an impending delivery.

The terriers led the way to the barn and
we all tiptoed in. I knew that Natasha
would not make anything easy for us. Gail
grabbed the foaling kit from the back of the
barn and we sat down quietly on the barn
floor, out of Natasha's sight, and waited.

She strained and grunted. Gail stood up
and peeked.

"I see the head and feet," she whispered.

Foals dive into the world feetfirst, their little muzzles tucked between their front legs. The foal was in position. We waited some more. Natasha stood up and began nibbling at her hay, unconcerned that her foal was dangling from her back half, semiborn. We still waited. Natasha finally stopped eating and pawed the ground again before throwing herself down. Gail gave me the signal and we moved quietly into position outside Natasha's stall.

But there was something wrong. There was blood in the sac surrounding the foal. It was nearly full born, but it was in trouble. Gail quickly opened the stall door and we knelt beside Natasha. I spoke softly to the laboring mare while Gail efficiently pulled the foal from her body. She broke the membranes and began vigorously rubbing its face. It wasn't breathing. She put her mouth to the small muzzle and puffed gently into its nostrils while I massaged its chest, pushing the tiny ribs up and down.

"Call Dr. Bulge," Gail ordered between puffs.

I dialed the cell phone, left an emergency call with his service, then dropped to my knees to help Gail.

It was a beautiful dark brown filly, strikingly marked with four white socks and a white blaze. She lay on the straw while Gail and I desperately worked over her. Natasha watched us, giving us an occasional worried nicker, her face filled with maternal concern.

Dr. Bilouge came within minutes and silently took over the work on the limp body. He gave her adrenaline, and, as was his style, said little to us, but fought desperately to save the filly. Finally, after examining her thoroughly, he looked up at us.

"PUDS," he said, and pronounced her dead.

The placenta had separated prematurely and there had been a hemorrhage into the membranes. It wasn't common, but it wasn't that rare, either. We called Kat, who came and looked her over with tears in her eyes, then instructed us to take her into a back field with the tractor and bury her first thing in the morning.

But Natasha had other plans for her baby. She stood between us and the stall door, her ears pinned, hind leg ready for firing. Every time we approached the foal, Natasha spun around in her stall and menaced us.

Gail decided there was nothing to do but leave the baby in the stall with Natasha until the mare settled a bit. Dr. Bilouge left some tranquilizers and Gail administered them. Later that afternoon, we were able to carry the little body away.

But Natasha refused to eat. She nickered over the stall door, calling to the foals as they passed by with their dams. She was in mourning, and I actually felt sorry for her.

I spoke admiringly to Patty about the way Dr. Bilouge had worked on the filly.

"He doesn't say much," I said to Patty, "but he's very keen. I think he's just painfully shy—probably that's why he's remained single. Maybe we should invite him up for dinner or something."

She jumped as though I had touched her with a cattle prod.

"Don't even think of it!" she exclaimed. "There've been attempts on his singlehood.

He's been engaged at least five or six times that I know of."

So Dr. Bilouge was a serial fiancé! There had to be a fatal flaw, and I wondered if it was because he was so emotionless with people.

Another week passed. All foals were on the ground and we were now rebreeding the mares. They were in their "foal heats," and this was the best time to breed a mare for the following year.

Unfortunately, the terriers thought it was an opportune time for them to become amorous, too. They were amorous all over the farm.

"They're disgusting," I remarked to Lenni.

"You know what?" she said with irritation. "They and you are the only ones getting it on a regular basis, so shut up."

Me and the terriers and the mares and stallions.

And Dr. Bilouge was the one who handled the stallions during the actual breeding.

My job was to get the mare ready for breeding while Gail held the foal. With her tail shampooed and wrapped up, her hindquarters washed, the mare was ready for her special date. She was put in a "stock," a special restraining stall in the breeding shed, while Dr. Bilouge brought the stallion in. It was the first time I had witnessed a breeding. The stallion trumpeted, pranced, reared, and in general let the mare know that he was feeling romantic. I watched as Dr. Bilouge walked the stallion up to the mare. The stallion was markedly aroused, and it was all too apparent that Dr. Bilouge was also. Embarrassed, I tried to avert my gaze. Dr. Bilouge was metamorphosing right before my eyes.

The mare nickered. The stallion screamed. Dr. Bulge groaned softly.

"Oooohhh," he said, "oooohhh, yeah, get her, ooooh."

The stallion thrust rhythmically, and I thought I detected a slight but duplicate movement from Dr. Bulge's hips.

"Mmmmmah, yea, go, boy, go," he whispered heatedly.

He kept it up for the duration, both physically and vocally. We knew it was over for both stallion and vet when we heard a loud grunt, though I wasn't sure of the source. Gail's face was flushed as she studied fascinating patterns in the sawdust on the floor. There was a moment of silence. Then Dr. Bulge sighed deeply and lighted a cigarette before leading the stallion away.

I looked at Gail. She nodded.

"Yep" was all she said.

"Eeeuuww," I said.

The next breeding, the following morning, went the same way.

The stallion snorted, Dr. Bulge moaned and breathed heavily. It was disconcerting to witness such vicarious pleasure.

"I don't know why Kat doesn't get another vet," I complained to Gail afterward. "He makes my skin crawl."

"He's the best vet around." She shrugged. "He's a good surgeon and a fast thinker. He's saved a lot of foals and mares in trouble."

"I don't know why Kat doesn't get another vet," I repeated to the women around the dinner table. We had been talking in euphemisms, due to Jillian taking one of her rare meals with us.

"He's a good vet" was the general consensus. "And he's really harmless."

"I hate him," I said.

And for the remaining weeks of breeding, Dr. Bulge got his year's worth of sexual release. He got his hair restyled. He dropped a few pounds and had a spring to his step. He whistled. He looked revitalized. But he was still abrupt and difficult to talk to, and I hated him even more.

"So, how's it going with Dr. Bilouge?" Lenni asked me.

"Bulge," I corrected her.

And Natasha continued to grieve. She barely grazed when she was taken out to the field, spending her time instead looking longingly at the foals that stood faithfully next to their dams. She was losing condition. She hardly bothered to make faces at me anymore. We wondered whether it was kinder to send her back to Speed and away from the maternity crowd.

Then a phone call came early one morning from Dr. Bulge. A mare had died the night before while giving birth to a frail colt. Dr. Bulge had worked all night keeping the foal alive, and now it needed to be mothered. Would Kat allow him to bring it over for Natasha? It was an Appaloosa colt—white, with black spots. We all looked at Natasha, who was standing in the field, brokenhearted.

"Absolutely not," Kat snapped. "She's a prize mare."

But Dr. Bulge called back again and again. Finally, he paid Kat a visit. He voice rang with never-before-seen emotion. His passion about the match surprised me. Finally, he was able to convince Kat that it would help Natasha's emotional and physical health. A time was set. Dr. Bulge gave Natasha some medication to produce milk again.

Later that day, a tiny spotted creature was carried off the horse trailer to Natasha. She sniffed it. He sniffed her. She squealed, insulted that this creature had been brought to her. Dr. Bulge gently held the foal upright and spoke softly to Natasha, explaining the colt's predicament. She picked up her hind leg threateningly, but Dr. Bulge persevered. He sat patiently with the foal draped across his knee while Natasha sniffed it again. He spoke to the mare and foal, caressing them both, moving them closer and closer to each other. He was there for nearly three hours. Finally, Natasha stopped squealing and just stared thoughtfully as Dr. Bulge closed the gap between the two animals in careful, gradual increments. The foal touched Natasha's flank and gave her a cautious lick. She nickered to it. Dr. Bulge nudged him even closer to Natasha's udder. She looked puzzled, then sighed happily as the foal took a few tentative sips. Natasha had a baby. No matter that she was a prize imported Warmblood with impeccable blood lines that stretched back to the Crusades, and that her adopted son sported tasteless loud black spots all over his white body. He was her baby now. Dr. Bulge stood up and looked away, surreptitiously wiping a few tears from his eyes.

Natasha and the colt both thrived, and there was much gratitude expressed all around to Dr. Bulge. Despite his unusual behavior in the breeding shed, I felt a new respect for him. He had redeemed himself to me and proved to all of us at the farm, beyond the shadow of a doubt, that he had strong feelings in his heart as well as in his pants.

Chapter Twenty-three

Foaling season was finally over, but it didn't exactly mean that we had free time on our hands. We had tack cleaning.

Tack cleaning is a necessary ritual at barns. Saddles are lined up as if they're at a car wash, dismantled of girths and stirrups, then rubbed with saddle soap and buffed to a sheen. Bridles are reduced to a pile of straps, cleaned diligently and then reassembled. The purpose is to remove damaging horse perspiration and dirt from the leather and to fill in those few precious moments of free time that grooms may be privy to. But it was an activity that was done sitting down, so I didn't mind it.

The day was cold and rainy and the mares and foals were left in their stalls for a quiet day of sleeping in. I fervently wished that I could enjoy such luxury and catch up on a month's worth of sleep deprivation, but Gail had planned an ambitious afternoon of cleaning every piece of leather on the farm.

I followed Gail to Kat's personal tack room in the back of the competition barn. The dampness had permeated even this little room, so she turned on the electric heater before handing out sponges and minibuckets of warm water for each of us to use. Anna-Helen, Anna-Sofie, and Anna-Helga were already seated on folding stools, chatting away happily in Swedish. Within a few minutes, the barn cats had rolled themselves into furry oblivion inside a stack of saddle pads, and the terriers, in a rare state of inactivity, sat together, swaying sleepily and trying not to succumb to the warmth of the heater, lest they miss a snack. I sat myself on the far side of the circle, away from them, always distrustful of their motives for sitting with us.

The tack room bespoke of Kat's penchant for order and tidiness, with its neatly stacked shelves and everything wrapped in plastic and labeled. Even we five grooms sat in a perfectly round circle, labeled along with the equipment, by dint of wearing our farm jackets with our names embroidered over our breasts.

Gail, though abrasive most of the time, was proving to be an amusing companion. Like the curator of a museum of people's lives, she relished stories concerning everyone around her. She generally kept herself on the outside of farm life, but she loved collecting anecdotes and gossip about the barn population, polishing them and storing them, to revisit and recount at will. She was a walking compendium of intimate information, and, of course, the Swedish girls and I were all ears.

Now she rested on her elbows while soaping up a saddle, warming her gossip muscles with some brief calisthenics about Kat's daughter, Bianca, from whom Kat had been estranged. They had argued over the sale of a horse that Bianca wanted to ride in competition.

"But you know Kat," Gail nodded knowingly, "money is thicker than blood."

"Ja, Kat, money," the Swedish girls concurred.

"Did her daughter ever compete after that?" I asked.

"Yep. She's competing. Doing good, too, with a horse named Nordik."

"Ja, Nordik, gut." The Swedish girls approved.

Gail moved on to Patty, filling in the blanks about Patty that I hadn't known. She was born to wealth, had married Dr. Benedicht Crumensko, a titled European oral surgeon, who died unexpectedly at a young age when he fell backward off a dental chair while self-administering a playful snoot of nitrous oxide.

Gail was hitting her stride now. She moved on to Candy Valesco. Born in the slums of Raleigh, she had opened an antique shop and, after several years, crowned her antique collection with her marriage to aged Brazilian industrialist Dominic Valesco.

"So she did some crossing over the manure pile herself," I mused.

"Yeah." Gail laughed. "She thinks she's one of the hootie palooties, but she is really just one of us slobs."

I secretly resented this last remark, as I felt I had little in common with Gail, except for our jobs at the farm. I was aware that the boarders as well as the other workers usually avoided Gail, with her huge girth and scruffy looks, her too-loud voice and booming, often inappropriate laugh. And I felt a little bit ashamed that I, too, sometimes shared their prejudices. I hadn't exactly considered myself a "hootie palooty," but I wasn't Gail material, either. Yet it was a pleasant afternoon. The room was comfortingly warm. The cats were purring, the electric heater glowed, and the terriers, finally falling victims to the warmth, collapsed into snoring comas. Anna-Helga hummed softly to herself in a sweet, high voice while the other two Swedes chatted softly. I liked the idea of sitting in a room within a barn within a farm, far away from Marshall, far away from problems, far away from all the things I wanted to get far away from. I fingered the moon and star earrings and smiled to myself. Gail stood up and poured hot chocolate from the barn thermos for everyone. It tasted funny, but I didn't care. I stretched out my legs and yawned. It was the closest I had come to complete peace in years.

Until there was a knock at the door.

It was Diana.

"Judy." She beckoned. "Kat wants you."

I threw on my jacket. The terriers leapt to their feet and rushed to either side of me, flanking me like two armed guards, as Diana led me to Kat's office. Kat greeted me with a smile and a puff of smoke from her pipe.

"Zhoody," she said, "I am goink to put you in competition."

"You mean a horse show?"

"Ja, ja," she said. "I haff too many horses dot neet showink. I am goink to Chermany in vun mont und Diana vill show Merkury und new horse I send von Chermany und you vill show Nero und Nairobi. Diana vill verk mit you."

"Nero!" I exclaimed. "And Nairobi!" I had seen Nero turn a perfectly ordinary training session into a ride worthy of Evil Knievel. And Nairobi was barely saddle-broken. "But they're both so difficult!"

Kat took another puff and blew a smoke ring past my ear.

"What about the Annas?" I asked. "Why can't they show those horses?"

"Dey are showink younk horses in younk horse clesses."

"Gertrude? She must be ready to show?" I said in desperation.

"She ist der groom. Zumvun must be der groom."

"But I have no idea what I'm doing," I protested, then added feebly, "I'm a crappy rider, and—I don't even have a level."

"Ja, ja, I know," said Kat. I wasn't sure which of my previous statements she was agreeing with. "Und you vill pay for all expenses," she added. "Uff course."

Uff course. Money is thicker than employees.

We left her office and I turned to Diana. "I'm fucked."

"Yeah," said Diana, "that's how I understood it. We've got about six weeks to get you competent. We're going to have to do some heavy-duty training to pull this out of the hat."

She was as good as her word.

My day off was quickly reduced again to no day off. And now my lessons with Diana incorporated morning lunge lessons.

A lunge lesson is a German riding torture that involves attaching the horse by his bridle to something that resembles a thirty-foot dog leash. The horse is then asked to trot or canter in a big circle around the person who stands in the center and holds the line. The rider, or victim, as it were, sits atop the horse, without benefit of stirrups or reins, or sometimes saddle, and rides around and around on the circle, until she achieves either a state of perfect physical balance with the horse or dizziness, whichever comes first. I was told it could take years for me to achieve the former.

Since Ivan was too ornery to be trusted on the lunge line, we used Stanley, an "easy-listening music" kind of horse, sort of a James Taylor in chestnut. Stanley usually closed his eyes and put himself on automatic pilot while cantering the circle, and Diana would have me hold my arms out to the side or up over my head in an effort to further challenge my balance. After several sessions, I was able to execute these useless movements with ease.

"In Germany, a working student is put through lunge-line lessons for sometimes three years before being allowed to ride solo," Diana declared one afternoon as we worked.

"Well," I replied, "that accounts for that inimitable touch of sadism so often found in the German sense of humor." I had been riding the circle for close to an hour by then and was getting wedgies from the saddle. My lower body had lost all sensation in the first half hour, and I was afraid to look down past my waist, lest my legs had disappeared entirely.

When Diana didn't have time for me, Gertrude took over. The tone of the lessons was entirely different with her. Gertrude made Stanley gallop madly on the circle while instructing me to ride facing sideways or completely backward. Sometimes she had me close my eyes, which inadvertently triggered the terror-shriek reflex from my mouth. All the while, Gertrude would be screeching at me in a language that bore no resemblance to any mother tongue on earth.

"Schulters beck Zurück und bleiben Sie die Hände ruhig!"

It was harder to understand her than to execute the impossible gymnastics she proposed, especially when their variations included having me touch my nose to Stanley's mane while kneeling on the saddle. It occurred to me more than once that Gertrude had a cruel streak and maybe I was ready to audition for Barnum and Bailey. When I was thoroughly exhausted, I was excused to finish my remaining barn chores.

And that was just my morning schedule.

I had no time anymore for lunch and had taken to chewing on strands of straw to break my hunger. My afternoon barn work was interrupted as well—by a second lesson. This was usually taught by Kat while I rode Ivan. I was to learn the Olympic dressage movements, all thirty-six of them, in one month. Since Ivan had been Kat's first Olympic horse, he made sure that I was reminded of his former status on a daily basis. If one muscle of mine twitched with fatigue, Ivan was ready to send me crashing to the arena floor. Thus, I rode and fell with alarming regularity. But over the course of the month, the novelty finally wore off for Ivan and my last fall found him standing over me like that oil painting of the Old West, **The End of the Trail.** He was looking down at my prostrate form with a look that could be interpreted as compassion, which inspired Kat to have Ivan further humiliate me by being just the horse to introduce me to the show ring.

"Yep, he's an old pro. He can show you the ropes," Diana reassured me when I told her, but she had a word of caution. "The only thing he's not crazy about is rain."

And so life was changing for me. My civilian days were over; it was all for glory now. I would be releasing the athlete in me. I would also be too tired ever to eat a formal meal again, as I now fell asleep before dinner. I would have no personal life. Lenni left sticky notes on my face that Speed had called, and I would call him back but have no memory of what we spoke about. One night he came up to the apartment and demanded to see me. Patty propped me up at the apartment door.

"Let's take a ride," Speed said, "I miss you."

"I miss you, too," I mumbled, and he led me to his car. I got in and leaned back in my seat, waiting for him to drive us somewhere. Suddenly, he was rocking my arm.

"Are we there yet?" I asked, straining to see the time. An hour had passed.

"We haven't gone anywhere," Speed said. "I've been sitting here and watching you snore like a jet." I stumbled out of the car and he led me back to the apartment.

I bought myself a copy of the **Farmer's Almanac** and circled the date, noting that the almanac page featured a few ominous clouds on the show date. I would have to watch the Weather Channel and calculate an average between the two. I polished my boots and bought myself the traditional white britches, white shirt, white gloves, and white "stock tie," which was really an ascot. I wondered what fashion genius had decreed white for dressage shows. Were they not aware that those pristine white britches would be **sitting on a horse**? And the white gloves would be holding dusty reins, patting sweaty horse necks, and in general becoming a disposable item before sundown?

Now the show was only a week away, and I thought I was ready. There was only one burning question left in my life, and now it would be answered soon: What level did I ride?

Chapter Twenty-four

"Second," Diana said. "You will ride second level."

We were sitting at the table in the apartment, filling out horse show entry forms.

"Then why was I killing myself learning all the fancy higher-level stuff?" I groaned.

"Because it's there," Diana said. "Besides, you'll only be starting at second; then you'll be moving up very quickly. Kat needs us to get these horses campaigned."

I looked up from the paper in front of me and shot her a beatific smile. I liked starting easy, and in an equestrian sport where the level you rode, or the level at which your horse was trained, practically defined your self-worth, I finally had a level, albeit a temporarily low one.

Diana sounded enthusiastic. "If you do okay, we can raise your level by your next show."

With a great flush of pleasure, I wrote down my level. Patty flapped out of her bedroom in her bunny slippers.

"Why don't you compete, Patty?" I asked. "You always said that it was something you wanted to do."

"I'm still in mourning, dear," she said. "I can't compete if I'm in mourning."

Diana shot her a baleful look.

"Patty, that's so lame."

"Besides, I wouldn't know what level to ride," admitted Patty. "I pretty much stink at all of them."

"Just do Training Level," said Diana. She pushed an entry form across the table. "It's the introductory level."

I tried to be encouraging. "Yeah, Patti! Do it! It's my first show, too! We can give each other courage."

She hovered on the brink of saying yes.

It wasn't hard to find a way to motivate someone who had just bought a new computer because she thought it came with free cookies. "I'll treat you to doughnuts," I said.

"What kind?"

"Cream-filled?"

I had her.

She started filling out the form. "Why do they need my age?" she complained less than a minute later.

"There's a Vintage Award, for riders over fifty," Diana said.

"Who said I'm over fifty!" Patty raised her head in indignation.

"You have a thirty-eight year old daughter!" yelled Lenni and Diana together.

"I forgot." She scribbled down her age. A moment later, she looked up again. "I need my registry number from the horse show association. It's in my purse."

"You sit right there and keep filling that out," I said. "I'll get it."

I went into her bedroom for the purse. I liked Patty's bedroom. She had moved in some of her personal furniture and the room was a reflection of her character: warm, comfortable, and slightly over-stuffed. It was so unlike Diana's, which was utilitarian, filled with bookcases, a desk, and riding clothes—spare, direct, and to the point. Even Lenni and Jillian's bedroom re-created its inhabitants: two single beds, always unmade, strewn with clothes and CDs, magazines, dirty paper plates and empty coffee cups, its occupants at odds with each other and the room itself. I wondered what my room said about me: Devoid of any decoration except for a bed I barely slept in and three pair of jeans hanging on a closet door, it had no personality at all. I brought back Patty's purse and she finished the entry form.

"Now we're all committed," Diana said. "We're ready."

Not quite. There were still a few things I had to learn before the show.

"I don't know all the etiquette for when I get in the ring," I said.

Diana gave me a booklet that was filled with horse show information. Each dressage test was ridden completely alone in front of a judge, in order for the rider to be the sole recipient of the judge's full scrutiny and amusement. There were seven more levels after Patty's, labeled counterintuitively by starting with "first level," then getting increasingly complex, until the highest level,

Grand Prix. There were four subtests in each level and twelve days of Christmas. Although I would be riding only second level, it had about twenty-four different movements. There were four different ways to trot a horse alone. It was all very intimidating.

"I'll never be able to memorize this," I complained. "Is there a Cliffs Notes version?"

"Don't worry," said Diana, trying to console me. "In the lower levels, you are allowed to have someone stand in the corner of the ring and read the test out loud, movement by movement. Just play Follow the Reader. Kat doesn't generally approve of readers—she likes her riders to look professional and memorize their tests—so you should really try to commit it to memory—"

"Diana, in the great scheme of things, how important is it for me to memorize this?" I barely had enough time to get my chores completed each day.

"Memorize," commanded Diana.

But I made her sign a blood oath that she would read for me if my memory failed.

The next thing I had to learn was how to braid a mane, since neatly braided manes were a sign that you and your horse had reached a certain level of haute couture.

Lenni was my instructor here.

"Why do horses have to be braided?" I asked her.

She shrugged. "It's just something we do."

I guessed that, like saddle sores and horse shit, it was all part of the tradition.

We chose Stanley as our subject, and he dozed peacefully while Lenni whipped in braids with mind-numbing speed. I tried my hand at it. My braids also looked like they had been whipped in, but by a tornado. Lenni was unbraiding them as fast as I put them in.

"Lenni, in the great scheme of things, is it really important for me to know how to braid a horse?" We were standing back and examining my eleventh attempt that afternoon, and Stanley looked like Medusa.

"Braid," Lenni commanded.

I mentioned the show to Gail. She was not impressed.

"So you're joining the hootie palooties at

the shows now," she sneered, as though it were a betrayal of her. "Aren't you just something!"

I knew that she had once dreamed of showing horses and becoming important in the horse show world.

"I'm only doing second level," I replied, as if that somehow would lessen my treachery in her eyes.

She snorted and, for punishment, assigned me to scrub down all the mare stalls with Lysol.

"Heard you were showing," Candy said to me in the indoor arena. She was riding her horse, Lexus, while I practiced on Ivan.

"Yes," I said warily.

"What level?"

It was so nice to have a level. I was like a bastard child who had been finally legitimized in the family's eyes.

"Second," I said.

"How cozy. That's the level **I'm** showing at," she replied, then added, "not that I'm worried. Lexus is a star. But I would certainly think that a horse like Ivan should be ridden at a higher level. Guess he had to sink to yours."

I could have said that I'd only been doing dressage for five months. I could have said that she had years of training on me and she and I were still doing the same level. I could have said that in the great, **great** scheme of things, what did it matter the level I rode at in a horse show? Ah, but that's the charm of **esprit d'escalier:** I was at my wittiest that night in the privacy of my bedroom, talking back to my mirror.

At least Speed was happy for me. He had caught me on a good night and we were sharing dinner at his house, where, if I dozed off with my face on my plate, I would only humiliate myself in front of one or two others.

"I'll come and watch," he promised. "What level are you doing?"

"Second," I said.

"A nice place to start," he said. "I'll cheer you on. Wear those earrings—they'll give you the power you need."

"I've never taken them off," I replied, and it was the truth. They had become my talisman. I had taken to touching them every time I needed a boost in morale.

The night before the show, Patti was popping cream doughnuts like tranquilizers.

"You're not going to fit in your saddle," I cautioned her.

"They won't count," she said, sucking the innards out of yet another one. "I'm burning them all off from nerves."

I knew how she felt. I couldn't sleep that night. I had given Ivan a scented bath, braided his mane under Gertrude's Teutonic scrutiny, laid out my clothes, and double-checked the Weather Channel. In opposition to the almanac, it promised a sunny, breezy day, which was good, because I remembered how Diana had warned me that Ivan didn't like the rain. I knew you could trust the Weather Channel because they rely on high-tech billion-dollar satellites hooked up to high-tech billion-dollar computers, unlike the almanac, which relies on rodent shadows and the thickness of caterpillar fur.

I was out of bed by 3:30 A.M. and then slipped into my show clothes: snow white britches, snow white shirt, and the snow white stock tie that had to be fastened around my neck in a special knot, whose execution was known to only six people on the planet, Diana being one of them. She fixed it for me and I pinned over the center a little gold horseshoe that Patty had lent me. Diana had let me borrow her light wool black jacket. I left it wrapped in plastic and on the hanger, slipping my gloves into the pocket. I would put it on just before I entered the show ring. Then I took a cue from Diana and pulled sweats over my clothes, which gave me all the grace and maneuverability of a three-year-old in a snowsuit, but at least they would keep me clean.

By four o'clock, we started carrying equipment to the horse van. It was like getting rock stars ready for a world tour. Large tack trunks heavily loaded with supplies were carried on, along with hangers of neatly folded horse coolers and sheets, and armloads of buckets, saddles, and bridles. We made a dozen trips from the barns to the van.

Finally, it was time for Diana to load the horses. Nairobi, detested by all, was immediately taken out of the mix and placed in exile, to be vanned solo, in a separate horse trailer that had been attached to Kat's Jeep, and to be driven by Kat. Seating the Security Council at the United Nations was easier than getting the remaining six horses placed into six stalls on the van. Merkury couldn't be stalled next to Allegretto because they were archenemies. Allegretto didn't like Ivan, and Lexus hated Merkury, but Sam, the buffer, could be put next to anyone except Nero. By 5:30 A.M., we were using pencil and paper to do math permutations. By six o'clock, we were up to second-degree integers from calculus. A solution was finally found and we were ready.

"I vill mek sure Kat is ready to leaf," Gertrude announced while I went back to the apartment to get Patty.

She was a nervous wreck, still dressed in her robe and bunny slippers.

"Ohhh," she moaned to me. "I don't think I can do this. I have cramps."

"We're going," I said, and threw her clothes at her. She looked a little green.

"In the great scheme of things, would it matter if I stayed home?" she asked.

Lenni came out of her bedroom.

"Shame on you, Patty," she declared. "Now get dressed."

Patty obediently got dressed. I wondered why Lenni was never that firm with Jillian.

Patty, of course, had bought her stock tie preknotted. She merely snapped an elastic band around her neck and was finished with it.

When we got back to the barn, both Candy and Kat were waiting with Anna-Helga, who was coming to lend an extra hand. Candy looked like a freshly groomed jungle cat. Her blond hair was styled in tiny wisps around her face and her fingernails were manicured into perfect rose-colored almond shapes. I wished I had fingernails. They had been my first sacrifice to barn life. Kat was groomed to perfection as well, but she still needed Diana to help her with her tie. She stood like a schoolgirl as Diana fussed with it.

"It's easy," Diana said. "It's just a square

knot. Left over right, right over left. I'm surprised you never learned how."

"Alvays I haff groom," said Kat. She gave her tie a satisfied pat, pinned on a diamond and gold horse head, and gave the signal for us to leave for the show.

The van, driven by Diana, would lead the caravan. Kat would drive me, Patty, the terriers, and Nairobi. Candy, driving her Jaguar, would be the last to follow. Kat got behind the wheel of her Jeep. The terriers jumped into her lap and began licking her face. I settled into the passenger side, wondering if she was going to drive with the dogs navigating.

"Poo, doggies," said Kat, "get in der beck tseat."

They grinned at me and obeyed.

CB radios were synchronized to the same channel. Patty ate a buttered roll to settle her stomach and we were on our way.

Chapter Twenty-five

Apparently, Willie Nelson is the music of choice when driving to horse shows. The strains of "On the Road Again" blared from the horse van as it pulled out in front of us. Kat started her Jeep, turned her Willie Nelson CD to a deafening volume, and careened down the driveway behind the van, lurching from side to side. I had never driven with Kat before and was getting more and more nervous as we squealed around turns and rocketed down the road, getting within kissing distance of the van in front of us. I wondered if Nairobi was getting car sick.

"Zo zlow," Kat complained. At least that's what I think she said, as I had to lip-read over a greatly amplified Willie.

She turned on her CB.

"Hallo? Hallo?" she was screaming into the microphone. I knew Diana was answering her, but we couldn't make out the words.

"Wie?" Kat screamed. **"Wie bitte?"**

I reached over and lowered the volume on the CD, thus solving the audio problem. Now Diana's soothing voice could be heard, affirming the route we would be taking, thus restoring Kat's tranquillity. She flicked off the CB and turned her head to me to continue our conversation. Since she showed no sign of facing forward anytime soon, I watched the road for her as she spoke. "You haff breakfast?" she asked.

"No," I said, "I was busy loading the trailer."

"I haff kaffee made. You haff fon thermos some." She gestured to a thermos by my feet and I scrambled to reach it before she decided to retrieve it herself. As I poured the coffee, I watched with some horror that it lubbed, rather than poured, into the cup. It tasted like it had been composted in the manure pile. I wondered how I was going to finish it.

"I make it myself," she said proudly. "I no vant to vake my housekeeper. Gut kaffee, ja?"

"Oh, delicious."

"I cook Cherman food, too. You like Cherman food?"

"Sure."

"Gut. I make pig knuckles for you."

Patty hiccuped in the backseat.

"Aach," Kat sighed, making a face at the van in front of us, "dey are zo zlow."

"They're going the speed limit," I said, but refrained from adding that since we were on their bumper, it might be wise for us to do the same. The van turned onto the service road of the highway, with Kat ricocheting behind them, the attached trailer playing Snap the Whip behind us.

"Vy is speet limit zo zlow in America?" she grumbled again as we catapulted onto the highway, cutting off an oncoming eighteen-wheeler. I left imprints of my fingers in her dashboard. I thought I saw the terriers hugging each other in the backseat. When I looked out through the windshield again, the van had disappeared. I think Kat had somehow launched us into the space-time continuum.

We reached the show grounds almost before we left the barn, thus proving Einstein's theory of energy, mass, and the speed of light. The van pulled in fifteen minutes later and found a good spot to park. Candy and her Jaguar pulled in behind the van.

The fairgrounds soon filled up with horse trailers. I got out of the car and looked around. As trailers and vans unloaded their passengers, I noted that the entire riding population was clad in the same black-and-white combo, which made it hard to distinguish men from women from penguins. Even the dogs matched one another—they were all Jack Russells. They came out of everywhere, jumping from car windows, spilling out of vans, bouncing down trailer ramps, frolicking and rolling and yapping and grinning. And each new recruit would introduce itself by way of sniffing the personal parts of all the other terriers before being welcomed into the convention. Kat opened her door and her dogs joyfully joined their henchmen. I made a silent vow that I would never again allow myself within five feet of dog noses.

Diana helped me unload Ivan from the

trailer and we prepared him for my first class. The bright morning sun started fading as wispy gray clouds blew across the sky. These were followed by thicker gray clouds.

"Did you say Ivan didn't like rain?" I asked.

"No," said Diana. "He doesn't mind the rain at all. It's the umbrellas he hates."

"I guess I'm safe." I let my breath out. "I mean, the Weather Channel predicted sun. It was only the **Farmer's Almanac** that said rain, and no one reads the almanac anymore."

I peeled off my sweats and put on the black jacket I had borrowed from Diana.

"Think it'll bring me luck?" I asked.

"You have to make your own luck," she replied.

I used the van window as a mirror and put on my borrowed black derby, tucking in my hair. I wished I exuded Kat's elegance, instead of resembling Charlie Chaplin. Finally, I pulled on my white gloves and asked Diana for a leg up into the saddle.

"Happy motoring." She slapped me on the leg and sent me on my way.

Once aboard Ivan, I walked him into the warm-up ring. Kat came over to give me a few last-minute instructions and I strained to remember everything she had taught me during the past five months. Then something hit my cheek. It was a drop. And another drop. I looked skyward at the first treacherous drops of a light rain. I wondered if it was too late to buy stock in caterpillar futures. More drops. Ivan looked up with interest. I had a feeling I knew what was coming.

"Remember, he doesn't really mind the rain itself," Diana had said, but she knew.

I sat very deep in the saddle and made Ivan trot in a small circle.

"Be wury firm mit him," commanded Kat. She knew, too.

A drop hit Ivan right between the ears and he caught his breath. Now **he** knew.

I rode him with great firmness as dozens of umbrellas suddenly sprouted up like dandelions on a front lawn.

"You will not care about umbrellas," I said firmly. "You will not look."

But he looked. He swung his eyeballs

from umbrella to umbrella, giving each new one a salutary snort. Then he planted his front feet and spun around like a maypole.

"Rite him **forvahrtz**," commanded Kat.

I could feel him trembling underneath me.

"Be strong," called out Diana, walking over to me and holding out a riding whip for me to take.

"What am I supposed to do with a whip?" I asked. "Beat his eyeballs out so he can't see the umbrellas?"

"Sometimes it's just good psychology to carry one," Diana said.

I took it.

I pushed him forward with my legs and made him trot rapidly around the warm-up ring. He leapt away from a red-and-blue-striped umbrella and then jumped in the air when he spotted a green one. He bolted from a yellow one. I could feel his teeth rattling on the bit. He kicked his back legs out, hopped up and down a few times, and did three routines from **Riverdance**. Then he spun us in ever-diminishing circles. One more circle and I was afraid we would reach entropy and disappear altogether. I thought

I saw the beginning of hives form across his neck.

I commanded him to be brave, but we all knew.

Ivan was having a nervous breakdown.

Suddenly, there was a disturbance in the horse van. It thumped and banged, squeals of equine anger emanating from within. Gertrude ran up to Kat. It seemed that Merkury had worked himself loose and had decided to start a commotion. Nero and Allegretto were more than up to the challenge. Only gentle Sam was in his corner, quietly eating hay and staying above the fray. Kat and Diana ran to help. Horses were ordered out of the van. Nero had to be rebraided because Merkury had ferociously eaten some of his braids, Merkury had a bloody nose, Lexus was limping, and Allegretto had a swollen eye. They came down the ramp like sullen middle school kids after a schoolyard brawl.

They would all have to be packed in ice, sprayed down with antiseptic, and tacked up and ridden to keep them separated. Which left me in the warm-up ring alone.

I rode Ivan with firmness and moral support, but he was practically biting his nails with anxiety.

"It's just you and me, kid," I said heartily, but neither one of us liked the way that sounded.

Kat, Diana, and Patty were now mounted. They joined me in the warm-up ring. It was obvious that none of them would be able to read for me, and though I had memorized my test, my mind was going blank.

"I can't remember my test," I whined to Diana while trying to keep Ivan from vaulting over her horse.

"I'm sorry," she called over her shoulder. "I can't help you. I wasn't planning to be mounted so soon."

"I don't know my test," I whined to Patty, "and my class is next."

She and Sam were walking around in slow circles, both clad in matching powder blue raincoats and exuding an enviable sangfroid.

"I'm on Sam," she said, "I'm not allowed to read while mounted."

"I forgot everything," I whined to Kat. Ivan had by now given up folk dancing and was executing the more sophisticated pliés from **The Nutcracker.**

Kat was warming up Merkury and doing the slow, collected trot of the passage, circling around me and Ivan, trying to set up a containment field.

The bell rang for me to begin my test.

"Chust go," Kat commanded, pointing me to the show ring.

"But I don't remember what to do," I said.

"I fix problem."

Ivan cantered sideways, punctuating it with little half rears. I aimed him for the show ring in-gate. Suddenly, Gertrude appeared, waving for me to follow her into the ring. **No, no, no,** I prayed, **anyone but Gertrude,** but she entered the ring ahead of me and went right to the reader's spot, standing there expectantly while giving me a big smile and a thumbs-up.

It was my very first show and Gertrude, Gertrude of the impenetrable accent and total lack of literacy in the English language, was going to be my reader. She cleared her throat loudly.

"Entair kollectet trat," she called out, stumbling over the printed words on the test sheet. "Halten und saluten und prochayeed kollected trat."

It was show time.

Chapter Twenty-six

As soon as we entered the ring, Ivan and I noticed that the judge was sitting at the far end, under a big orange-and-turquoise-striped beach umbrella decorated with diving dolphins. Ivan gasped and bolted to the left, ending up in the approximate vicinity where Speed and Candy were leaning against the fence rail. Candy had her arm through Speed's and was snuggled against him to stay out of the rain, even though her other hand was holding a big bright red-and-white-polka-dot umbrella. Not holding it exactly. More like twirling it. She apparently knew, too.

Ivan shied violently away from them and to the right, toward a lovely floral-print umbrella. Left, twirling polka dots; right, floral print. Left, twirling polka dots; right, floral print. Not to mention directly in front, diving dolphins. There was no place left for him to go, so he leapt straight up in the air like a whale breaching water.

Gertrude waited patiently for us to finish executing our unscheduled airs above ground before proceeding to read in that gibberish so peculiar to her. Within a matter of seconds, she was reading several movements ahead of me. I could hear a bell ring and dimly remembered Diana explaining to me that it was a judge's penalty. I was supposed to stop whatever I was doing and let the judge explain my mistake before I could continue. I would have given anything to stop what we were doing. Ivan had become a surface-to-air missile.

The bell rang again. Now the judge was waiting for me, Gertrude was waiting for me; Kat and Diana and Patty were all mounted and standing ringside, waiting for me. The crowd who had collected around the ring out of morbid curiosity were waiting for me. Speed and Candy were waiting for me. Ivan was waiting to die. I was waiting for him to kill me. I squeezed my eyes shut for a moment and, summoning the power from my moon earrings, pulled myself together, took my whip, and gave Ivan a mighty thwack across his rump. He startled and gasped and then stood there, blinking, as though emerging from a nightmare. Apparently, pain left more of an impression than umbrellas. He actually moved forward with his feet close to the ground and we finished our test, I saluted the judge and left the ring.

I immediately jumped off Ivan and handed him to Gertrude.

"Ich put chim in fan," she said.

"Please put him in a van heading for hell," I said.

"Tough ride," Candy came up to me, brimming with schadenfreude. "Too bad, darling. Well, I better mount up." She turned to Speed. "My class is in a few minutes. We can leave right after that. We're still on for dinner, right?"

Speed nodded.

"See you later, then," she said, waving her first two fingers at him. She walked over to Anna-Helga and her waiting horse.

I looked at Speed, full of questions that I didn't give voice to.

"I'm her lawyer," he said to me apologetically. "We have some business to go over."

"Mmm," I said.

Candy put in a respectable ride, and when she was through, she left the show ring and handed her horse off to Anna-Helga before reattaching herself to Speed. I busied myself helping Gertrude polish Merkury for Kat's ride and took great pains not to look up.

"They're gone," said Patty, riding over to me a few minutes later. "You can come up for air now."

"They're having a business dinner together," I said to her.

"Mmm," she said.

"Is your daughter coming to see you show?" I asked, anxious to change the subject.

"No." Patty shook her head. "She doesn't approve. For some reason, she thinks I'm obsessed with horses."

"Why would she think that?" I asked. "Just because you packed up everything you own to live in a barn for seven years? So, how are your nerves?"

"Look," Patty said, extending a trembly

hand. "The doughnuts are wearing off. I need to take something stronger. Maybe a cheeseburger." She headed her horse for the snack stand. I continued to groom Merkury. Diana rode up on Allegretto.

"I did miserably," I said, barely able to look her in the eye.

"Don't worry." She flapped a hand at me. "Just think of it as your 'first waffle' class."

I looked at her, puzzled. "Waffles? What are you talking about, my first waffle class! You mean I will have other waffle classes?"

"No, not first as in inaugural, first waffle, as in how the first waffle you make never comes out right—it sticks or it falls apart—so you throw it away. By the second one, you get the formula right. Never worry about your first waffle. It's just a practice run for your second waffle. It's destiny. That's part of my philosophy of life."

I understood right away. My first class had been my first waffle class, like my first marriage had been my first waffle marriage. I shouldn't sweat it; my destiny would make the next waffle better.

"Wow, Diana," I said, "that's profound!"

"I know," she said. "That's what I like about myself. Well, gotta go, gotta show."

She put in a magnificent ride. It was apparent that her waffle-making skills were well honed.

Patty was next. She rode up to the in-gate, chewing gum at a furious pace. I looked up at her.

"Patty, you can't ride and chew gum."

"You mean I can't walk and chew gum. Thanks a lot."

"No, I mean it looks tacky."

"Ugh, you're right." Patty spit the gum into her palm, rolled it up, and stuck it under the flap of her saddle. "But how am I going to stay calm?"

"Just think of your last cheeseburger," I said. "Focus on the taste, the texture, the bun. . . ."

It worked. Patty rode conservatively, having a studied air about her, but made no mistakes and left the ring glowing with pride. For the next hour, she babbled on, relentlessly reliving every moment.

"We were all **there**," Diana finally snapped.

Now it was Kat's turn. She slipped into the special clothes worn for the upper levels—yellow vest, the ubiquitous white gloves, black top hat, and black cutaway "shadbelly" jacket, which had formal tails. Like doctors' jackets in medical school, the jackets of dressage riders lengthen as the expertise of their owners increases. There was a hushed crowd of spectators collecting around the ring before she entered. Her name was announced over the loudspeaker in clipped British tones, courtesy of an imported announcer. Her music started with the strains of the "Triumphal March" from **Aïda.** She sat regally on Merkury at the entrance gate until their cue. Even Merkury seemed to understand the seriousness of the occasion, and he stood totally immobile until Kat signaled him to move. And then they entered the ring like a king coming home. Merkury's strides were huge, yet he moved with a lightness that belied his size. His legs crisscrossed beneath him in lateral precision from one side of the ring to the other, each hoof touching the ground in perfect time to the music. Then like the metal he was named for, he was all quicksilver flash as he collected himself in a slow prance before exploding down the long side in a brilliant extension. The crowd gasped with delight. Now up the center line in a canter, changing his lead every stride, so that it looked like he was skipping along of his own accord, slipping into a pirouette and then the pièce de résistance, the piaffe, a slow prance in place. Enthusiastic applause greeted their exit from the ring. I still had goose bumps an hour later as I helped Gertrude settle Merkury down in the van.

The show was over.

Kat had won her class, Diana had won hers, and Candy had won mine. My score was appallingly low. If they were giving a hundred honorable mentions in a class of twenty, they wouldn't have mentioned me. I helped load the van and wondered if I should just go home to Long Island. Competitions didn't seem to be my forte. Not in the show ring, not in the Speed division. I couldn't even beat down a pair of terriers.

Kat whistled for her dogs and they sorted themselves out from the hundreds of others and jumped into the Jeep. Or maybe they weren't the same ones. Maybe they were all related. Maybe they all hated me. Maybe everyone brought a few of those damn terriers to the shows and took random ones back home and then just exchanged them again at the next show. Who would know? I was in a foul mood. I would never show again. I would fill my pockets with rocks and walk out among the sea of terriers and drown.

"Vee leaf." Kat nodded toward her car and Patty and I got in. Kat got in, too, and turned the car on. My fingers found their previous indentations in the dashboard as she sped away from the fairgrounds.

Patty was in a great mood all the way home. She had gotten a respectable score and had taken third place.

"I don't mind third place all," she chirped several times. "It's kinda like being a bridesmaid instead of the bride, only better. You get to have all the fun without worrying about fitting into a white dress." Apparently, it had slipped her mind that she should have worried about fitting into her

white britches, but she was on a cheeseburger high and kept chattering on: She
loved Sam, she loved the judge, she loved
Kat, and she wasn't in mourning anymore.
I sat morosely in the front seat and said
nothing.

"Zhoody," Kat began. I couldn't look at
her. "You did ferry vell. Eevan ist full of
temperament! The chudge vasst my olt rival
und alvays he hates Eevan."

"Really?" I said in a lugubrious tone.

"Aach ja," Kat said gaily. "He tell me
vonce to send Eevan to meat factory." She
chuckled at the thought. "You haff ferry gut
geritten. You rite him next show und dann
you rite Nero. You are vunderbar riter."

I was **wunderbar!** Me! **Wunderbar!**
Nothing else mattered! An Olympic gold
medalist had called me **wunderbar.** I loved
her. I loved Ivan. I loved Patty. I even loved
the "chudge."

We pulled into the farm. It was late afternoon and we had a lot of work to do. The
horses had to be unbraided and rubbed
down before their dinners, and then the

equipment unpacked—a reversal of our early-morning routine.

Anna-Sofie came over to me as I was leading a spent Ivan back to the barn.

"You haff hier einer mann."

Einer mann? It took me a minute to realize that she was saying a gentleman was waiting. I peered ahead through the drizzly afternoon light. Leaning against a wall inside the barn was Marshall.

"Hello, Judy." He smirked. "Guess the party's over."

Chapter Twenty-seven

He had put on some weight and his hair was a little longer, but he was still the same sneering, arrogant, self-serving, self-possessed, self-important, self-satisfied, egotistical, overconfident, presumptuous, conceited, smug, blue-eyed Marshall I remembered.

"Pack," he said. "I want you to come home."

Gertrude passed by, leading Merkury into the barn. She glanced sideways at us.

"What's the point?" I said. "Just give me the divorce papers. I'll gladly sign them."

Gertrude was followed by Diana, who was leading Lexus. She gave me an upraised fist behind Marshall's back.

"The point is, you're my wife," he said. "You belong by my side."

"No, I don't," I said. "I gave that position to Grace Cairo by default."

He opened his mouth to say something, but Anna-Helga passed him, leading Sam. Sam turned around and blew his nose on Marshall's jacket.

"Grace is history," he said, wiping off his jacket.

Gertrude passed us the other way.

"Too bad," I said. "I thought it was a nice match. Probably your best one so far."

"You misunderstood my relationship with Grace," he said. "She was helping me with my business."

"And I'm only away at summer camp," I said.

He tilted his head and tried on the old Marshall charmer smile. His blue eyes cried in the rain. In the back of my mind, I could hear Willie clearing his throat for a song. Marshall's voice dropped to a seductive whisper. "We had a nice home together, didn't we?" Then he made a sweeping gesture toward the farm. "Your boyfriend own all this?"

"This farm is owned by a woman," I said. I didn't mention that Speed's farm was even bigger.

Diana squeezed past us to go back to the van.

Marshall stepped closer to me. It was the horse dance, like the mares in the field fighting for dominance, for a position of power and control. Natasha fighting me when we first met. Natasha finally obeying me.

"We can talk about this when we get home," he said.

"I'm not going anywhere," I said, and stood like a defiant mare, defending my territory. But it wasn't working.

His face turned red with anger. He opened his mouth to say something, but now Gertrude was leading Allegretto. Allegretto gave Marshall a gentle nudge as he passed by. Marshall wiped off the dusty nudge mark. I could see that he was struggling to keep his charm burners fired up.

"I don't want to lose you," he said, his voice soft and supplicating. "You were the best thing in my life."

"It took you five months to figure that out?" I retorted, but he acted like he hadn't heard me.

"I need you," he murmured. I started to feel bad until I remembered that he'd probably said those very words to each of his girlfriends.

Diana carried in a tack trunk.

"It's too late," I said, "so just send me the papers."

We waited until Anna-Helga passed with Nero. Then Diana came over to me and took Ivan. Marshall eyed her up and down.

"Can't we work things out?" he asked after Diana led Ivan away, "We have eight and a half years invested. This is not the way to end our marriage. Come home. We can talk things through, and if you want a divorce after that, I'll give it to you. My lawyer has the papers ready, if you still want to go through with it." He actually looked a little sad.

Gertrude passed us, carrying a tack trunk. Anna-Helga passed the other way.

"Jesus," said Marshall, his voice suddenly rising in frustration. "This is like standing in Grand Central Fucking Station!"

Anna-Helga passed us with an armload of blankets. Diana passed the other way.

"As you can see," I said, "I'm busy. We'll be here the rest of the afternoon doing this."

Diana squeezed past him with another tack trunk. Anna-Helga passed the other way.

Marshall pursed his lips. I could see that his patience had run out.

"I'll be back late tonight, when this circus train is finished. And you'd better be packed and ready to leave. I won't let things end like this."

I wanted to tell him about the first waffle theory of life and how we both needed to start over and make new waffles, but he suddenly reached over and grabbed my wrist, squeezing it hard. "Do you hear me?" he rasped.

The good thing about Natasha was that she had given me more strength in my arms than most mortals need. I snapped my wrist out of his hand and spun around to face him.

"Don't ever touch me like that again."

He blinked his eyes in surprise a few times. They flashed like the little blue lights on emergency vehicles. I gave him the Natasha Defiance Stare and waited.

Anna-Helga and Gertrude passed us with an armload of saddles. Diana came up behind me, holding several riding whips. She handed them to me and gave Marshall a big smile. He eyed the whips now in my hand. I flapped them around a little for effect.

"You think that's funny?" he asked.

"No," I answered truthfully, "not at all."

He stood for a minute or two, looking at me, looking at Diana, looking at the whips.

"I'll be back later," he said, "and you better be ready to leave." He stomped off, disappearing into the gray mist. Diana came over to me and together we watched him go.

"As I said," Diana nodded, "sometimes it's just good psychology to carry a whip."

Chapter Twenty-eight

"Maybe you shouldn't stay here tonight," Diana said to me after Marshall left.

"I don't have anyplace to go. Speed is having a business dinner with Candy."

"Mmm," she said.

Gail sidled over and stood next to Diana.

"Why don't you come home for dinner with me tonight?" she asked. I suspected that her invitation sprung more from a driving ambition to get an update for her collection of hot gossip than from hospitality, but since the barn scene had just removed every shred of privacy from my life, in the great scheme of things, dinner with Gail was preferable to another public confrontation.

"I appreciate your invitation. Thank you."

Gail was pleased. "I'll just give my mother a call and tell her to throw a few things together for dinner. You won't mind, will you, if it's potluck?"

Since potluck was the menu of choice in the apartment most nights, I didn't mind at all.

By early evening, we had finished settling the horses and were ready to go. I decided to follow Gail in my car so I could come home later.

Gail lowered her bulky frame into her faded blue station wagon and waved out the window for me to follow. Marshall's car was nowhere in sight. He had probably gone back to his motel to ratchet up his anger for his performance in the sequel—**Round Two: The Showdown.** I planned to check in with Diana by cell phone and come back long after he was gone.

Gail drove along miles of highway before finally turning onto a winding, secluded road, darkened from old trees with branches that dipped so low, they scraped the roof of my car. We passed a weedy, overgrown field, then crossed a narrow, hobbly bridge over a dried-out streambed. Gail's old car jounced and swayed, and after an hour or so, I wondered if I should have left a trail of oats behind me.

She finally turned down a rutted dirt driveway that sent clouds of dust toward my windshield. A small brown sparrow of a house sat at the end. Curtains hung askew inside the tiny front windows that flanked a broken storm door. The porch light, a bare bulb hanging from an overhead socket, cast a dim glow against the peeling brown wooden porch.

"There's nothing like coming home to your castle at the end of the day," said Gail, leading me inside.

The living room was small and worn but clean. A large marshmallow of a faded pink velvet couch slouched against one wall. Against a second wall was a shabby pink-and-green floral chair that sagged under a grossly overweight Jack Russell. He lowered himself to the floor and stretched luxuriously before lumbering over to meet us.

"This is Sunny," Gail grunted, dropping to her knees and giving the dog a hug.

I started to say I used to ride a horse

named Sunny, but the dog sighed deeply and threw itself upside down onto my feet.

"He wants his belly rubbed," said Gail.

Having learned my lesson about staying on the good side of dogs, I complied immediately.

"Don't tell me—one of Kat's puppies?" I said.

"How did you know?"

"Lucky guess."

"Are you hungry?" An older, even heavier version of Gail appeared in the doorway. She had a green bandanna on her head and was beaming at us.

"I'm pleased to meet you, Mrs. Brace." I extended my hand.

"Oh, please call me Ellen. The pleasure is mine. Gail so rarely brings friends home." She was gracious, her voice sweet, with a generic southern accent. "Dinner's ready. I know Gail's as hungry as a bear when she gets home, so I always make sure it's ready. Just a quick dinner, since it was kind of a last-minute deal, but I'm so glad that you came."

The kitchen was obviously the heart of the house. Scrubbed clean, it was old-fashioned, with both stove and refrigerator up on legs. A creaky wooden fan rotated slowly above an old yellow Formica table.

"I made these," Mrs. Brace said modestly as she set the table with three crocheted yellow-and-white place mats that looked like lumpy daisies. "They're my special-occasion mats."

I felt obligated to admire them profusely.

"Since my accident, when I hurt my back, I have lots of time to do my crochet work," said Mrs. Brace, bustling over to the stove. "Come on, Gail, get them dishes out."

"So, Judy," Gail said as she busied herself setting the table, "guess you're gonna need a divorce lawyer."

"She don't need a lawyer; she just needs dinner," Mrs. Brace called out before I could answer. "So hustle your bustle." She was at the stove, forking what had apparently once been a whole flock of chickens, now southern fried, onto a large platter. She carried it to the table. It was followed by a vat of gravy, thirty pounds of mashed potatoes, an entire cornfield on the cob, enough salad to fill a tractor bed, a bucket of green peas, and, in case that wasn't enough, three dozen homemade biscuits. The table wobbled a bit.

"It's always an honor to cook for Gail's friends," said Ellen Brace with great sincerity. "I always encourage her to bring friends home. She has a man friend that picks her up in his car, but he don't come in."

"That's enough, Ma," Gail said firmly.

"I always tell you to invite him in, don't I, Gail? Having folks in is a diversion for me, too. I was so thrilled when Gail called to tell me you were visiting us. I don't get out much, due to my hurt back. Please sit right down."

I took my place at one of the yellow daisies and a hubcap-size plate piled high with food immediately appeared in front of me.

"Now, don't you be shy," Mrs. Brace admonished. "I always tell people not to be shy, don't I, Gail?"

Gail, already submerged in her dinner, nodded her head.

"Well, I may not see many folks, but I have Gail. She puts up with her cranky old ma." Ellen Brace smoothed her place mat with a plump hand and patted her daughter on the arm. "I don't work, due to my hurt back, so she supports us. And we do okay."

"You're a wonderful cook," I said, and meant it. I liked southern fried chicken. Somewhere in my past life, it had become an integral part of my karma. Maybe I was once a chicken.

"So you live at the farm," Mrs. Brace said.

"I share an apartment with three other women," I answered, now digging into the mashed potatoes, which were oozing yellow rivulets of butter.

Gail came up for air. "She's going back to New York with her husband," she declared before disappearing again behind a large chicken leg.

"No, I'm not," I said and took another forkful of mashed potatoes.

"So, Gail tells me you were a teacher?"

"Yes, I used to teach English."

"Mmm." Mrs. Brace shook her head. "Well, I sure don't see the need to teach

English to them what already knows how to speak it. It ain't practical. Now, I can see the idea behind teaching somethin' you don't know. Like arithmetic, maybe. You ain't born knowin' arithmetic, and it's good to know how to count on things. Do you know how to teach arithmetic?"

"I guess I could, but it's not my specialization."

"Specialization." She laughed. "Everybody gets so special, they can't do nothin'."

"No," I began, "it's not like that at all. It means—"

But she was just warming to her subject, so I continued eating my mashed potatoes.

"When Gail went to college, I told her to study somethin' practical. 'Be somethin' useful,' I said. Didn't I, Gail? Somethin' useful." Mrs. Brace paused, and, seeing as how I was enjoying the potatoes, put another two pounds on my plate before resuming her musings. "I said be somethin' useful like a beautify-tician or a practical nurse. I myself was a practical nurse until I had to lift old man Parker. Deadweight, he was, and the nursing home knew it. Still had to lift him all by myself. Deadweight! Then we found out he was really dead. Passed on during the night." She gave an ironic laugh, but she was watching my food intake like a hawk. My plate was defying all known principles of modern-day physics: The more I ate, the higher the piles on it grew.

"That's sad about Mr. Parker," I said.

"Yep, I thought he looked a little blue when I tucked him in the night before, but nobody listens to me. Even Gail don't listen to me. Went and studied horses, she did. She got into them specializations and studied horse sense."

"It was equine science, Ma," Gail said, sucking down a whole chicken leg at once.

"And does that make you an equine scientist? I guess not! But if you had studied hair, you could be doin' mine," Ellen Brace reminded her. The hair in question was well hidden under the Brace signature soiled bandanna.

Gail sighed and took another pound of peas.

I tried to explain. "Specialization just means—"

"Equine science! If that don't beat all," Ellen Brace went on. "What'd they teach her? A horse has four legs. You feed one end, it all gets processed and comes out the other. Everything boils down to poop. 'Fore you know it, they'll be havin' a specialization for every kind of animal poop." Ellen Brace noticed that I had just eaten the last pea on my plate. Her hand was faster than the eye, and suddenly my plate was overrun with green peas. "So, Judy, what made you leave teachin' and come to the farm?"

"She left her husband," Gail said helpfully. "And he just came to get her."

"I needed a change," I said.

"From her husband," said Gail.

I wished she would disappear into the Everest-high mound of mashed potatoes that she had just heaped onto her plate.

"I never found husbands too useful, myself," Mrs. Brace agreed.

"We did have some problems and I needed a change in my life."

"Guess you realized that specializin' in English wasn't too practical, eh?"

"Ma!" Gail admonished her.

"Well, practical nurses and beautifyticians are always needed," Mrs. Brace said. "That's why them call 'em practical nurses. 'Cause it's a practical thing to be. Teachers aren't. And neither are equine scientists."

My energy was focused on battling the mashed potatoes. I couldn't finish them fast enough. Like snowdrifts in an arctic storm, they were piling up rapidly, but I felt compelled to defend Gail.

"Gail is very important at the farm," I said. "Kat depends on her. She handles the mares and trains the foals, and I'm learning a lot from her." I looked down at my plate. To my horror, the mashed potatoes were now accompanied by a whole fried chicken. When had that arrived? I wondered in desperation. I hadn't seen Mrs. Brace's hands move except once, when she stripped the meat from three chicken legs and sent it downward to the waiting dog.

"Well, Gail is my mainstay." Mrs. Brace nodded. I watched in fascination as she ate a whole chicken breast in two bites. "She's a good daughter. I'll give her that. If it wasn't for her, I'd be living in a dog shed. And that

Kat woman should appreciate what she's got here. Gail's a real treasure. Kat should let her ride and train up some of them horses. Then she could sell them off. Get rid of them. That would be practical. She don't need so many horses when one or two will do."

"Mmm," I said through another mouthful of chicken, declining to mention that if Kat sold all her horses, Gail would be out of a job.

"Ma, Judy doesn't want to know about my riding," Gail said. There were sparks flying from her knife and fork. "She has enough to worry about."

"She don't look worried to me."

"She's going back to New York tomorrow."

"No I'm not," I said.

"Leave the girl alone," said Mrs. Brace.

I successfully finished another chicken leg, but the next time I looked down at my plate, everything had been completely replenished.

"Judy should know how valuable you are," Mrs. Brace was saying, " 'cause then she could tell Kat."

"Ma, let Judy eat in peace," Gail said.

"I'm just saying, Gail," Mrs. Brace declared. "I'm just making pleasant conversation."

I put down my fork. My stomach was now trying to arrange for storage facilities in other parts of my body.

I finally sat back and admitted defeat. "It was all delicious, but I can't eat another bite."

Mrs. Brace was not to be fazed. "Hope you saved room for dessert. Chocolate cream pies. Two of them and a banana cream pie. I'll clean up and Gail can show you a picture of her riding days."

The multitude of pies sounded ominous. I wobbled to my feet and followed Gail into the living room. We sat on the sagging sofa, Gail at one end, Sunny in the middle, me at the other end, the three of us too stuffed to move. Mrs. Brace waddled over, holding a framed picture for me to admire. It was Gail, younger and slim, smiling happily on a horse.

"That was at one of those whatchamacallits—competitions. Gail used to go to competitions."

"Oh yes," I said, recalling my experience from that morning. "They're great fun."

"I wouldn't know," said Ellen Brace, "being as how I have a hurt back. I never got out to one."

She served dessert. Each of the pies were smothered in two feet of whipped cream. I took a small piece on my fork and ate it slowly, taking minuscule bites.

But Mrs. Brace was not to be fooled.

"Don't you like chocolate cream pie, Judy? How about a slice of banana cream instead?"

"No, no, I love it. I'm just savoring it."

I finally finished my piece of chocolate cream pie. No sooner had I put my fork down than Ellen Brace had another piece at the ready. "You're as thin as a piece of paper," she lamented. "Have some fruit salad, too."

A fruit salad worthy of the Garden of Eden appeared on the table. It was impossible to eat any more. I spent the rest of

dinner slowly peeling a grape, hoping Mrs.
Brace wouldn't notice that it never made it
to my mouth.

The evening passed quickly. I tried to sti-
fle an attack of yawning. Mrs. Brace noticed
and I apologized.

"No need to apologize, dear. Your day
starts early, just like Gail's. You're welcome
to stay over, so you don't have that long ride
home all by yourself."

The drive back! Exhausted from the long
day and the massive digestive process that
was now under way, I knew I would never
be able to remember the tortuous route
home.

"You can sleep on the couch," said Mrs.
Brace.

I eyed the pink marshmallow. It actually
looked inviting.

"Thank you."

I called the apartment on my cell phone
while Mrs. Brace trundled off to find a
clean sheet and an extra pillow. Diana answered. Marshall had been there earlier,
pounding on the door and shouting, and
she had sent him away, scolding him for

waking up the horses, but she couldn't be sure he had really left.

"You'd be better off staying over at Gail's," she said, "and getting a good night's sleep. We'll help you handle things when you get back tomorrow morning. He was in a pretty foul mood."

I wished she hadn't said something that sounded exactly like **fowl.**

"Okay," I agreed. "I guess you're right. He'll be back, twice as obnoxious."

"Please don't mind the crooked curtains in here." Ellen Brace pointed to the windows. "Gail has to get the right screws and put the curtain rods in better. You know, with my hurt back, I can't set them straight. Gail does all the maintenance around here, but sometimes she don't get to things."

"Ma, Judy doesn't want to hear about maintenance."

"Well, I'm just saying, with my hurt back and all."

I settled down on the couch. Sunny stretched himself over me from knee to ankle. My legs were turning blue.

"Well, I'm goin' get some shut-eye," said

Mrs. Brace, checking in with me a final time. "I've been up and around too long. I'll certainly be feeling it tomorrow in my back. I guess I'll leave Sunny with you, being as you both look so comfortable."

Sunny, snoring loudly, opened one eye, then closed it. I was too tired to care. I pulled the pillow over my face and fell deeply asleep.

The smell of bacon and eggs woke me up early the next morning. I washed up and went into the kitchen. Mrs. Brace was awake and busy making breakfast.

"I usually just have coffee," I said, hoping to deter her. I could still taste chicken.

"Nonsense. A girl has to eat something to handle those beasts at the farm. I always make sure that Gail eats right. She's already finished a nice big breakfast and is getting herself dressed. I'm sure you've noticed how good she looks. Hearty! Now you sit right down."

I sat, but as soon as Mrs. Brace turned away, I grabbed the food off my plate and sneaked it down to Sunny. He gave me an appreciative look.

"Guess you like bacon and eggs," Mrs. Brace said as she faced me again. "I'll just wrestle up some more."

"No, no." I jumped to my feet. "I appreciate it, but I don't want to be late. We have a long drive ahead of us."

Gail appeared in the kitchen doorway. She looked no different from the day before. She still had the same bandanna and clothes on. Mrs. Brace walked over and gave her a hug.

"There's my baby. Want me to make you girls some sandwiches?"

"Save yourself the trouble," I said, "I have yogurt in my apartment."

"Nonsense." Mrs. Brace was back in breakneck speed with two large brown paper bags. Mine weighed as much as a sack of horse feed.

Sunny walked us all outside. He rubbed himself against my leg. I knew he was marking me—a doggy way of sending a letter home to his folks.

Mrs. Brace stood in the doorway. "Is that nice gentleman picking you up tonight?" she asked Gail.

Gail shot her mother a look. "Dunno," she said quickly. "Gotta go."

"Gail has a nice-looking gentleman pick her up in his car every once in awhile. Late at night. They go out—heavens knows where—so late, but I don't pry. I'm just glad she has a gentleman friend."

"Enough, Ma."

"Drives a black BMW. Fancy car. Nice-lookin' man, too. I think he probably has some money, driving a car like that. Poor people don't drive BMWs. Wears a cowboy hat, too."

I felt a shock run through me. How many men in rural North Carolina wore cowboy hats and drove black BMWs? But Gail had wedged herself between her mother and me and was practically pushing me toward my car.

"You didn't answer me, Gail?" her mother called. "Is he coming tonight?"

Gail said nothing and got in her car, waving for me to follow. She drove quickly down the dusty driveway, leading the way. As I drove behind her, my mind was spinning. Was Speed seeing Gail? Weren't things serious enough between Speed and me for me to expect him to be monogamous? And then there was Candy. Was Speed being a trigamist, one up from a bigamist? Did I have legitimate gripe, since technically I was still married? I made myself two important promises. First, I would find out exactly what was going on between Speed and Gail, Speed and Candy, Speed and me, and me and Marshall. And secondly, I vowed that I would never, ever eat southern fried chicken again.

Chapter Twenty-nine

There were three police cruisers in the parking lot when we got back to the farm. A small crowd milled near the boarders' barn, where two policemen were setting up yellow tapes that read CRIME SCENE. I paused for a moment to take it in, then raced toward the barn. Had Marshall done something irrational? How irresponsible of me to have run off the way I had! I should have stayed and settled things when I had the opportunity, instead of letting his wrath fall upon my housemates. A cop resembling an aging Boy Scout was standing next to the yellow tapes and sending away curious boarders and riding students. He had the square jaw and square crew cut of his profession, as well as square hips from being accessorized with the usual cop fashionista walkie-talkie–gun–nightstick combo. Kat was talking to him, and I could see the strain on his face as he tried to decipher her fractured English. The three Swedish girls and Gertrude stood next to her, excitedly adding to his confusion.

He stopped me right outside the barn.

"You can't go up there, ma'am. It's a crime scene."

"But I live here! What happened?"

"We got a murder."

Kat patted me on the arm. "Ja, ja," she said. "It vas Lenni."

My heart felt as if it had stopped beating. "Omigod! Lenni?"

The Swedish girls concurred. "Ja, Lenni, ja. Ja. Lenni und der mann. Ja. Ja."

Square Cop shook his head. "Yep, some guy named Lenny."

"What happened to Lenni?" I could barely manage to say the words.

"Das war furchtbar," said Kat. That meant it was terrible, because I had heard it often enough about my riding.

"I have to go in there. I have to see what happened to Lenni."

But Square Cop blocked me.

"No one goes in there," he said. "There was a stabbing."

"Did Marshall do it?" My voice was shaky.

"All I know is that it was some guy named Lenny. Now move along."

"Furchtbar," Kat added.

"Is she okay?" I asked, straining to see into the barn.

"Like I already told ya, lady. It was murder." He looked at me and blinked slowly.

"What **happened** to Lenni?" I was standing an inch from his face and shouting now. I wanted to reach into his brain and pull out the information.

"Furchtbar," Kat said again, clearly upset. "Mein poor farm."

"Ja, Lenni und der mann," the Swedish girls added.

I made a move toward the barn.

"You can't go in there," he said, grabbing my arm. "Can't you see? It's a crime scene."

"I **live** here!" I tried to pull away.

"Why don't you just move along home, missie."

I realized his square jaw was just the outward indication of the cement-block brain trapped inside. I pulled away, freeing myself with the quick Natasha snap that was becoming my trademark move, and raced up the stairs.

Lenni was alive. She was sitting at the kitchen table, pale and weeping, while three huge cops stood around her in a circle, grilling her like a cheeseburger. Every question brought a fresh outpouring of tears from her.

"I don't know what more to say," she wept. "I've told you everything."

Patty was standing behind Lenni, rubbing her shoulders in an effort to comfort her. "It's okay, Lenni," she kept saying softly. "They know it was an accident. Hush."

"Lenni!" I shouted. "What happened?"

"Marshall." Lenni's voice dropped to a broken whisper. "I killed him."

"Omigod!"

"Did you know the victim, Marshall Van Brunt?" one of the cops asked me.

"My husband," I stammered. A wave of ice was traveling up into my chest. "I mean, almost ex-husband. I'm divorcing him. He came here from New York."

My left eye started going into a spasm.

One cop looked at me sympathetically. One looked menacing. They apparently subscribed to the old good cop/bad cop routine and were playing it to the hilt. The good cop nodded and wrote something down on his pad. The bad cop scowled at me. The third cop, not having any particular character designation assigned to him, moved to the window and rocked back and forth on his feet while gazing out at cloud formations.

My legs shook uncontrollably. The good cop helped me into a chair. I looked up at him through twitching eyelids, which made him look wavy. The bad cop planted himself in front of me.

"What do you know about this?" he snapped.

"I don't know anything. I don't even know what happened."

The bad cop demonstrated with a snipping motion of his fingers. "She cut off the tip of his—"

"Omigod!" I gasped.

"—thumb."

"A fatal thumb wound?" I had a sudden mental picture of Marshall doubled over in agony, clutching his thumb and slumping to the floor. "Is that possible?"

"It's possible. And we know she's the perp. Now why did she do it?"

I stared up into his squinty eyes. "Lenni's not a perp. She's a good person."

"Those are the worst kind," he snarled.

"Actually," said the good cop, "the EMTs did file a preliminary report that it might have been a myocardial infarction."

"But we don't know for certain," the bad cop added.

"Yes, of course," I said, my mind spinning. "From the cheese omelettes."

"You mean she poisoned him?" Three cops leaned toward me.

"No, no. It was his cholesterol."

I could see that they weren't following me.

"Cheese omelettes," I repeated a bit more loudly. "He always ate three-cheese omelettes." Why were they looking confused? It was all so obvious.

"I'll bet he even had one this morning for breakfast before he came here."

"Cheese omelettes," said the good cop, and wrote it down.

"Cholesterol?" the bad cop asked.

"Yeah. It was close to three hundred," I said, then added helpfully, "and sometimes he even had a side of bacon with it."

"So, you think he was poisoned?" The bad cop planted his hands on the table in front of me.

"I didn't say that. **You** said that."

He straightened up.

"She's being hostile," he said to the other two cops. They all wrote it down.

I reached over to touch Lenni's hand.

"Don't touch it," she moaned, pulling it away. "That was the hand that killed him."

Patty shook her head with exasperation. "You were supposed to kill Bill, not Marshall."

"This is not a joke," the bad cop said sternly. "We can put this whole apartment under arrest."

"Maybe we should call Speed?" Patty suggested. "He handles all the farm business."

"Yeah," said Diana. "Ask him for a group discount."

"How did you get him in the thumb?" I asked Lenni.

"I was peeling sweet potatoes," she explained, "for a sweet potato pie. I still had the knife in my hand when he kicked the door in."

"He kicked the door in?"

She nodded. "Just two hours ago. He was yelling for you and pounding on the door. I was going to open it, but I had to rinse the potatoes off my hands, because they were orange. Then he kicked the door in and came right into the kitchen."

"If you had baked the sweet potatoes first, you wouldn't have needed a knife," the bad cop said.

"That's what I keep telling her," said Patty. "It's easier to bake them first."

"I slice them in half first," said Lenni defensively. "Then I peel them, and then I simmer them with a touch of nutmeg and brown sugar. Then I mash them."

Everyone agreed that she was making too much work for herself that way.

"My mother always put allspice in hers," said the good cop. "Do you use allspice?"

"No, just the brown sugar and nutmeg," said Lenni.

They wrote it down.

Diana brought over a cup of tea. Lenni took the tea with shaking hands and turned to the neutral cop.

"He just broke right in," she explained. "Yelling. And I was peeling the sweet potatoes, and he came into the kitchen and I stabbed him and he dropped—it happened very fast." She took a sip of tea and spat it across the table.

"Unhh! What's in the tea?"

"Mostly bourbon," said Diana. "With lemon juice. I thought it would bring some color back to your face."

It had. Lenni's face was purple now.

"Judy, you look like you could use some, too." Diana handed me a cup.

I pushed it away. "I'm a widow," I said. "I'm too upset to drink anything."

"You shouldn't waste good bourbon like that," said the good cop, licking his lips. Diana got the message and poured him and his partners generous shots.

"I always keep bourbon in the house in case someone gets murdered," she said.

"I didn't mean to make you a widow,"

Lenni moaned. "I was worried about dinner tonight. I was planning to make southern fried chicken and put the pie in later while the chicken was frying. He kicked the door right in the middle of my pie." We all looked over at her pie, but she was pointing at the door.

Sure enough, there was a Marshall-size foot hole in the bottom of the door.

"What's that powder?" The bad cop pointed to brown powdery footsteps that made their way across the kitchen floor.

"He knocked over the can of nutmeg when he died," said Lenni.

"Oh Lenni." Patty shook her head. "You shouldn't put nutmeg in the pie. No one likes it with nutmeg."

"Patty, I **sweeten** it with brown sugar," Lenni said. "I don't use just nutmeg alone. Besides, I always thought you liked my sweet potato pie."

"I do, dear," Patty reassured her. "It's wonderful, but I really think a hint of cinnamon would make it absolutely divine."

"Corn syrup," said the neutral cop. "Corn syrup goes with nutmeg."

"Yeah, everyone knows brown sugar goes with cinnamon," said the good cop.

"And a drop of bourbon," said Diana.

The good cop wrote it down. The bad cop turned to me.

"And where were you when they were murdering your husband?"

"I was staying overnight at a friend's house."

"Pretty convenient, eh?"

"We sent her away," Diana protested.

"Ah!" The bad cop got it now. "You-all sent her away so you could do your little crime and she would be in the clear."

"It was big crime," Lenni wailed. "And I'm the only one who did it."

"Why would I want to be in the clear and let Lenni get in trouble?" I asked. "It was my husband. She didn't even know him."

The bad cop pushed his face close to Lenni's. "Why don't we ask Ms. Griffin?"

Lenni broke down sobbing. She was getting close to hysterical. Diana turned to Patty.

"You studied medicine. Can't you do something for her?"

Patty moved toward Lenni. "I'm a chiropractor. . . . I suppose I could give her a back adjustment." The good cop waved Patty away and handed Lenni a tissue. She used it to dab at her eyes and blow her nose, then wiped the table with it.

"So you were making a pie," said the neutral cop, prompting Lenni to finish her account.

She emitted a small sob. "I just sliced out. In self-defense, I mean. I only got his thumb, and he staggered into the kitchen, and then dropped. Just like that." She snapped the fingers on her guilty hand.

The cops finished their bourbon. Diana poured some more. They wrote some more. But now there was a definite atmosphere of relaxation in the room.

"You bake a lot?" The good cop asked Lenni.

She nodded.

He nodded, too. "I like sweet potato pie. You can't get good sweet potato pie in the supermarket."

"I bake my own, from scratch." She sniffled, then added modestly, "I even put pecans in it. It's a very good recipe."

Now all three cops were nodding. They looked like a trio of those bobble-head dolls that sit on dashboards.

"A homemaker gone bad," said the bad cop. "They're the worst kind."

"You know, you could start a cottage industry," mused the good cop.

"Killing husbands?" Lenni looked at him, bewildered.

"Naw, baking pies. Everyone loves pies." He gestured to the other cops to gather around him. "Excuse us for a moment."

The three of them went into a huddle that lasted a few minutes before they turned back to us. The good cop cleared his throat.

"We feel this was self-defense. The victim in question most likely succumbed to a heart attack." He gestured toward his colleagues. "We've agreed that we don't need to take Ms. Griffin in, but you will need to talk to the district attorney."

The bad cop drained his bourbon. "And we will keep the knife."

"Oh no," said Lenni. "It's my best paring knife."

"Just stay where we can find you," the bad cop said.

"Okay," said Lenni. "I won't even finish baking the pie."

"You can finish the pie," said the good cop. "You might want to save us some."

They ran out of questions and there was an awkward pause.

"So," said the bad cop, draining his glass, "you girls live alone here?"

"All alone," said Diana.

"With only one another for protection," added Patty. I thought I detected a waver in her voice.

"Must be tough," said the bad cop.

"And Lenni's the single mother of a young girl," said Diana. She poured another round.

"Unfortunate circumstances," he agreed. "It can be pretty scary to have someone kick a door in." He gave Lenni a smile. He was transforming right before our eyes.

Lenni rose to the occasion. "Oh, I was terrified." She clutched her hands to her chest to emphasize her terror.

"I'm sure," said the cop formerly known as bad.

Now we had two good cops and one still neutral.

"Well, I guess it does look like self-defense," said the neutral cop. "Three attractive ladies living alone . . . one the mother of a small child . . . some guy who comes breaking in . . ."

This last round of bourbon induced a strong wave of sympathy. Now we had three good friends.

"And it was a minor thumb wound," the original good cop pointed out. He snapped his pad shut and tucked his pencil back into its holster. "We'll know tomorrow what the coroner has to say." He turned back to Lenni. "One of us will call you." Then he gave Diana an appreciative leer.

"Thanks for the bourbon, honey."

She smiled and fluttered her eyes.

He liked that.

"Anything you want to add?" He turned back to Lenni.

She nodded, "One half cup of brown

sugar, and a teaspoon of nutmeg," she said. "You make sure you write that down, too."

• • •

The phone call came the next afternoon from the bad cop turned good. According to the coroner, Marshall's arteries resembled the New Jersey Turnpike at rush hour—fatally clogged, with little or no traffic flow. And one small blood clot had inconveniently wedged itself in the wrong place at the wrong time. In the great scheme of things, he had been doomed before he left New York. Lenni was free to make sweet potato pies to her heart's content.

He also wanted to know if Diana or some of the "other girls" would like to go for dinner with the "boys." She demurred and passed the phone to Lenni, who accepted.

"Just tell them to leave us the yellow crime-scene tape," Patty called over. "We're going to rope off the kitchen whenever Lenni cooks."

Chapter Thirty

As soon as we got the coroner's report, I knew I had to call Ruth.

She was shocked.

"I knew it would come to no good," she exclaimed. "You running off to nowhere! And now you're living with a bunch of murderers!"

"Just one," I said. "And she wasn't a murderer until after I got here."

"The whole thing is unspeakable! I hope you're at least coming home for his funeral!"

"Of course I am. I also have to come back to settle the estate. I've arranged to have the coroner's office send the body back to his family. He should be arriving sometime tomorrow, postage due."

"I can't believe you would joke at a time like this."

She was right. Suddenly, I felt exhausted and overwhelmed.

"I'm sorry," I said, and began to cry. "I'm new at being a widow."

"Pull yourself together, darling," she said, trying to console me, "and let me know what time you're getting in. I need to pick up some new linens for the guest room. Something stripy, I think."

That was Ruth. Always extravagant in her emotional support, this time she had allotted me her full six seconds before we hung up.

As Marshall's widow, I had business to settle. I knew that I would have to return to Long Island and arrange for the sale of the house, Marshall's boat, and all of Marshall's businesses, which included partnerships, investments, franchises, and Grace Cairo's spanking new condo in the Hamptons, which was in Marshall's name.

Speed called late. "I heard you've been widowed," he drawled. "Rather flamboyant way to end a marriage, wasn't it?"

"I wasn't the one making the pie," I said. "I wasn't even home."

"Do you want to stay here with me until things settle down? Maybe we can even get away somewhere. I'll take some time off."

"No thank you," I said, then added pointedly, "I wouldn't want to crowd your schedule. I know you've been very busy lately. Besides, I'm leaving for New York first thing in the morning."

"I can accompany you."

"Oh yeah, that'll console both families, me bringing you to his funeral."

"You sound . . . abrupt. Did I do something wrong?"

"No."

"I'm assuming by the tone in your voice that means yes."

"No it doesn't. But if it did, we can talk about it when I get back."

"There's something I need to discuss with you, too, when you get back."

"What?"

"When you get back."

"Aren't you being a bit mysterious?"

"No more than you."

It was a tie. Things would have to wait.

Before I went to bed that night, I scrutinized my face in the mirror.

"How are we doing?" I asked the reflection, but I wasn't sure of the answer. I tried a variety of mournful faces, including demure and outright tragic, but the truth was, other than a bit tired, I looked the same.

I crawled into bed in a contemplative mood. It was hard to believe that Marshall was dead, courtesy of his quirky physiology and Lenni's quick reflexes. I felt guilty about all those evenings that Patty, Lenni, and I had spent creatively killing him and Bill off. Now that Marshall was really dead, it was a pretty tasteless way to unwind at night. He was never again going to be part of my life, either as a husband or an adversary, and it left an oddly painful void, which surprised me. Ending a bad marriage was like taking off an ill-fitting pair of shoes. Then there you were, all barefoot, bruised, and vulnerable.

But I wasn't going to be financially vulnerable. His death was going to leave me well-off, and that, too, was going to change everything. I was tired of mucking and cleaning and feeling tired. Would I become one of the hootie palooties? Would it change things between me and Speed? And considering how crowded his social life was becoming, did I want my relationship with him to move forward? Would I always think of Kat screaming "forvahrtz" when I thought of that word?

Early the next morning, Patty and I were having breakfast together. Kat, in an uncommonly generous mood, had given me time off to attend the funeral.

"Do I look like a widow?" I asked Patty.

"You look fine," she reassured me. "Being a widow doesn't create exterior damage. How do you feel?"

"I don't know," I said. "I mean, we were married eight years. I did love him once. Then I hated him. Now I feel sorry for him. Shouldn't I feel more . . . mournful?"

"It takes practice before you get good at it," Patty observed. "Besides, the relationship was already dead. There's not a big difference between divorce and death, except that now you have a body to contend with."

We drank our coffee in silence.

"I have to leave in an hour for my flight," I said.

"Do you want me to get a flight for the funeral?" Patty asked. "Lenni told me that she would go, too."

I put my hand over hers. "Thanks, Patty. You can both come if you want to, but it's not necessary. I'd appreciate a drive to the airport, though. Right now, I just want to get through the funeral and come back."

I was carrying my suitcases to Patty's car when Candy Valesco pulled into the parking lot. She looked sympathetic and even friendly. It might have had something to do with the newspaper coverage, which described Marshall as a self-made multimillionaire and famous New York business entrepreneur. I knew he wasn't either, but I let it pass.

"How terrible for you, dear. Now you'll probably want to get back to your life in New York." Candy took my hand, her features carefully arranged in faux sympathy.

"I'm leaving for New York now. Patty's driving me to the airport. But I'll be back soon."

She looked surprised. "I thought you'd

want to go home permanently. Isn't your life there? With your family and friends?"

"My life is here," I said.

She withdrew her hand and her sympathy.

"See you soon," I said cheerily.

• • •

Though Ruth greeted me with a consoling hug, she didn't exactly roll out the red carpet. Yellow throw rug was more like it.

"Leave your shoes on that," she commanded. "I don't want zoo dirt all over my floors."

I kicked off my shoes and followed her into the kitchen. I had forgotten what perfection looked like. The granite gleamed, the marble gleamed, the stained-glass cabinets gleamed, the coffee gleamed, the scones gleamed.

"Guess it's your first time in a long time in a decent house," she said, pouring me a cup of fabulous coffee.

"They have houses in North Carolina," I said, settling in and buttering a fabulous scone.

"Outhouses?"

"Ruth, the last time I checked a map, North Carolina was still in the United States. It's not a Third World country. You are being a New York snob, and you don't even live in Manhattan."

She rolled her eyes and got up from her chair. "Who cares about a state whose motto is Uh, yes, we wear shoes."

"You're mixing it up with Mississippi. North Carolina's more like Tobacco is a **brown** vegetable."

She gave me one of her well-practiced disdainful looks. "Well, the only place that's important to me is where I am at the moment. Now, come on, let me show what I've done to the house while you were gone."

I was glad to let her. If I kept her busy with the house, maybe she wouldn't remember that she'd lent me the dress for the brunch. I had yet to replace it.

We walked through the house, room by tedious room, all of which had undergone two style metamorphoses and three color changes since I had left. She showed me the guest room. It was all satin and pouf and pink marble and ferns and stripy fabrics. I eyed the bed with some longing.

Ruth looked me over. "Where'd you get those earrings?"

My hands flew to my ears. "I got them as a gift from a friend."

"They're—"

"A wealthy friend," I added.

"—very nice." Then she looked over at my suitcase. "Do you have something appropriate to wear. Maybe something navy? Black is so harsh for daytime."

"I have a dress with me."

She squinted her eyes. "Let me see it."

"God, Ruth, you think I'm going to show up in a red flamenco costume? I know what to wear!"

"Let me see it anyway."

I opened the suitcase and took out the plain navy suit that Patty had made me buy from a little boutique on our way to the airport. Ruth heaved a sigh of relief. It apparently passed the Widow's Dress Code.

Later that evening, Ruth, Henry, and I had a quiet dinner. Henry kept peering at me in that sympathetically intrusive way common to psychiatrists.

"What?" I finally asked.

"Nothing. Just wondering if you might need something to help you sleep."

"Believe me, I won't have trouble sleeping."

"Maybe an Ambien?"

"No thanks, Henry, I'll sleep fine."

"How about a Halcion?"

"No, really. I'm fine."

"Valium? Valium is quite innocuous."

"No! Thanks."

"Maybe a few—"

"Henry, why didn't you just become a pharmacist?"

"You are suffering from a classic case of denial," Henry said, shaking his head and readjusting his glasses.

I excused myself to retire early. The strain of months of sleep deprivation had caught up with me. I showered and settled into the luxuriously soft bed in the guest room. My mind began drifting off into an alpha state dotted with smiling terriers.

"We need to talk," Ruth startled me up-right when she came in and settled down on the edge of the bed.

The terriers suddenly morphed into Ruth. I tried to focus. I was sure she wanted to talk about the dress.

"You can't keep living down there," she began. "You need to come home. You have college degrees, though God knows why they are in creative writing. Teaching is a nice career. You could you get back to it. There's always a need for teachers."

"Do we have to talk about this now?"

"Absolutely. I want you to come to your senses. I worry about you. You **are** my sister, you know."

"The pretty one?" I asked, but she seemed not to have heard me.

"Now that you are a widow, you have the chance to start a different life," she contin-ued. "Henry and I think it's best if you come back to New York, finish your Ph.D., and teach on a college level. Stay with me for a while. And Henry can put in a good word at Hofstra University. Henry really thinks that you are suffering from some kind of obsessive neurosis, all this fooling around with horses. Henry says horses are symbolic of other issues in your past that you haven't resolved. Maybe something phallic. He is worried that you are over-compensating for some early deprivation. Henry says it's time to face your problems and stop drifting through life."

I was trying hard not to drift off to sleep.

"Henry thinks that—"

"Oh, Henry!" I interrupted her, "What is this, analysis by proxy? How could he diagnose me when he's barely held more than a two-minute conversation with me since I've known him? Hasn't it occurred to him that I'm happy doing what I'm doing?"

"And what is that exactly?"

I sighed and laid back on a stripy pillow. How to explain? I reviewed the past five months in my mind. Visions of Natasha rearing over my head, little foal faces squealing over stall doors, braiding Stanley, cleaning saddles, Ivan nuzzling me after a good ride. Patty and Lenni and Diana and Kat. Even the terriers.

Okay, maybe not the terriers.

"I do a lot," I said.

"Mmm," she said.

"Ruth, I . . ." My voice trailed off. It would all sound so trivial, so inconsequential. I didn't think I would be able to make her understand.

"I don't want to be stuck in a first waffle life," I finally said, "I want the **second** waffle, because when you make your second waffle, it has to be the best waffle you can make."

"Waffles? Is someone actually teaching you to cook?" Her voice rose. "Don't ever learn to cook, or you will be **expected** to cook! That's what housekeepers are for! Haven't I taught you anything? Besides, who makes **waffles**? You can buy them frozen and just put them in the toaster!"

"Oh." I hadn't thought of that. I began to cry. What was the point of trying hard to make perfect waffles when you could buy them frozen? It was all too sad! I couldn't stop myself from crying. Ruth handed me a tissue.

"I think this is affecting you more than you want to let on," she said, getting off the bed. Then she leaned over and kissed me on the forehead before she headed for the door. I was asleep before she left the bedroom.

• • •

Like his penis, Marshall's funeral was well attended and consummated quickly. I made myself peek into his casket. He still looked arrogant, conceited, unfaithful, controlling, smug, self-satisfied, and now dead. Present were his family, Ruth and Henry, some cousins I hadn't seen since kindergarten, a few mutual friends, his business associates, and three of his ex-girlfriends, who came to gloat, until discovering they were all wearing the same token-of-affection diamond heart necklace. His parents barely spoke to me, but they shot me so many daggered looks, we could have gone on the road with a knife-throwing act. His lawyer, Walter Furst, of Furst and Furst, came, too, dressed in navy blue and crisp white, with gold-rimmed spectacles, gold cuff links, a gold bracelet, and a gold watch big enough to be the monetary standard for a small nation.

"Mrs. Van Brunt," he said in an unctuous

voice. "I am so sorry to meet you under these circumstances."

"It does kind of preempt things, doesn't it?" I said. "I'll bet it took all the fun out of the divorce for you."

He put a hand on my shoulder. "It's never anything personal. I am just the hired gun."

He handed me his card. "Why don't you come to my office tomorrow? We do have to probate your late husband's estate. I was the one handling all his business."

I took his card and wrapped it in a tissue so it wouldn't contaminate my handbag.

Grace Cairo, Marshall's last girlfriend, came dressed in black, her face showing the strain of realizing she needed to find another potential husband. Her birdcage earrings had been replaced by heart-shaped diamond earrings, small replicas of the necklaces, displaying Marshall's decided lack of imagination when it came to giving gifts. Or maybe the earrings were an upgrade from the necklaces. She paused a moment by the coffin to offer a short prayer on her knees, an obviously well-practiced position.

Lenni and Patty showed up, too. I introduced them to Marshall's family, although I conveniently left out the fact that had it not been for Lenni, none of us would need to be there. Speed surprised me by slipping into the back of the chapel. He signaled me with a wave of a finger, then gestured to a plastic-wrapped item draped over his arm. It was strange to have him standing in the back of the room while Marshall was lying in the front. I felt disjointedly caught between two worlds.

Later, when I was asked to speak a few words at the service, I declined. I had come to bury Marshall, not to praise him. I sat quietly in the front pew and listened to the eulogies from his family and business associates, realizing that no one had really known him. Had I?

Did anyone really know me? Was I wasting my life seeking the perfect waffle? Was the whole thing in the seeking, or in the obtaining? Could the quality of Kat's happiness over winning her gold medals have been any greater than mine the day she complimented me? Would anyone know or appreciate the difference between frozen and real waffles? And finally, was there one perfect waffle for each of us, or did we sometimes just have to settle for a cheese omelette with a side of bacon?

After the service, I realized that there was a certain responsibility that came with Widowhood. Like being gracious and not snickering when condolences were being offered by his ex-girlfriends, who didn't think I knew who they were. Like resisting the impulse to shove Grace Cairo into the coffin with him and slam the lid down on both of them. Like agreeing that he looked natural, although he would have looked more natural if they had laid him facedown on top of a woman.

"His time was over so quickly," his father lamented to me.

"It was a theme with him," I agreed.

Speed passed down the receiving line and solemnly shook my hand.

"Nice service," he said. "I'm glad they were able to reconstruct his thumb."

"Thank you," I said. "His family wanted him to look good."

Ruth was at my side in a flash. Speed does that to people. I introduced them and she clasped Speed's hand to her bosom.

"I'm taking good care of my little sister," she said. "I always try to be there for her. I want everyone who's important to her to become part of **my** life, too."

"Well, this is for you. Judy forgot to bring it back with her," he said, and handed her the plastic-wrapped package. He touched me on the chin and returned to his seat at the back of the chapel.

"He's gorgeous," Ruth whispered after he walked away.

She opened the plastic and peered in. I peeked over her shoulder. There was her dress, in perfect condition.

"Well, I'm glad **someone** remembered," she said. "Though I can't imagine how he got the dress."

"I took it off after the brunch," I said.

"They must do brunches differently in North Carolina," she remarked. "Who is he?"

"He's the one I'm hoping to make the perfect waffle with."

"Oh! Why didn't you say so? Do you

think he would fly to New York to cater a private party?"

Before I could answer her, she trotted to the back of the room and proceeded to monopolize Speed's attention for the rest of the day. I overheard her asking his advice on the best way to stuff cream puffs.

And so the day passed. I shook six dozen hands, accepted one hundred murmurs of condolence, forty-nine pats on the arm, and twenty-two insincere hugs.

And when I was asked what had been wrong with Marshall, I answered truthfully.

"He had a bad heart."

Which was certainly true. He had a very bad heart.

Chapter Thirty-one

There was one last duty I needed to perform before I could leave for North Carolina. I had to visit with Marshall's lawyer, Walter Furst, of Furst and Furst, to sign papers and start getting the estate probated.

I hate attorneys who wear gray sharkskin suits, because for them, it's a little like wearing your kinfolk. I hate light pink shirts with perfectly matching pink-and-silver-striped ties. I hate pink pearl tie tacks. I hate black patent-leather shoes, gold cuff links with big monogrammed initials, perfectly trimmed thick white hair, and the faint odor of Paco Rabanne. Which, of course, exactly described Marshall's attorney. Apparently, he had underdressed for Marshall's funeral, because now he was adorned with an additional three bullion of gold. His firm should have been named Furst, Furst and Fort Knox.

"Judith!" He extended a manicured hand with shiny fingernails and a gold pinkie ring with another monogram, in case he forgot his name. I hate obvious manicures on men. I hate being called by my first name by someone who has just met me on a business basis and then expects me to address him by his last name. I was already holding Walter Furst in contempt before he even gestured for me to enter his expensively furnished office. I hate lawyer's offices that are filled with tasteful modern sculpture—plus a large tank of tropical fish. I began hating fish.

"Would you care for some coffee, Judith?" he asked, pulling out an overstuffed chair that faced a huge carved baroque walnut desk. He waved for me to sit down. "I can have my secretary bring you some."

"No thanks, Walter," I said.

He looked momentarily surprised by my familiarity.

"Well, it's very nice to have this opportunity to speak with you privately," he said in a hearty voice, then sat himself down in his ergonomically expensive chair and flashed me an ergonomically brilliant white smile. I wondered if he had sharpened his teeth for our appointment.

This man, hired by Marshall to represent him in our divorce, had been the major architect in planning my evisceration for the last three months, and now he was trying to exude sincere bonhomie and gracious hospitality.

"Let's just get things started, shall we?" I snapped.

He looked disappointed that we weren't going to be best friends.

"Uh, well . . . okay," he said, and reached down to pick up a large carton of files.

"Judy, these all belong to you." He gestured grandly to the carton. Then he pulled out a file and slid it across the desk to me.

I scanned through some of the contents. They read like cuneiform inscriptions from Hammurabi.

"I'm sure they look intimidating to you, Judy."

"Well, Walt," I said, "they're just legal contracts, but I will have my attorney look them over before I do anything."

"I wasn't informed that you had an attorney," he said in a hurt tone, as though I were betraying our friendship.

"Marshall died before I was able to give him any papers."

"Ah yes. Poor fellow." He gave a sad sigh and started tapping a gold mechanical pencil on his desk. I hate pencil tapping. "Marshall was having such a bad time of things after you left him and moved to North Carolina."

"Poor Marshall," I said, "but it was that old kindergarten thing. You know, 'She doesn't share well with others.'"

He pursed his lips and pressed his fingertips together. I hate when people purse their lips and press their fingertips.

"Well, little lady," he finally said after a moment of gravitas. "You know, there's a lot of complicated business in those files."

"I'll bet there is, Wally."

His lip twitched a bit.

"I'm sure you're quite upset at the moment. It's all been a terrible shock. But, might I say, you're going to be a wealthy woman. I happen to be very familiar with these papers, since I represented Marshall during all of his business deals. I'd be more than happy to get everything straightened out for you."

I got up from my chair, threw a piece of paper onto his desk, and walked to the door.

"Thanks for your generous offer, but I think I want my own attorney to handle it from here. There's his address; you can send everything on to him." Ruth had given me the name of her attorney, while making sure she mentioned several times that he was single.

"Mrs. Van Brunt?"

"Yes, Mr. Furst?"

"You know, his family isn't happy with the way he died. I might be able to run interference for that."

"Isn't happy?"

"The circumstances were a bit suspicious."

"It was cleared by both the district attorney's office and the coroner. There's nothing suspicious about it; it's not like he committed suicide and hid his own body."

"He died so suddenly. Out of state and all."

"You don't become immortal when you leave New York. People die out of state."

"I'm the one who helped him draft his original will, which leaves you everything."

"You didn't do me a special favor. He just never changed it after we broke up, and you probably overlooked that little detail. Now everything goes to me. And I'll thank you to—"

He raised two manicured hands and changed tactics like someone shifting gears on a race car. "Whoa," he said. "Don't get all sensitive now. I only meant to offer my services to you as a goodwill gesture. You may want my investment advice. There's a lot of money at stake."

I put one hand on the doorknob. "Thanks but no thanks, Mr. Furst. And by the way, please inform Gracie Cairo that she has two weeks to vacate. She's a squatter, as far as I'm concerned. I think I'm going to use the condo as my New York home."

"Only two weeks' notice? That's hardly enough time for anyone to find another place to move. You don't need it right away—you have a house. Doesn't it bother you put the poor woman out so fast, to take over the condo just like that?"

"Not nearly as much as it bothered me when she took over my husband."

I tried to slam the door behind me for emphasis, but it had air brakes, and shut itself slowly.

I hate doors like that.

Ruth drove me to the airport.

"I don't know why you're in such a hurry to leave; you have nothing to run away from anymore."

"I'm running toward something, Ruth. There's a big difference."

She was quiet for a few minutes. I was hoping she'd offer something profound in the way of advice and big-sisterly concern. She looked contemplative for a few minutes. I waited.

"Well," she began, and then stopped, and reached over to pat me on the hand before she finished her thought. "If you don't mind, get me some recipes from that good-looking guy who was at the funeral."

"Oh, right," I said.

"And"—she gave me a peck on my cheek—"be happy."

Chapter Thirty-two

Landing in Raleigh was a little like landing in the bathroom after Jillian had been in there all day: hot, unbearably humid, and oddly fragrant. Patty picked me up at the airport.

"Speed sent you flowers," she said, "I didn't know when you were coming back, so I put them in my bedroom. But I didn't read the card."

"Thanks. It's okay about the flowers." Then something struck me. "Patty, how did you know who they were from if you didn't read the card?"

She cleared her throat. "Oh yeah. Well, it said, 'Please call me as soon as you get back. Love, Speed.'"

"**Love,** Speed?" I repeated.

"His very words."

• • •

"So what did you want to tell me?" I asked Speed as soon as he answered the phone.

"Glad you liked the flowers," he said.

"What was so urgent?"

There was a pause. Finally, he spoke. "First, I have a question for you. Are you staying in North Carolina, or is New York calling you back?"

"I've decided to stay. I've already spoken to Kat. I'll work part-time for a while and still take lessons from her. Why?"

"I want to talk about us. You probably know I haven't been good with making commitments, and there are some things in my life you should know about."

"Oh, is this the 'why I can't commit' speech?"

"Just the opposite. I want to let things get serious."

"Are you kidding?"

"I'm serious," he said. "Don't I sound serious?"

"Then I need to discuss some things with you, too."

"Good. I want to see you tonight for something special. I'll pick you up late. We can talk a little bit, and then there's a place I want to take you."

"Where?"

He took a deep breath. "Well, a gathering. Of sorts. Try to take a nap today, because you'll be up very late."

"Why does it have to be tonight? I just got back from New York."

"It's a full moon."

"Should I bring garlic?"

"Only if you plan to eat it. And wear your earrings."

"I never take them off."

We hung up.

Patty was at my side in a flash. "I wasn't listening in, but what do you need garlic for?"

I sat down on the couch, trying to sort through a dozen thoughts. "He wants to pick me up late tonight. Some kind of gathering under a full moon. I don't know what to think."

She sat down next to me. "Well, does he go for your neck when you make love?"

"Not usually."

"Judy, it's time to break out the good wine. Strictly for fortification, of course.

This may be the thing all women dread: The Night He Reveals the Fatal Flaw."

She went to her bedroom, brought back a bottle of Carruades de Lafite and poured us each a generous glass.

"What happens if he's an alien?" I asked morosely.

"Don't be silly, I know his father. Besides, have you ever seen crop circles on his farm?"

"No, but his workers dress like little green men."

"Means nothing. You'll just have to wait and see. And you'd better tell me everything."

I took a long drink. "Damn! I had hopes for this relationship," I said. "I knew things were too good to last."

"Honey," Patty said, "not all flaws are fatal. Some just make you wince a little, and then you go on. Be patient. A full moon could mean maybe he's one of those sunbather-naturalist types who like to tan their willies."

"You can't tan in moonlight, Patty." I poured myself some more wine. "Think! What kind of people meet late at night?"

She thought some more, swirling the wine in her glass. "I'm not sure," she finally said. "But if they start howling, I would make tracks."

Speed's news of a midnight gathering started to trigger some grave misgivings in me. He hadn't specified exactly which category his gathering belonged to, but I was getting worried. I still had a suspicion that he might be involved with Candy, and it was going to be touchy enough to raise objections about that; if he was also socializing with members from more unorthodox realities, I wasn't sure how I would handle it.

He picked me up promptly at 10:30 P.M.

"It's so late!" I complained as we walked to his car. "Where are we going?"

"You'll see."

"Why are you being so mysterious? It's not like you."

He took a deep breath. "I've always told you that I believe in controlling one's destiny. Even **you** wished for that when we first met. And I'd like to bring you into another area of my life."

"What does it have to do with the full

moon?" I asked, wondering if I should have stuffed a silver spike into my handbag.

"A full moon is at peak light," he said. "And we can use its power to move forward in our lives. Achieve success! You want to be a great rider. I'll show you how you can get what you want."

He went on to talk about how to release the energy indigenous to the cosmos, and about dynamism and transformation, and controlling the direction of one's life journey. He sounded like a space-travel brochure.

"Glad you cleared it all up for me," I finally said.

"I'm not allowed to tell you more than that."

" 'Not allowed'?" I was puzzled.

"It's a secret. Will you come?"

Now I was puzzled and intrigued. "I suppose so. But I won't get white sizzle marks at my temples, will I?"

"No sizzle marks," he promised.

We drove back to his house and he made some coffee. He looked so handsome, leaning with one arm against the wall, his hair falling across his forehead; I was almost tempted just to come out ask him what his fatal flaw was and get the suspense over with.

"Now, what did you want to ask me?" He squinted his eyes with curiosity.

I took a deep breath. First things first. "Are you seeing Candy?"

"She's married."

My irritation flared. "You said you wanted to get serious, and before you do, you need to know this about me. I demand exclusive rights to only three things in my life: my toothbrush, my pint of Cherry Garcia, and the man I am currently sleeping with."

"I'm not sleeping with Candy. I promise you. Everything will be explained tonight."

Ripper barked from under the table, and Speed glanced at his watch.

"It's time to go," he said. He left the room for a moment and came back carrying a small suitcase. I followed him outside to the BMW. He threw the suitcase onto the back-seat. Ripper jumped in next to it.

"What's the suitcase for?" I asked. If we

were going to be abducted by aliens, I at least wanted to take along my cell phone and a change of underwear.

"You'll see. We're going to the lake— where we went on our first date."

"A moonlight swim?"

"No."

But he grew more talkative as he drove us down the private road that led to the lake from the other side of his farm. "You wanted to conquer the universe, didn't you? Well, I'm giving you a rare opportunity to join others in exploring the true nature of success."

" 'True nature'?"

"You don't think it's good luck or talent, do you?"

"What else is there? I mean, besides good looks and money."

"It's how you **arrange** the forces of the universe."

"Speed, I can't even arrange my bedroom furniture, so how am I going to arrange forces of the universe?"

"I can't say anymore. It's a secret."

"Secret is a deodorant," I muttered.

• • •

He pulled off the road and onto the shoulder, where there was a break in the trees. I could see, with the help of the moonlight, that cars were already parked there. I caught a glimpse of a cream-colored Jaguar.

Speed led me into the thicket of trees behind the cars and put the suitcase down. He snapped it open and pulled out two blue robes. "Here," he said, handing me one and slipping into the other.

"You're kidding!" I exclaimed, holding it up. "I haven't worn one of these since graduation."

"Please put it on," he encouraged. "You can't come to the meeting without it."

I looked over at him. "I guess we're not going to a church social. Unless you're part of the choir."

"Hurry. We're running late."

I pulled it over my clothes; the hood flopped onto my hair. "I hope I don't get hood head," I complained.

"Let's go." Speed walked ahead of me

along a narrow path that led through the woods. "I'll show you where to sit and watch," he whispered over his shoulder. "But you can't talk."

I followed close behind, holding on to the back of his robe. "Can I snicker quietly?"

"No."

Ripper barked and ran off. Speed said nothing more as we passed between the trees and came out in a clearing. Thirteen robed figures were standing in a circle, their heads covered. The candles they were holding gave dim flickers of light, and I could see that each person was wearing a robe of a different color; red, yellow, dark green, baby blue. They looked like human Crayolas. One figure, dressed in a lovely cream robe, was holding a long flat-bladed knife and summoned us forward.

Speed showed me to a flat tree stump where I could sit down and watch.

"What about popcorn?" I asked. "I can't watch cults without popcorn."

"Not another word," he hissed.

The figure with the knife took Speed by the hand, faced the circle, and made a

Judy Reene Singer

gesture as though cutting an invisible gateway into the ring of people, then beckoned Speed to take his place in the circle.

I waited for them to put their right foot in and shake it all about, but they stood quietly. The gateway was closed by the ritual knife, a key obviously being too mundane for them. I looked around. Robes. Candles. A large urn standing to the side, burning incense. I wasn't in Kansas anymore.

Now someone in a green robe walked into the center of the circle. "I declare the meeting open." He gave a modest bow and looked in my direction. "I see we have a visitor."

I jumped up, ready to introduce myself, but Speed made the introduction for me.

"This is a friend of mine. She doesn't have a name yet."

"I do, too," I snapped.

"A **secret** name," he emphasized.

"You can pick one later," the leader said to me, reaching out to shake my hand. "I am Bravo."

"Bravo is your secret name?" I asked. He nodded. I would have kept it secret, too.

"Now let's give our handshake and secret sign," Bravo announced. Everyone shook hands, then raised their other hand and made some kind of sign with their fingers.

I was disappointed in Speed. Generally, I try to avoid werewolves, mummies, aliens, ghosts, witches, vampires, or any other denizen of unearthly spheres, and though I couldn't place which phylum these multi-colored figures belonged to yet, I knew I wasn't going to hear three choruses of "Kumbaya." I sat down again, shifting myself to a comfortable position on the stump and wondering what kind of nonsense Speed was involved with. I sighed loudly. Why couldn't his fatal flaw be something innocuous, like wearing corny boxer shorts or always leaving the toilet seat up? Then it hit me: That's why they're called **fatal** flaws. Otherwise, relationships would just be put on the critical list.

"Any announcements?" Bravo asked.

The knife-wielder interrupted him. "Wait! We can't talk with **her** here!" It was a woman, and her voice had a familiar ring. Candy! Candy, who was always in the thick of society functions, had finally picked the proper fashion accessories to complement her personality. I loved how her robe matched her Jaguar. It was sheet chic.

"She has to promise to keep this meeting secret," someone called out.

Bravo turned to me again. "Do you?"

I looked from him to Candy. "Of course," I said. It's so hard to say no at knife point.

Bravo questioned me further. "Do you believe in secrets?"

I thought about that for a moment. This was obviously a trick question. Marshall had spent our entire marriage operating at top secret. But would I have been happier to have known everything about his affairs? And now here was Speed, all decked out in a dashing navy blue robe. Was he hiding something, too? Or just revealing his bad taste in fashion?

"Well, I guess some secrets are okay," I agreed reluctantly.

"Then we will discuss adding you as a member."

They huddled together and chatted for a

few minutes before resuming their circle. Apparently, I passed the screening process.

"We decided to let you observe the Society of the Secret Seven," Bravo continued. "You can stand up again."

I stood up. Secret Seven? I had counted thirteen people. Maybe their secret was that they didn't know how to count.

Candy spoke. "You have to promise not to reveal our secrets to anyone."

"Okay," I promised, but I crossed my fingers. They surely didn't mean that I couldn't tell Patty and Diana. Or Lenni. Or give Ruth a quick call. Did crossed fingers work with witches? Were they witches? Should I have crossed my fingers backward? I'd have to take my chances on the technicalities.

The knife was passed ceremoniously from figure to figure and they started a chant while someone produced a platter and a chalice. The platter was piled high with food. I peeked over. Southern fried chicken.

"You will partake of this, the Platter of the Dominion of Good Food. Having eaten of it, you will have officially shared our hospitality. Then we can start your initiation."

Like the good hostess she was, Candy passed the platter around and everyone took a piece. She didn't hand out napkins, but then, I realized, they could wipe their hands on their robes. The platter was finally passed to me. I remembered the food at Candy's brunch had been pretty good, so I took a chicken leg and bit in. The recipe tasted familiar. I scanned the figures for a triple X, double-wide robe. There was one in sky blue. It couldn't have been Mrs. Brace with her hurt back and all. . . . It had to be Gail.

"Drink this."

Now the chalice was passed around. I took a small sip. It tasted like sweet beer. I took another swig to wash down the fried chicken, then handed the chalice back to Candy.

I grinned. "Secret recipe?"

She didn't answer. The figures began circling counterclockwise.

"I, Bravo, command that you must now undergo the Initiation Ordeal to test your sincerity."

I protested. "I really don't do ordeals."

"She is just an observer tonight," Speed interjected for me. "She has to decide first whether to join us."

"Then we shall save the Ordeal for another time." There was a general murmuring of consent around the circle. This seemed like a good idea to me, too. Ordeals are always better when they are postponed. I sat back down on the stump again.

The group resumed their chant about achieving power and success, about the Tree of Life, Seven Basic Secrets, and the Thirteen Members of the Inner Circle, from which new people apparently rotated in and out, like in a volleyball game.

"You will cross the great road and come join us," Candy intoned at me. I waited for her to mention about crossing over the Manure Pile, but I guessed that was a private philosophy.

Someone came forward carrying a large pointer and a flashlight, then illuminated a spot on the ground. The pointer was used to draw seven circles with the number 7 inside of them. I know it's important to have a logo, so you know who your friends are. I shifted back and forth on my tree stump, trying to keep my legs awake. I checked my watch. It was nearly 1:30, it didn't look like they were going to break for a commercial anytime soon, and I was very tired. And impatient.

"Excuse me." I finally stood up and cleared my throat. "It's been fun, believe me, but I have to be up early tomorrow, and I think I'll just be running along now. Thanks for the chicken." I marched toward the trees, looking for the path.

"You can't leave," Bravo protested. "The meeting's not over." They were giving the hand signal again.

"It's over for me," I said, giving them a hand signal of my own—the middle-finger one. I found the path and started to go. I turned and added, "By the way, my secret name is Cheerio."

I waved good-bye, pulled the robe up around my knees, and started briskly down the path. Speed was behind me in a flash.

"Where are you going?" He took my arm.

"I'm not big on satanic rituals." I pulled

my arm away. "I don't even eat candy on Halloween. I want to go home."

"This isn't satanic," he said. "It's a secret society. I wanted you to join."

"What's the secret?" I asked.

"I can't tell you until you join."

I picked up my robe again and strode down the rest of the path. Somewhere not too far off, a hunting horn blew long, wailing notes. Wolves howled. Maybe it was Ripper. No, there was more than one. Ripper was probably in his own circle, most likely with those hounds from hell, Kat's terriers.

"Please don't go," Speed said, following close behind me.

"Then tell me what this is all about." I whirled around, pulled the robe off, and tossed it at him.

"I can't. It's a secret. You have to join first."

"I can't join something until I know what it's about." His car was just ahead. I could hear voices behind us. I guessed the meeting was over. One by one, people threaded through the woods, got into their cars, and quickly pulled away. A minute or two later, Speed and I were standing alone next to his car.

"You find out after you join," he said.

I was exasperated. "The secret is that you eat bad food and drink cheap beer in the woods?"

"It's a society that brings success to its members."

"So I could be successful like Gail?"

"You don't know that it was her. Our membership is secret."

"Are there other size-forty-six chunkies around here who make a life out of fried chicken? She ought to start the Secret Church of Chicken."

"Okay. Gail joined to bring some changes into her life."

"And what about Candy?" I tried to keep my voice from rising. "She's pretty successful. Why is she here?"

"How do you think she found her husband?"

"That's no secret. She found him in an antique shop. Maybe they were running a two-for-one special. Old chair with old man."

"Judy, this is very important to me. I really want you to join."

"I don't know why you need this," I admonished. "You have everything you want."

He took off his robe and rolled it up with mine, tucking them neatly into his suitcase. "Everything I have is from my father," he said. "I want to show him that I can be successful, too."

His face was set with determination. I knew we had come to an impasse. There it was, the Flaw, glaring in hopeless finality. And I didn't even know what it was about. It was a secret.

"I wish you luck, Speed, but this isn't for me." I opened the car door and turned to face him. "Let's go."

"My place?" he asked hopefully.

"Just take me home." I said. "Unless you want me to click my heels and catch a ride with a flying monkey."

"I meant, I was hoping you'd spend the night."

"I can't," I said. "I don't even know your secret name."

He whistled for Ripper, who bolted out of the woods and stood alert as Speed opened the back door and threw his suitcase onto the seat. Ripper jumped in and grinned at me. Speed murmured, "I really wanted us to move forward in our relationship."

There it was again. **Forvahrtz.**

"Not while you're committed to stuff like this."

"I haven't **totally** committed myself to this."

We sat in silence as he drove. Once in the apartment, I raced to the bathroom, tore off my little moon earrings, wrapped them in a piece of toilet paper, and threw them into the garbage. Then I jumped into a hot shower, dried off, and threw myself onto my bed. I finally dozed off just before dawn.

There were figures encircling my bed when I opened my eyes the next morning. I sat up and screamed. But it turned out to be just Patty, Diana, and Lenni.

"Must have been a fun night," said Diana. "I see you're still in a party mood."

"Get up," Patty demanded. "I made coffee. You've got to tell us everything."

They pulled me into the kitchen and we took our places at the table. Patty poured coffee.

"So what's the story?" she asked. "I don't see fang marks."

"Well," I groaned, "he dresses up like a wizard."

"At what?" she said.

"Not what. He's part of a cult."

Patty gasped. "You mean he's committed his soul to the devil?"

"No," I said. "He still has commitment issues."

"Omigod," Lenni blurted out. "Speed's an evil sorcerer!"

"No, a sorcerer is a magician," explained Diana, "like a necromancer."

"I thought that's what sprays steam," said Lenni.

"No," said Diana, "that's a nebulizer."

"I don't think so," said Lenni. "Nebulizers make love to people who are sleeping."

"No, you're thinking of narcoleptics," said Patty.

"No," said Lenni, "those are necrophiliacs."

"Necrophiliacs make love to dead people," said Diana.

"Omigod," said Patty, turning to me. "Did you see dead people?"

"It was hard to tell," I said. "Everyone wore robes."

"Actually, this whole thing doesn't surprise me." Diana shrugged. "I've always thought getting a law degree is sort of like joining a satanic cult."

"It wasn't a satanic cult," I said.

"What was it, then?" Lenni asked.

"It was a secret."

"Oh." Patty looked disappointed. "I hate secrets."

"She'll tell us when she's ready," said Lenni soothingly.

I looked from one to the other. My circle of friends, grinning like idiots. "Thanks for the sympathy," I said. "I wanted some comforting words about the end of a relationship, and you are not helping."

Now all three looked contrite.

Patty apologized. "I'm sorry. I know you wanted some warm and fuzzy words of comfort, but I might not be a good mother figure. My own daughter has labeled me an obsessive neurotic because I live with horses."

"Above horses," Diana corrected her. "But you are still an obsessive neurotic."

Lenni frowned into her coffee. "All I can say is, if Speed brought me to something like that, I'd kill him."

"You're allowed only one murder a year," Diana pointed out to her.

"Well, thanks for the input." I got up from the table, trudged back into my bedroom, and threw myself across my bed. A few minutes later, there was a knock on the door. It was Diana. She came in and sat down on the bed.

"That must have been a bit of a shock," she said.

"I really wanted this to work, Diana. I was kind of falling for him."

"It might still be okay. There are a lot of mixed marriages these days."

"Right." I snorted. "And when he goes out once a month during the full moon, I can pretend it's his bowling night."

"Well, it depends on what you want from a relationship. What you are willing to tolerate. If he's worth it to you, it may not be such a fatal flaw."

"It's fatal. How could I ever be with someone who has secrets from me?" I wailed.

"If he tells you, it's not a secret," Diana pointed out. "So that actually makes sense."

I wiped my eyes and sniffled. "I was so hoping Speed was the One. My second waffle. I wanted it to be a really good waffle."

Diana leaned over and gave my hair an affectionate ruffle. "That's the way things go sometimes," she said. "You just have to accept him for what he is. It's something that you learn as you go through life, Judy. Some of your waffles are going to have a few nuts in them."

Chapter Thirty-three

It was about a week after the full moon, and Patty started spouting a mangled version of Spanish. We became **mis amigas**, or **compañeras**, and had our names given a Hispanic flavor. Diana's and Lenni's names barely changed from their English version, but my name once again underwent a transformation—to Hoodee—which was the sole reason I'd dropped Spanish in high school. I hated that my name sounded like something a bird makes when it gets sick.

Patty gave no reason for her sudden Latinization, and we remained mystified until she finally hung a pamphlet on the refrigerator. Apparently, Gabriel-Rafael Valderone de la Valderone would soon be arriving at Easton Stud to hold a clinic. He was a Rider among riders, the brochure proclaimed, a Trainer among trainers. A Classicist, a Purist, a Phenomenon. Only the foolish would miss the opportunity to work with him. Our horses deserved this rare chance to enhance their Equinehood, to relearn how to move in their most naturally balanced state of mind and body as they were ridden toward supreme Enlightenment. The fine print at the bottom of the page stated that an hour with Master Valderone de la Valderone was only $250, and for this paltry sum you were entitled to a 10 percent discount on Master Valderone de la Valderone's upcoming privately published $75 book, **Riding Into Your Destiny,** as well as the $150 soon-to-be-released private video, **Primordial Equitation.** For those who wished merely to audit from the sidelines, the fee was only one hundred dollars—per day. And Master Valderone de la Valderone strongly urged all attendees, equestrian and pedestrian, to take advantage of his three days at the farm. Anything less would compromise one's karma.

"I can't believe you've never heard of Gabriel-Rafael Valderone de la Valderone!" Patty exclaimed. "He **must** have come to New York to hold clinics."

I vaguely remembered him from Candy's brunch. He had been the one holding court in her dining room, wearing the black satin pants and ballet slippers, but I had been too overwhelmed with the social scene to pay much attention.

"Is he like an Olympian or something?" I asked.

Patty was indignant. Gabriel-Rafael Valderone de la Valderone was beyond the Olympics. He had no need for mere horse shows. His riding was like a great ballet or a fine painting, and one didn't put exquisite works of art into **contests.**

"He's very deep." She sighed. "Very complex. You may not even understand anything he says, he's so advanced. Way beyond mere mortal riding. He's . . . transforming."

I was dying to see someone who would transform beyond mere mortal riding. Maybe he would transform into a centaur, with the head and shoulders of a man and his bottom half that of a horse, except for the problems it could create when he had to buy himself underwear.

"Two hundred and fifty dollars an hour."

I whistled, reading the prices over Patty's shoulder.

"It's not even an hour." She laughed. "It's an instructional hour—forty-five minutes."

"Like the psychotherapeutic hour," I said. "Are you going?"

"Of course. All the boarders are."

That meant twenty-five women and their horses, which now created a very big problem for Diana. As farm manager, it fell to her to help smuggle twenty-five horses off the farm, along with the entire population of student and workers, since the riders would need grooms. And it would have to be accomplished without arousing either the suspicion or ire of Kat, who always maintained a strong proprietary interest in her riders and their horses. A secondary problem was purely personal: It involved my seeing Speed again. I had been avoiding his phone calls since the last full moon.

I worried about it over dinner.

"We can take care of Speed," Diana said between bites of salad. "Lenni and I can hover around you at all times, like guard dogs. He won't get a minute alone to talk to you."

"Yeah," agreed Lenni. "Just call us the Devil Dogs."

With my problem settled, the conversation turned back to the strategy for the clinic.

Diana was exasperated. "You think Kat won't notice her entire farm emptying out?"

"How about if we tell her it's a trail ride?" Lenni suggested. "That we're taking the horses for a little spin out in the countryside."

"Lenni!" Diana exclaimed. "We're living on three thousand acres. Kat **owns** the whole fucking countryside!"

"Kat respects you," Patty said to Diana. "She might not mind us all going if you told her that you were interested in riding with Gabriel-Rafael, too."

"Thanks, but I wouldn't spend ten minutes with that charlatan!" Diana pushed away from the table with a look of disapproval. She retired to the shower, but Lenni, Patty, and I stuck it out, trying to come up with a reason for twenty-five horses to leave the farm.

It was almost impossible. Vets and farriers, saddle makers and blanket fitters—all came to the farm. There was no reason for a horse to leave. Ever. Horses don't have sick relatives to visit, nor do they need a day off for shopping in the city. There was no logical reason for an entire barn population to emigrate anywhere. We eventually gave up and went to bed.

Patty was in a funk for days. A Spanish funk. "**¡Ay caramba!**" she took to groaning. "**Es un problema grande.**"

A **problema** without a **solucíon.**

Kat solved it unwittingly, all by herself. She announced a few days later, during an early-morning lesson, that she was going out of town to judge a few horse shows and would be back at seven o'clock Sunday night. Since the clinic ended at five o'clock, twenty-five horses had to be back in their stalls by the time Kat came home. It was going to be tight.

"**¡Excelente!**" Patty was ecstatic when she heard the news.

"¡Ay, ay, ay! ¡Qué crapola!" said Diana. That remained her only concession to the current trend in Spanish.

But Patty happily made enchiladas for dinner. She put a rose in her hair and was given to choral outbursts of "Sobre las Ollas."

The morning of the clinic, we had **huevos rancheros,** whipped up by Patty, to put us all in the mood. Plus, Diana, diplomatically acknowledging Patty's general cowardice about riding Sam, suggested giving the horse a minute dose of a tranquilizer to take the edge off Patty's nerves.

We made several trips with the van, got all the horses settled at Speed's farm, and set out to find Gabriel-Rafael V. de la V.

He was already in the indoor arena, surrounded by a coterie of swooning, cooing women, all of them expensively dressed and bejeweled. Gabriel-Rafael wore black velvet boots that came up past his knees and were decorated with big silver buckles across the ankles. His white ruffled shirt was open at the neck to reveal a gold chain heavy enough to tie down a boat in a hurricane.

He had a goatee, and his long dark hair was pulled back in a ponytail that curled out from under a plumed hat. His signature black satin cape fell from his shoulders. All he was missing were the other two Musketeers.

Patty looked mesmerized as she poked her way through the murmuring women to gaze adoringly upon his countenance.

"Gabriel-Rafael," she said, sighing, "I'm ready to ride."

He bowed low and flashed his dazzling teeth.

"Señorita Patty, it weel be my extreme pleasure."

His special volunteer assistant had been chosen from one of the boarders from our barn. She was wearing a little beige Narciso Rodriguez number with mink draped all over it. Not exactly riding clothes, but then, I had never seen her equitate, since the extent of her activities when she came to the barn was to feed her horse carrots. She clapped her hands and brought things to order. Riders were to enter the ring mounted and wait in the middle while Señor

Valderone de la Valderone mentally contacted and engaged each horse's inner horse. Thus, G-R would be able to ascertain exactly what complaints were being harbored by the horse and could determine if the horse's psyche had been damaged from its enslavement to the human race. This information would be passed along to the rider, along with some helpful suggestions, from either G-R or said horse, thus fostering an agreeable communion between the two species.

One of Speed's farmworkers entered, dressed in his green uniform and carrying a drum. He looked a bit bewildered, but G-R gave him a signal and he began beating the drum in a slow rhythm. The volunteer assistant picked her way gingerly around the dirt arena in her new Pradas and then, with great ceremony, lighted white candles in each corner, after which she lighted incense pots and hung them near the bleachers. Over the speaker system came the soft fluty sounds of New Age Indian pipe music. The drummer left. Twenty-four bosoms heaved with anticipation.

The first rider entered. It was Patty, her face pale.

Mounted on Sam, she waited in the center of the ring, as expectant as a new bride. Sam, efficiently tranquilized, seized the moment to close his eyes and grab a quick nap. Gabriel-Rafael approached them slowly, his eyes closed, too, his arms straight out in front of him. When he reached Sam, he laid his hands on the horse's body. Sam napped on. Gabriel-Rafael stood motionless.

"**¡Caramba!**" he finally said. "He ees soo blocked. I can barely feel hees spirit."

He poked Sam a bit in the neck to rouse him from his slumber, then waited for a few more messages.

"**Sí, sí,**" began Gabriel-Rafael. "He weeshes—" But he was apparently interrupted by Sam, who suddenly became quite talkative—a complainer, really. Gabriel-Rafael nodded. "I weel tell them, **mi amigo. Sí, sí.**"

He turned to the audience, which was leaning forward, holding its collective breath.

"He wants hees rider to come to heem

softly, to be gentle weeth heem, to touch heem weeth love, to caress hees body. . . ."

Twenty-four women shuffled in their seats and sighed luxuriously.

"He wants her to ride heem weeth respect for hees horsehood."

I glanced at Diana. She was biting her lips and carefully studying the arena lighting.

Now Master Valderone de la Valderone had Patty pick up a trot but without touching the reins at all. The horse, sans navigator, lumbered every which way in a slow, draggy trot. Patty looked over at Gabriel-Rafael with some anxiety.

"He must be freeeee," G-R sang out. "Let heem go where he must."

Sam made a 180-degree turn and freed not only his spirit but also his body of his rider. Patty tumbled into the dirt.

I leaned over and hissed to Diana, "What exactly is he trying to do?" She didn't know.

Twenty-four pairs of eyes turned to me, giving me reproachful looks for whispering while Master V. de la V. concentrated. I slunk down onto my bench.

Sam, who was never a fireball and was

now blissfully tranquilized, trotted for half a minute or so before deciding that a life of freedom was a total snore. He trotted back to his nap spot so a disheveled Patty could be helped back into the saddle by two farm-workers.

"Join your horse," Gabriel-Rafael sang out. "Be one weeth heem."

But now that Patty was remounted, she held her reins in a death grip. She didn't want to become one with the floor again.

"You **must** release your horse," G-R urged. "Only then can you have a true rela-tionship weeth heem."

But Patty was hanging on to Sam's mane for extra ballast.

"Try harder," G-R commanded. "You must wa-aaant it."

"Oh yesss." Patty threw her head back and inhaled deeply, but she was still covered with dust from the arena floor. "I do waaant it." She coughed hard.

She threw her reins down and gave Sam a definitive kick in the ribs. Sam grunted. His inner horse was drugged and wanted to sleep it off. After much prodding, he finally allowed himself a slow-motion trot around the ring while Gabriel-Rafael chased behind him, cape afloat, to keep him going.

"Be freeee," panted Gabriel-Rafael, displaying a surprising lack of physical fitness for a horse trainer. "Be freeee!"

"Ride into the light," I snickered sotto voce, and Diana elbowed me.

After several near misses of the candles in the corners, and one pass that came dangerously close to a quivering auditor, the undirected Sam trotted himself back toward the center of the ring, nearly running into G-R, who had taken refuge there, his eyes closed as he gasped for air. Patty's eyes were squeezed shut with terror. Sam came to a satisfied halt and closed his eyes, too. For a moment, the three of them looked like an ad for Sominex.

His breath finally restored, Gabriel-Rafael was pleased with the results. **"¡Sí, sí, sí!"** he shouted. "Success is yours! **¡Magnífico!"**

Twenty-four pair of hands obediently and fervently applauded.

A relieved Patty dismounted. A relieved Sam squatted his hind legs forward and peed.

We met Patty outside the indoor arena.

"It was wonderful," she declared. "Absolutely releasing! I have never ridden better."

"Interesting ride, Mizz Crumensko." Speed was behind Patty. He smiled at me. I smiled back. Lenni and Diana took the cue and squeezed flanks against me, the three of us standing there like a human sandwich. Speed gave me a questioning look, a half bow, and walked away.

The clinic finally ended Sunday night, and by 6:45 the van had completed its final trip. Kat got back to the farm promptly at seven o'clock.

She was never the wiser.

But Patty couldn't stop talking about her experience. She clasped her hands to her breast and sighed, saying how Gabriel-Rafael had opened her channels to higher spiritual planes, ones that she hadn't even known existed within her. He was marvelous. He was beyond marvelous. He was sublime. When Diana pressed for an explanation of exactly what was so compelling, Patty paused for a moment to think.

"It's the accent and the clothes," she said. "I can't resist a man in uniform!"

She wondered aloud if she should call him, just to thank him, to convey the extent of her gratitude. And to let him know that because of his divine intervention, she was now embarking on a life of new possibilities for the first time in twelve years. Aside from transforming Sam, Patty had done a bit of transforming herself: She was now the new available Patty.

The phone in Gabriel-Rafael's motel room was busy for days, and Patty fretted by the apartment phone. No doubt G-R had opened a lot of other channels, too, and the other twenty-four women who had attended his clinic were all letting him know just how open those channels were. Finally, Patty got through. She spoke in dulcet tones, giggled like a schoolgirl, and then hung up, her face glowing.

"I'm taking him out to dinner tomorrow night," she announced.

"Shouldn't it be the other way round?" Lenni asked. "Big Jim always pays for me when we go out." Big Jim was the former bad cop, and he and Lenni had hit it off well since Marshall's death.

"Gabi is not your average man," Patty said loftily. "It's my **honor** to treat him to dinner."

Patty was a generous benefactor, and within two weeks, she and G-R had become an item. He was attentive and courtly. She picked him up at his motel, because he was too transcendental to drive a car. He even deigned to extend his stay in North Carolina—for her benefit, of course. She paid for his meals. She bought him another gold chain. And she was the envy of every woman who had fallen under his spell.

"He is divine," she told us nightly. "He knows just how to treat a woman. I've never been with a man who has such sensitivity." Though we did our utmost to pry, she refused to share any more with us.

Now, Patty and Gabriel-Rafael were constantly in each other's company. They went to dinner and to shows. Mostly, they shopped. And Patty paid for it all. Apparently, teaching the path to ecstatic equitation, though esoteric, wasn't lucrative.

Sometimes, G-R even came to the barn to help Patty seek metaphysical inspiration as she sat motionless on a motionless Sam. The other boarders would stand at a discrete distance and sigh with envy. Kat watched it all with amusement.

"Hass he ever reit a horse?" she asked Patty.

"Gabi?" Patty was taken aback. "Oh, no! He never rides. It would interfere with his aesthetic sensibilities."

During their time together, Patty was positively incandescent. "He has consented to be my partner for the Hunt Ball," she gushed one night after dinner at News and Bruises time. "I will be the envy of every woman around." An overstatement perhaps, but Patty was expansively happy. "He is a divine dancer," she said, "and he has consented to escort me while he's wearing his riding clothes. He looks so special in them, don't you think?"

None of us answered her.

She started making plans for a ball gown that would complement his attire.

"Not too flamboyant," she demurred, "but it will definitely have to have a cape."

And then came the day of the Terrible Announcement. It was on the radio and television. It hit the newspapers. A local horse trainer had been arrested for exposing himself in public. He had chosen the produce section in a Piggly Wiggly, right between the cantaloupes and the strawberries.

"Now, if he had chosen to do it between the bananas and the cucumbers, probably no one would have noticed," said Diana.

"He didn't do it," said Patty.

But other people stepped forward with similar complaints. Patty's Hunt Ball partner would be permanently unavailable. She was devastated.

"It is a terrible mistake," she kept repeating. "I know he will be vindicated. I'm sure they misinterpreted his intentions."

"There're not too many ways to interpret someone with his knickers open, diddling his winkie in public," commented Diana.

"I'll get the scoop from Big Jim," Lenni volunteered.

Big Jim sent his profound apologies. Apparently, Diana's assessment had been correct. There weren't too many ways to interpret someone's intention when he had his knickers open and was diddling his winkie in public.

Patty took to her bed with an ice pack.

A few weeks went by, but she heard nothing from G-R. He refused to come to the phone when she called the county jail, and he refused to see her there when she went to visit him. She was bereft. She had planned for her moment of triumph at the Hunt Ball and now not only was she dateless but her companion extraordinaire was in public disgrace, as well.

The day after a speedy trial and conviction, she put in a sympathy call to Gabriel-Rafael. After insisting to the sheriff that she would not hang up until she personally spoke to G-R, he was forced to the phone.

Was there anything she could do to help him? she asked. Deliver special food? Go to his motel and pack his things so he didn't run up a big bill? No, no, no. Gabriel-Rafael was adamant. He was fine. His nephew Gonzalo would be flying up from Florida any day now and would do whatever was required.

No, no, **no,** Patty insisted. It wasn't a problem for her. She would pack up everything and Gonzalo could pick them up at the farm.

No, **no, no,** Gabriel-Rafael insisted right back. His nephew Gonzalo . . .

No, no, no. Patty wouldn't hear of it. It would be much better to have his clothes, his boots, his cape, safe and sound in her keeping. She didn't mind at all helping him in his moment of need.

G-R was outdone by her resolve and persistence. She was going to help him whether he was receptive or not. She would pack up his personal things and keep them safe until the arrival of Gonzalo.

I drove a determined Patty to G-R's motel room that afternoon. The clerk gave us the key after Patty paid the delinquent bill. We went upstairs to pack his things.

His room was extraordinarily neat. His swashbuckling boots were in a corner, side by side, his feathered hat neatly stored in a faux-velvet hatbox. I packed the contents of his dresser drawers into the suitcases we found. Then I heard Patty gasp in the bathroom. I went in. There on the counter, alongside the typical men's toiletries, were typical women's toiletries; lipstick, blush, mascara, an eyelash curler, face powder, cheap perfume, and hair spray. A nearby box neatly held panty hose and silk slips. Another box, neatly stacked under the first one, held a big blond wig. We were silent as we dutifully packed it all up.

His closet was next. A grim-faced Patty opened the door. Before us lay an assortment of Gabriel-Rafael–size women's shoes: white satin pumps, red leather sandals, slides with white feathers, and pink satin wedgies. On the rack hung dozens of Gabriel-Rafael–size dresses: ball gowns, slinky feathered numbers, satins, and silks. A few tastefully tailored day pieces, too. And his cape, of course.

Patty moaned loudly.

It was all too terrible. I realized right away that G-R was not only a connoisseur of public displays; he also seemed to have a voracious appetite for dressing in women's clothes. I started to console Patty, but she was beyond consolation.

"He betrayed me," she sobbed. "I trusted him. I never pressured him for sex. I thought he was too pure. How could he do this to me? Tell me that he cared about me, and all the while he—he had another girlfriend!"

Chapter Thirty-four

Kat was leaving in just over a week for Germany, and everyone wanted to say good-bye. A notice was posted on the bulletin board in the lounge. "We are giving Kat a big send-off party," it read. "Margo's beach cottage!" This was followed by the usual addendum: "Boarders Only."

"We'll have our own party," Diana announced. "Strictly for workers."

"But then Patty can't come," I reminded her. "And I would have to leave halfway through because I'm only working part-time."

"Okay," Diana agreed. "Workers and slackers. But no one else."

We made it for Friday night, and everyone was to bring their specialty, except for me, since my specialty was toast. The Swedish Annas purchased a whole salmon and marinated it somewhere in their apartment for a whole week, using the secret ingredients that Swedes like to put in everything: dill, salt, vodka, and lingonberries. This, they claimed, would transform the entire fish, head to tail, into gravlax, a Swedish delicacy. Gertrude brought a few cases of that German delicacy, **flüssiges Brot,** or "liquid bread," otherwise known as beer. Lenni made a vegetable lasagna, Gail commanded a squadron of fried chickens, and Patty, Diana, and I filled in the gaps with a variety of cheeses and crackers and salads.

The guest list grew to enormous proportions. Patty invited Countess Ronzerilla, who brought along two spiral-cut hams and Charlotte, her housekeeper, lest the countess actually have to sully herself by carrying a tray of food. Kat invited Speed and Candy. Lenni invited Big Jim. Some of Kat's riding students showed up and were quite democratic in allowing themselves to mix with the rest of us while they ate our food.

Kat arrived in jeans, ebullient and ready to party, and carrying a box of puppies from the terriers, who followed her into the lounge, beaming with pride and the knowledge that they had fulfilled their annual duty of increasing the world population of obnoxious dogs. Patty stood over them and squealed to me. "Joodles! Lookit this cutie wootums, just weaned from her mama." Now apparently fluent in gibberish, she picked up one of the puppies and kissed it lavishly. "I'm taking one home!"

"Come away, Patty." I took her hand.

"I **need** this puppy," she insisted. "I'm on the rebound."

There was no talking her out of it; she had chosen a small female, whom she immediately named Ruth. I tried to point out that I had a sister named Ruth.

"I am not going to live with the by-products of that evil union." Diana protested, but Patty was unmoved.

"Ruth will be raised as my surrogate daughter," she explained. "Maybe this time I'll get it right." She opened the top button on her blouse and tucked the puppy inside to keep it warm.

Speed brought a case of champagne,

372 Judy Reene Singer

enabling us to toast Kat's departure several times over. The champagne made me giddy; several beers did the rest. Within the hour, I had sung three choruses of "Bier Hier," harmonizing with Gertrude in flawless German.

The food was plentiful and enjoyable, except for Lenni's vegetable lasagna. Diana had been suspiciously picking at it for a few minutes before she finally slammed her fork down. "Jesus, Lenni," she said, "what the hell is rolling around under the noodles?"

"Brussels sprouts."

"No one puts brussels sprouts in lasagna!"

Lenni became defensive. "You weren't supposed to know they were there."

The only one who had no problem with it was Patty. She heaped her plate to heroic proportions, and then came back for more. I raised my eyebrows at the amount.

"I'm eating for two now," she explained.

Charlotte deftly carved the spiral hams. "I tried to set them out so the spirals go the same way," she announced. "I didn't want to make anyone dizzy."

The Swedish Annas laid out the gravlax in the middle of the table, where it cast its flat, glassy eyes over the festivities. A few tentative tasters agreed that it was not as disagreeable as its visage would lead us to believe, sort of a cross between a strong drink and tuna salad. But the eyes were problematic, seeming to follow us around the room. I was about to drape a napkin over the head, when the countess grabbed me by the arm.

"I remembair you," she said in a French accent. "Shoodith Van Brunt of the royal Dutch Van Brunts. Vee met at Candy's brunch."

The title sounded so real, I was impressed with myself. We shook hands again. She peered over my shoulder, then threw her head back and took a deep breath, which had the effect of changing her accent. Now it was Dutch.

"Ahhh, zo much aura around you. I mast reet your fortune. Pliz, kamm to my home and let me reet your leafs!"

I took another sip of beer from the bottle

I was holding. "I don't think so," I said. "I shed my leaves last winter, and I've kind of sworn off the supernatural stuff."

"Yesh," she said. "You vill kahm. Vee vill learn vaht your future brinks." She looked down at her plate, where brussels sprouts were rolling perilously close to the edge. I took the opportunity to slip away while she focused on rebalancing her plate. Grabbing another beer, I decided to hang out next to the only place that could offer me any comfort: the dessert table.

I could hear Candy holding court on the other side of the room. She was in an expansive mood and discussing the finer points of finding Mr. Right. "You have to evaluate your prospects," she was telling Anna-Helen and Anna-Helga. "Men are like horses. You always want to marry one who's Grand Prix level, but always remember to keep a nice young horse in the wings for when the first one gets too old. Something trainable."

The Annas just smiled and sipped their beers. It was a revealing philosophy, but I knew they hadn't understood a word.

I felt a touch at my elbow. It was Speed.

He leaned over and whispered into my ear. "Are you ever going to call me back? I've been lonely."

"Yeah, thirteen is such a lonely number."

He took my hand.

"Don't be so narrow-minded," he said peevishly. "We both know you're going to call me. You may as well do it sooner than later. How about we get together after the party?"

"Please pardon the expression"—I looked him straight in the eye—"but you can wait till hell freezes over. I leave you to your rainbow coalition."

"We'll see." He clicked his champagne glass against my beer bottle and walked away.

I spent the rest of the evening brooding over a pecan pie, while Speed spent the rest of the evening with Kat, talking earnestly about the sperm count of certain German stallions. I couldn't help but notice that Patty was a frequent visitor to the desserts and was perilously close to finishing an entire triple-layer chocolate mousse cake all by herself.

"Patty!" I said.

"Rebound!" she replied, putting the last slice on her plate and walking away, Ruth now tucked under her arm.

Diana sauntered over to me, carrying a bottle of beer.

"What are you so pensive about?" she asked in a low, conspiratorial voice. "The fluffy wedding you lost out on or the three adorable daughters?"

"None of that," I said defensively, and took another drink.

"Joodles, if I may call you that, you did the right thing." She was earnestly drunk. "Think of the guest list. Would you really want some of your guests showing up in long robes? Where would you seat them?"

"Next to the air conditioning," I said. "Listen, I'm getting over it. And you can call me Joodles. I kind of like it."

We drank to that.

Before long, the main topic of conversation moved on to the Parade of Injuries. Every party that includes equestrians features this parade, where injuries are brought out like rare jewels and compared in terms of size and bedazzlement. Equestrians crack more bones than a southern barbecue joint and are not shy about comparing dents. Shirts are lifted, pants are dropped, scars are exposed, and disaster stories one-upped until they reach near-death proportions. Since I had been relatively lucky thus far, I listened with fear and awe. It was just a matter of time, I was reassured, before I'd get initiated into the carnage.

The party had come to life, owing to the high level of inebriation that most of us had reached. Lenni and Big Jim were dancing in a corner, despite the fact that we had forgotten to bring music, Patty and Ruth were nose-kissing, and Diana and I were now standing in another corner, splitting a case of beer between us. Gertrude had Candy pinned by the door, preventing her exit while explaining in German the European system of measuring horses. And the three Annas merrily shrieked and chased one another around the lounge with the head of the gravlax. By all accounts, things were going well.

It grew late. Kat clapped her hands for

attention and announced that she had officially passed the audition to train with Herr Reiner Schlutermann, the current coach of the German Olympic team.

"Herr Schlutermann ist ferry mean," Kat related. "He has no patience and screams all der time. Und he valks like dis."

She puffed out her chest and swaggered bowlegged across the lounge, to a round of cheers.

"Aach ja," she continued, "he makes everyvun cry. Und verks you to horrible death. I can't vait to rite mit him!"

Things were winding down. Diana brought out the gifts we had all chipped in for, new white leather gloves and a black silk top hat, since Kat's old one had taken on an oddly tilted shape.

"Viel danks, viel danks!" Kat modeled the hat and gloves, then gave us her parting words. "Zo, I vill be gone for tree monts and I trust you mit my farm." She gave Diana and the rest of us hugs and held up her beer in a salute.

"Pliz," she said. "Be ferry careful venn I

go to Churmany." She looked around at us. "No more murder."

We swore it would be our last one. Everyone clicked mugs, sang a round of "Auf Wiedersehen," and the party was over.

Chapter Thirty-five

"I am not going!" Diana protested for the third time. "And you shouldn't be listening to that crap, either. You're both too gullible and impressionable. Look at how you got taken in by that Valderone guy, Patty. And we won't even mention Judy sleeping with Darth Vader."

"Please come with us," Patty begged. "You know we can't be trusted to go alone. We're too gullible and impressionable. You said so yourself."

"I won't waste my money on a fraud."

"I'll pay for it, Diana," Patty offered. "And for Lenni, too. We'll go as a group."

"She charges?" I was surprised. The countess, in her generous offer to investigate my past and future lives, had neglected to mention that there was a fee for services.

"Of course she charges. It's like Pay-per-View."

Patty made an appointment for all of us for the next morning.

• • •

The countess lived in a large Gothic manor with goddess statuary dotting the landscape. Charlotte met us at the front door.

"The countess is in the stables." She directed us to the back of the house.

We followed a gravel road to an ivy-covered barn decorated with spires and griffin heads and black wrought-iron fixtures.

"I'm beginning to think that North Carolina is one big insane asylum," I muttered to Diana.

"Not that big," she said.

"Countess?" Patty called out.

The countess glided out of the barn, wearing a long dark green dress. She extended her hand to Patty.

"Patrizeeah Crumensko, I am looking forvahrtz to our leetle session." They exchanged air kisses, after which she turned to Diana and me. "Come zee my beauties."

We followed her into the barn. It was immaculate. In each stall stood a gleaming white Lipizzan horse. They nickered over the doors, and the countess gave us carrots to hand out.

"What magnificent animals!" I exclaimed. Lipizzans are a baroque breed that feature beautifully arched necks and noble faces, and these were apparently some of the finest. We followed the countess from stall to stall as she announced the name and pedigree of each, ten in all.

"All trrrained to zee highest level," the countess proclaimed, rolling her triple r's like bowling balls.

"Do you ride all of them?" I asked. She looked at me in horror.

"Nevair! Nevair!! I buy zem to admire." She clapped her hands and a groom appeared.

"You may now put zem outside for exaircise."

Her groom gave a little bow and began putting halters on the horses to take them out for the day.

"Come to zee house. Vee hoff business."
The countess briskly led us back.

Walking into the house was like entering
an aorta—all red velvet drapery, red flocked
wallpaper with dark woodwork, and gold
lamps with red tassels. The couches were
red-and-gold paisley. All the rooms needed
were white lace around the door frames and
the whole house could have been sent off as
a Valentine card.

We followed her down a long hall to a
carved black door with an arched top. It
creaked as it swung open.

"Go in and zit down." The countess
motioned us to go ahead of her. "I vill
find Charlotte to prrepare ze tea." Then she
left.

The walls of the room were a golden tan.
One wall was covered by an Egyptian mural
featuring a large pyramid with an eye in its
center. A second wall had an open mouth
painted on it, the tongue slightly pro-
truding.

Diana looked around. "Interesting decor.
Sort of Early Fun House."

There were five chairs upholstered in dark gold tapestry and arranged in a circle. In the center of the circle was a brass table.

We all took our seats. Lenni happened to look up.

"The ceiling is mirrored," she said.

We all looked up.

"It's creepy to look down on yourself." Lenni shuddered.

"I almost expected to see the top of my head when I looked up," I said.

"If you're looking up, you're not actually looking down on yourself," said Diana. "You're looking up at yourself looking down. You wouldn't see the top of your head unless you have eyes in your scalp. All you should see is your exact reflection."

"Golly gee, Mr. Wizard," I said. "Thanks for the science."

"I don't agree," said Lenni. "You can't look down and up at the same time."

"Sure you can," I said. "I see my face."

"Wow," said Patty, turning her head from side to side. "I haven't looked this good in ten years. All my wrinkles are gone."

Lenni was confused. "If it's a perfect reflection, I don't understand how it's not looking up, too."

This conundrum was interrupted when the countess entered the room.

"Vee vill hoff tea now," she announced. Charlotte followed her, staggering under the weight of two platters, one stacked with gold teacups, a teapot, and a jar of tea leaves; the second laden with bagels and cream cheese.

While we eyed the food, the countess settled into a chair and handed each of us a teacup.

"I reet tea leafs," she said, "und I'm a clairaudient."

"Eclair?" asked Patty. She looked toward the tray of food.

"Clairaudient," repeated Diana. "When you hear things."

"Well, I **heard** her say éclair," said Patty. She grabbed a bagel.

"Der food iss for later," scolded the countess. "Vee begin." She raised her arms and lowered her head. "I call upon der spirits of der leafs to refeal all! In fact, I chust heard a voice."

"That was me," said Lenni. "I asked for the sugar."

"Silence pliz, und put tea leafs in your cups."

We obeyed, and Charlotte poured in the boiling water.

The countess instructed us to drink all our tea, swirl the remaining leaves until they coated the sides of the cup, and then revolve the cup three times counterclockwise.

"Now holt hants."

Diana took my hand and Lenni's. Lenni grabbed for Patty, but Patty was buttering her second bagel.

"Aahh!" The countess leaned forward and waved her hands over each of the cups. "I commant you to refeal to me der future of all who ist here!" She gestured to Lenni.

"Pliz giff to me your cup now."

Lenni handed her cup to the countess, who closely examined its contents. "You vill marry a man mit letter **B** in first name. You vill hoff daughter mit a **J** name, und I see a kite. Ja, it's wery clear."

"But I already married a man named Bill. And I **have** a daughter named Jillian,"

Lenni protested. "And Big Jim and I went kite flying last night. That can't be my **future.**"

The countess studied her for a moment. "Vich vay you turn your cup?"

"Clockwise, like you said."

"I said **counter**clockvise!"

Poor Lenni had turned her cup the wrong way and the countess had read her past. Lenni sighed and took her cup back. Patty was next.

"Shh," the countess cautioned us. "The leafs refeal to me"—she pointed toward Patty—"you vill hoff flat tire venn you go home."

"I meant to get them rotated," Patty said, "Can the leaves recommend a good mechanic?"

The countess held the cup closer to her eyes.

"Very hart to reat. Strange markinks on der leafs."

Patty got up and peeped in. "Oh, those are bagel crumbs," she said. "I was dunking."

"No dunking!" the countess snapped. "Der food throws off der whole future."

"Sorry. Can you find anything in there about my love life?"

"It says loff vill kam from zee east. Dot is all. Too much junk in your cup."

She took Diana's cup next. "I see leaf shaped like a bridge. Loff vill kam to you, but you mast bridge der gap to find it."

"What gap?" asked Diana.

"You vill know venn it is time to know."

"Oh," said Diana, "that gap."

I wondered what my leaves would reveal. Was there a third waffle in my future? Would it be half-baked, like my last one? It was finally my turn.

"Ahh!" the countess said softly after glancing in. "Sooo, you haff been vit der evil pipples?"

"I broke off with that pipple," I said. "Does it say anything about my future?"

The countess nodded. "The leafs varn you to bevare of . . . of underpants on a bleck horse."

Patty and I looked at each other.

"We don't dress horses in underpants," Patty said.

The countess blinked at her. "You air beink too literal. You mast interpret thees."

I was impatient. I could figure the underpants thing out later. Now I wanted to know what else my leaves had to say.

The countess rubbed her temples and took another look. "It says you vill find loff venn you haff broken wision."

"Does it mean my glasses?" I asked. "Do I need a new prescription?"

The countess shook her head at me. "Allow the leafs to spik to you wizzout trying to figure eet out. You vill understand venn der time comes. Now vee eat."

She rang a small bell next to her chair and Charlotte appeared with clean cups and a pot of coffee. Then she passed around what Patty had left of the bagels and cream cheese.

"Where did you get these from?" I asked, taking a bite of bagel. "It reminds me of home."

"A nice little shop in Brooklyn. A friend of mine flies them in once every two weeks and Charlotte freezes them," said the countess in perfect English. "You can't get a good New York bagel around here."

I looked at the countess in surprise. She seemed totally unaware that her speech had just undergone a radical transformation.

"Hey," I said. "What happened to your accent?"

"Vot accent?" she asked.

It was time to leave. Charlotte showed us to the door while the countess retired to her bedroom to rest.

"Thanks for the bagels," I said to Charlotte. "It was like being in New York again."

"Oh yes, the countess knows her bagels," Charlotte agreed. "She was from Brooklyn before she married her first count, you know."

"Her **first** count?" I asked.

"There were three."

We piled into the car and waved good-bye.

"What a fake!" I exclaimed to Patty as we drove home. "I don't believe she's even really a countess. She probably once had a husband named Earl."

Patty defended her. "But she's very sincere."

"And she was accurate about my past," Lenni pointed out.

"Oh yeah," snorted Diana. "You know how hard it is to guess the past."

Two miles later, the car wobbled and shook. Patty pulled over.

The front tire was flat.

Chapter Thirty-six

Kat had been in Europe just one week when Diana got her phone call. She had purchased another stallion, jet black, named Magneto, and he was already on a transatlantic flight to the States. After a stay in quarantine, he would be joining us at the farm.

"Magneto? Wasn't he a comic book villain?" I asked Diana.

"Don't prejudge him," she cautioned me. "It's only a name."

A week later, she got another call. It was the quarantine station in Miami Springs, Florida, informing us Magneto was ready to be picked up. Diana hitched a horse trailer to Kat's Jeep and asked me to accompany her for the three-day round-trip.

"We'll have fun," she promised. "Not like our usual budget trips. We'll have good food, nice places to stop and rest, a relaxed time. Kat said I could put it on her expense account."

"Wow," I said. "I'm in."

No fried chicken and flat soda for us. We had decent meals in real restaurants, and now we were having a very nice dinner and planning to stay overnight in a classy motel.

"Sleep well," Diana warned me over a glass of wine. "Once we get the horse loaded, we're going to take turns driving straight back to North Carolina. And we'll have to sleep in the Jeep."

It had definitely been a bait and switch.

The Miami quarantine station was set up by the federal government to regulate all horses coming into the States. Getting through the locked gates required paperwork and signatures and an authorization from God.

"Can't be too safe," said the station manager. Magneto had already spent the week getting examined from muzzle to tail, lest he try to sneak in diseases, parasites, flowers, cheese, or oil paintings without declaring them.

"Do you think this is the black horse that

the countess warned us about?" I whispered to Diana as the manager walked us across the gravel parking area to the stalls.

"You've got to stop believing all that nonsense," she snapped.

"Here is his shipping certificate and his pedigree papers," the manager said, handing me a large envelope. Then he took a step back and nodded to a stall in the corner. "He's in there. Good luck."

A huge black head appeared over the top of the stall. Magneto rolled his eyes, fixed a fierce gaze upon us, and trumpeted loudly.

"Whoa!" whispered Diana.

She slipped a halter onto his head and the lead-line chain across his nose and then led the horse out.

He was magnificent, a luminous ebony, tall and muscular, and he moved like a panther.

"Look at his body," Diana exulted. "I can't wait to ride him." I could see love sparkles starting to form in her eyes.

"Magneto!" The manager tapped his chin. "Wasn't that the name of some villain in the comics?"

"It's just a name," I said. "Don't pre-judge him."

"Well," the manager retorted, "he's been here a week and already he's knocked down two of my grooms. He's a tough bastard."

I shot Diana a raised eyebrow. She remained expressionless as she handed me the lead line.

"No thanks," I said, handing the lead back to her.

"Or you can be the one to get underneath him to wrap his legs," she said.

I held on to the lead while she bent down to wrap Magneto's legs quickly for the trip home. He screamed again and suddenly reared up, clacking his front hooves together. Diana and I both jumped back to give him clearance.

"He's got a bit of a temper," the manager said.

"Not unusual for stallions." Diana shrugged.

It was very unlike her. Normally, she would have pinned the horse to the ground by his ears after his first wrong move.

I opened the trailer ramp, waited as

Diana led him into the trailer, then shut the ramp behind them. She quickly tied him in and ducked out the escape door. Magneto kicked hard against the closed ramp and gave another earsplitting scream.

"Hope you gals are strong enough to handle that boy!" The manager chuckled as he walked to the front gates, waiting to close them after we left. Diana and I stood there for a moment and watched as the trailer bounced and rocked as if it was about to leapfrog over the Jeep.

"He'll settle down, won't he?" I shouted to Diana over his neighing.

"Of course," she shouted back. "He'll stop as soon as we start rolling."

Magneto kicked and screamed for nineteen hours, all the way back to North Carolina.

• • •

"Meet Magneto," Diana announced after we reached the farm and unloaded him. Patty, Lenni, Gertrude, and the rest of the farm crew collected in front of Kat's show barn to see him. She unloaded him in all his ebony splendor, to a chorus of oohs and aahs.

Then she walked him around to settle him after the long trip, but Magneto pranced next to her, tossing his head and whinnying mightily. Everyone agreed that he was spectacular—until he threw out a kick, his back legs coming within centimeters of Gertrude's nose. She grabbed for her nose and jumped back, then shook her head gravely.

"Dot vas ferry bot," she said, then shook an accusatory finger at him. "Und Churmany alvays sells der bot horses."

"I don't think he's bad," said Diana, defending him. "He just has to settle down."

Magneto had no intention of merely settling down. He bucked several times and stamped his feet with temper. I pulled his breeding papers from the envelope in my pocket and scanned them quickly.

"Hey," I announced. "His sire's name was LadyKiller. His dam's name was Misery-Three. Maybe that inspired them to name him Magneto."

"Hmm, Magneto," mused Lenni. "Sounds

familiar. Wasn't that the name of some comic book villain?"

But Diana had already led him away.

Magneto proved to be a difficult horse. He was rigid about his dinner routine, ripping his feed bucket from the wall and tossing it in the aisle if his food was late; he sulked if he thought he missed a snack and nipped the hand that fed him. He was impossible to ride when the other horses were being fed, and he was jealous if Diana showed attention to any other horse in his presence. Sometimes he bucked and reared in his stall for the sheer pleasure of being ornery.

Gertrude greeted him the same way every morning as she stood outside his stall waiting for a safe moment to enter and feed him. **"Guten Morgen, verdammter Idiot."** Then she always turned to Diana and commented, "Churmany alvays sells der bot horses."

"He's not bad," Diana would retort. "He's brilliant."

And he was brilliant. In the way that some scientists are brilliant and just over the line into madness. He was strong and impetuous under saddle and often bolted Diana around the arena, challenging everyone within earshot with his powerful screams. The muscles in her arms would strain as she fought him for control. But Diana continued to love him.

"I wish Gertrude would stop calling him a 'damned idiot' every morning," she complained to us at the dinner table. "It's not good for him to hear that all the time."

"She doesn't always call him that," Lenni said. "Sometimes she calls him a **'verdammter Scheissekopf.'** "

"Well, Kat bought him for a reason."

"Knowing Kat," said Patty, "he was in the bargain barn. Just be careful around him."

"I know," said Diana. "I love him, but I don't trust him."

"Sounds like marriage," I said.

And she continued to ride him faithfully—every day.

"Isn't he wonderful!" she would crow as riders fled the ring and visitors cowered behind the gates. "What a challenge!"

He was arrogant, and it showed when he

moved. He trotted as though he had no use for gravity, taking huge lofty strides that floated him across the ring. But Diana persevered, matching temper for temper, challenge for challenge, and will against will.

"What power!" she would exult when he reared and twisted as she mounted. "He's going to be my Olympic horse!" Then she would take her whip and bash him on the rump to discipline him.

"What talent!" she would enthuse as he flew around the ring in his great jumping canter, trying to unseat her with a tantrum. Then she would take her whip and bash him on the rump to discipline him.

"What persistence!" she would say admiringly as he stamped his feet and snorted just before bucking her off. Then she would grab her whip, remount, and bash him on the rump to discipline him.

She never rode him without her weapons of spurs and a whip. Sometimes she even carried two whips.

Despite himself, he began to advance in his training. And I enjoyed watching them, always making sure I stood safely at a distance.

In just a few weeks, they seemed to reach an understanding between them: Diana was the rider in charge; Magneto was relegated to being the horse who followed orders. Until one day when he suddenly reared, slamming Diana in the mouth with his head and loosening two of her front teeth.

"You might need a bridge," Patty said, examining Diana's mouth later that day. "As the widow of a dentist, I know these things. Maybe you should leave him for Kat to ride."

"But I love him," Diana said. She swallowed some painkillers, put herself on a diet of poached eggs and yogurt, and resumed riding him. And I always watched.

I made it a point to stand a distance from the ring when she rode him. He was an extravagant mover, animated and elegant. He inspired animation in Diana, too, especially when she screamed "NO, NO! NO!" just before he threw her across the ring. There was even a betting pool among the Swedish girls as to how long each ride would last.

Yet he fascinated me. He was going to make an extraordinary show horse. And I just knew he would be a thrilling ride.

"Would you like to try him?" Diana asked me one day as I stood in my usual spot six feet from the gate. Their ride that morning had been unusually soft and cooperative.

"Thanks, but I like to eat solid food," I said.

She made a wry face. "He hardly rears anymore, and he's being very mellow today. You've been riding a long time now. And you've had some tough rides. I know you can handle him."

"But I'm not dressed to ride," I protested. "I'm only wearing jeans and shoes."

She dismounted and held the reins out to me.

"Just for a minute or two," she said. "Come on. I'll be right here."

There he stood, gloriously coal black. I really did want to try him, if only for a few minutes. Then I remembered the warning from the countess.

"Well, okay," I said, "but first I have to do something."

I ran behind a secluded part of the arena fence and slipped off my shoes and jeans, then my underpants, then quickly pulled my jeans and shoes back on.

"What are you doing?" Diana called over. "Throwing up? He's not that bad."

"Taking off my underpants," I called back. "Remember what the countess said about danger and underpants on a black horse?"

I walked back into the ring, my underpants folded neatly in my back pocket, took the horse from Diana, and swiftly mounted. "I'm not taking any chances."

"How do you know she didn't mean you would be in danger if you **didn't** wear underpants on a black horse? Wouldn't that make more sense? Or underpants with treads on them? You know, the slippage factor. Underpants prevent slippage."

"I think she meant no underpants."

"I think you're making a big mistake riding commando."

Magneto settled the argument by prancing a circle around Diana and trumpeting loudly. He was impatient, and I realized that I had better get his attention back on work.

"Get him **forward**," Diana urged.

"Riding forward is the best approach with a stallion," I reminded him, trying to keep the waver out of my voice. He didn't seem to care. One of the boarders started to enter the ring on her mare.

"Is that Magneto?" she called in.

Diana affirmed that it was.

The boarder turned her horse around. "I think I'll ride outside. I wasn't planning to breed her for a few years yet."

It was a great vote of confidence.

"Forward! Right away!" Diana yelled. I didn't like the urgency I detected in her voice. In a moment, I knew why. Magneto reared up, squealing with rage at the mare leaving his presence.

"Take your whip and smack him on the ass," Diana shouted.

I took her advice and snapped the whip against the horse's rump. He leapt forward with resentment, then reared again. It was like sitting on a rocket. After a long moment in the air, we landed. I struggled to stay astride, trying to balance into the power of his body while it coiled and uncoiled underneath me in an enormous trot.

"Keep him going **forward**," Diana called to me. "Remember, he's a stallion, and they like to rear."

She didn't have to tell me that rearing was one of the most dangerous things a horse could do. That had been Natasha's first lesson with me.

"Whoa." I let my breath out slowly, my legs urging him to move forward.

"Now canter him," said Diana. "Before he gets bored with you."

I gave him the signal and Magneto responded instantly by surging into a bounding canter. We sailed around the ring; I could barely contain him. I gasped for air as the g-forces plastered my nostrils shut. He was an incredible ride.

I didn't think to ask what to do when he got bored at the canter, because in a flash, he was already bored. He bolted sideways and then reared.

"Forward," Diana yelled. **"Now. Now!"**

I had a quick mental picture of myself at the pearly gates, with Saint Peter shaking his head at me and remonstrating, "You were supposed to go **forvahrtz.**"

Magneto reared yet again.

It was too late to stop him. He reared so high, he lost his balance and slipped backward, falling over in slow motion. I had two thoughts. One was to wonder if I should have put Ruth in my will; the other was, Shit, this is gonna be so **bad.**

The second one turned out to be prophetic.

Chapter Thirty-seven

I guess it was inevitable. I had been on the sunny side of luck since I'd started at the farm, but now my luck had run out. Magneto and I hit the ground at the same time and almost in the same spot. All went black. It seemed like a mere second later that I was wondering who had put so much dirt in my bed. It didn't matter—you make your bed and you sleep in it.

"Can you answer me?" Diana was calling to me through a hollow tube.

"Whooooaa," I said.

"Don't move," she instructed, which was fine with me. It was still dark out, way too early to get up. I went back to sleep. I could straighten out the dirty bed thing later.

Sirens.

I sat up to grab the phone.

"Don't move," someone said. "You probably have a concussion."

"Whoa," I replied.

"Man, look at this," someone else commented. "That horse threw her right out of her underpants! They're lying next to her."

"Whoa," someone said.

Something was rolled underneath me and I floated up into the air. I tried to open my eyes, but purple-and-yellow squares of light were spinning and weaving into one another. They started pulsating in time to the loud ringing in my ears. It had to be one of Jillian's new music CDs. I'd have to talk to her about the volume. How can anyone get any rest like that?

"What happened?" I heard a voice ask.

"Horse went over backward on her," said Diana. "That black one."

"Black is too harsh for day," I said. "Navy is better."

"She's speaking nonsense," said a second voice.

"Not unusual for her," said Diana.

"Diana, I'll go with her." Now I heard Patty's voice. "You take care of Magneto. I'll call you from the hospital. You can drive there later."

"Why is everybody in my bed?" I complained.

"I'm going with you, hon," Patty whispered into my ear. Then she chuckled. "Hope your mama taught you to always wear clean underwear!"

The siren grew louder and we bumped hard onto the road. The ambulance was going over backward.

"Noooo!" I said, trying to sit up. "Forward! You've got to use more leg." Then I realized there was a sharp pain below my knee. "Forget the leg," I said, "It just fell off."

"Jeez, she's really out of it," someone said.

"Whoa," I agreed, and let the spinning squares take over. People spend a lot of money for special effects like that. Then the darkness closed in.

"Come to the light." A gentle, soothing voice was calling to me. I felt myself moving headlong into a tunnel that had a white light at the end, glowing softly. I was nervous. It was my first near-death experience. I thought I saw Elvis. Then I was afraid I'd run into Marshall, and I worried about how embarrassing it would be to have to explain my sudden arrival to him. I wondered if I ran into Marshall, was I heading for the wrong place?

"Come to the light," the voice repeated.

"Okay, Lord," I whispered back. "I'm coming."

Wondering just what my spirit guide might look like, I forced my eyes open.

"Come more to the **right,**" the nurse instructed. "And don't look so worried; it's only a CAT scan. We need to get you into a better position."

Since my afterlife was going to be put on hold for the moment, I again drifted off to sleep.

The searing pain in my leg woke me up. I moaned loudly.

"We're going to have to cut her jeans off; her leg is swelling three times its size," someone said. I felt the scissors against my leg and then coolness as they removed my pants.

"Whoa," said a voice. "She doesn't have any underwear on."

Someone threw a sheet over my lower body.

"Must be an athlete thing," said the first voice. "I once read that hockey players don't wear socks, something about bonding to their skates to prevent slippage."

"Judith? Judith?" Someone was calling me. I opened my eyes again. There were three identical handsome men standing over me. Six identical beautiful blue-gray eyes looking down at me with concern.

"How many fingers am I holding up?" one of them asked loudly. I tried counting and lost my place after twenty-seven.

"I'm Dr. Nicholas Hartwell, the neurologist on call," one of them said. "I think you have a torn meniscus and a skull fracture."

"Unusual that triplets should go into the same profession," I mumbled. "Your mother must be so proud."

"Just me. Are you having trouble seeing?"

I thought I was seeing phenomenally well. Overseeing, in fact.

"How do you do that voice trick?" I asked them.

"What trick?"

"Where you all speak at the same time, but I hear one voice."

"Still just me."

"I guess it's like synchronized swimming."

"I'm going to give you some tests. Judith? Don't fade out."

"Am I allowed a reader?" I asked. "Otherwise, I won't remember the test."

The tests were trick questions about obscure things that I hadn't studied for. How did I spell my name? How did my accident happen? Where did it hurt?

"Judith?"

I squinted my eyes open again. The three neurologists were still there.

"So many doctors to take care of me," I murmured. "I'm very flattered."

"It says here you live at Sankt Mai Farm," they said. "Isn't that where they had that Thumb Murder?"

"That's how I got widowed," I said.

"You didn't want to pay for a divorce?"

"Takes too long."

They all took their penlights and shone them deep into my eyes.

"Hmm," they said. "I think I'll send you for an MRI."

"Am I what?"

"MRI," they said a little louder.

"You are not I," I said firmly. "There are too many of you." Having established that, I went back to sleep.

• • •

Three Pattys came to visit the next day. My vision was still blurred and making me nauseated.

"Do you mind if I keep my eyes closed?" I asked her. "Looking at you is making me sick."

"Thanks," she said. "You don't look so hot, either. If I had been there, I never would have let you ride Magneto. You realize, of course, that you still had underpants on a black horse?"

"But I took them off."

"And then you put them in your pocket."

"Oh no, Patty! You're right!"

"Well, it took me a while to figure that out. God, I am so worried about you."

"Thanks, Patty."

She squeezed my hand. "That's what surrogate mothers do, dear."

The Drs. Hartwell came in. "You can have just a few more minutes," one of them said to Patty. "She needs to rest."

She leaned close and whispered into my ear. "Lucky you! What a cute doctor."

"They're triplets," I said.

"No kidding." Patty sighed. "If I were a little younger, there could be one for each of us."

"Then we'd need someone for Diana," I said. "Ask them if they have a sister."

"You really need to go," said one of the Drs. Hartwell. "She's not very oriented yet."

"I just have to tell her one more thing," Patty said. "Ruth is finally pooping on newspaper."

I fought to stay awake. "You . . . must . . . be . . . so . . . proud . . . of . . . her."

"Yep," she said happily. "Before long, she'll be doing her business right outside the barn. Judy, she's redeemed me! I'm a good mother again! She's the best daughter a mother could have!"

Once again, I had been bested by Ruth. Patty kissed me on my cheek and left.

"So who's Ruth?" asked one of the Hartwells.

"My . . . older . . . sister," I said, then fell asleep.

• • •

I slept for three days. On the fourth day, I woke up to the smell of roses. Apparently, Speed had sent enough flowers to cover a float in the Rose Bowl. Three Dianas came in that afternoon.

"Thpeed wanth to thee you," they said.

"Who?"

"Thpeed."

"Why are you talking like that?"

They leaned over me and smiled, pointing to where their two front teeth had fallen out.

"Magneto," they said. "God, I love that horth."

I fell back to sleep. When I woke up, three Dianas were still there.

"Tho, I've been thtanding here for an hour. What thould I tell Thpeed?"

"Tell him 'thorry,' " I said.

The next morning, I was down to seeing doubles. Two Gertrudes and six Annas came for a visit. I opened my eyes long enough to say hello. They looked like an alpine baseball team, grinning around my bed.

Gertrude leaned close to me to impart a bit of wisdom.

"Churmany alvays sells der bot horses," she said gravely.

Then they played with my IV, drank up my juice, and finished all the chocolates that Patty and Lenni had brought me.

"Be vell! They waved a cheery good-bye after also polishing off the two baskets of fruit I got from Ruth and Kat.

Two Drs. Hartwell came in later that morning.

"How're all of you doing" I asked.

"Good. How are you feeling?"

"Terrible headache," I complained.

"I'll put some more painkiller in the IV."

"Breakfast of champions," I murmured gratefully, and fell asleep.

By the end of the week, there was only one Dr. Hartwell. He was standing at the foot of my bed, looking at my chart.

"So, where are your brothers?" I asked.

"One brother. He has a pediatric practice in Durham."

"That was fast—I'm sorry he left neurology."

"Actually, my sister left neurology some years ago. She's a dentist now, not too far from here. Why do you ask?"

"Just trying to do some matchmaking."

"Well, my brother is already married. And my sister is gay, so—"

"A gay dentist?" I grew excited. "It's too perfect! The countess was right! I knew it all along! Now Diana will be able to bridge the gap!"

"I might reduce your pain meds," he said thoughtfully.

• • •

Another few days and I was ready to go home. Dr. Hartwell came in for his usual morning chat. I was sitting on the edge of the bed, testing my balance.

"So, is it true? You actually had a horse fall on top of you?" He turned on his penlight and peered deep into my eyes. "Was it a klutz?"

"No, just crazy," I said. "I'm the klutz. I should have jumped off his back when I had the chance."

"Well, you should be fine with some rest," he said, pocketing the flashlight. "Unless, of course, you use your brains for a living."

"No problem there," I said. "I went to college to become a writer."

"Ah!" He smiled. "I like creative people." He had a sweet smile. I decided that I liked him. I watched as he scribbled a few things on my chart.

"Dr. Hartwell," I asked, "with that name, shouldn't you be a cardiologist?"

"Well, my original name was Dr. Brainwell, but I wanted to be more subtle."

I shrugged. "I always thought doctors followed their names into their specialties. I had a gynecologist once named Dr. Finger."

"Coincidence," he said. "By the way, your orthopod should be in soon to plan surgery on that knee you busted up." He reached over and squeezed it gently, as if it were an overripe melon.

"I don't remember him." I said.

"He's been to see you twice. He's the Korean guy," he said, smiling slyly. "Dr. Lim."

Then he held his hands out to me. "Come on, try standing. Just don't put too much weight on that leg."

I stood up. My knee buckled and he caught me in his arms.

"We can't keep meeting like this," I whispered.

"Well, get some rest." Dr. Hartwell blushed as he helped me back to bed. "You may have headaches for a while. Do you have someone who can take care of you?"

"Patty," I said. "She's my surrogate mother."

"Ah yes. I remember her. The mother of Ruth. Well, no horses, no driving. And come back to see me in a month."

"Okay."

He turned to leave, then stopped at
the door. "I can make farm calls," he said
shyly.

"I'd love that." I smiled back. "I'd really
love that."

Chapter Thirty-eight

"How's your head?" It was Nick Hartwell. I'd been home only two days when he called.

"It doesn't feel like my head," I complained.

"I'm pretty sure we sent you home with the right one," he said. "We made a mistake only once in the past, but now we double-check nose prints. What I meant was, are you up for company? I can cook dinner."

"I never turn down dinner. Especially if someone volunteers to cook."

"Good. How many people actually live with you? Seems like you had a cast of thousands visiting you at the hospital."

"Just five of us, if you include Lenni's daughter, Jillian, but she never eats anyway. And sometimes Big Jim, who eats enough for three. Oh, and Gertrude, who eats enough for the entire Balkan region."

"That's what? Thirteen thousand or so? I'll have to make sure I bring enough."

"Good. Or we turn into the Donner Party."

"Oh, and I forgot. You have to also allow for TheDogRuth. She eats with us, too."

"Ruth the dog?"

"No, her name is TheDogRuth. That's what we call her to distinguish her from my sister."

True to his word, he came over late that afternoon, laden with bags and packages, and a large box of chocolates for me.

"You certainly look better," he said when I met him at the door.

"Now that I can focus, you do, too."

I led him into the kitchen, where he made himself right at home. He seemed to know what to do with pots and pans and large sharp knives. I was appointed assistant chef, and while he busied himself preparing his secret signature dish, I was given a task commensurate with my culinary skills: the washing and tearing of lettuce for the salad.

"Do you cook?" Nick asked me as he sautéed vegetables in a pan.

"I cook good toast," I said.

"You don't cook toast; you toast toast," he said. "It's different."

"Actually, you toast **bread,**" I corrected us both. "It becomes toast when it turns brown, and turning things brown is what it's all about, isn't it?"

"No," he said, "the motivation is entirely different." He flipped the pan up and down and half a dozen multicolored and perfectly cut vegetables leapt about before falling back into the olive oil. "Didn't you cook for your ex-husband?"

"He died before we got exed, so he's my late husband. And no, we ate out. Almost all the time. Except for my French specialty, which I made on holidays."

"Aha! So you did cook something! What was your specialty?"

"Duh! French toast."

• • •

The apartment door slammed. It was Patty, coming home from an afternoon of shopping. She immediately discovered the chocolates and reduced their number by half before sniffing her way into the kitchen.

"Something smells interesting!" she said, grabbing a fork en route to the stove, where she came to a delighted halt.

"It's Nick's secret signature recipe," I said. "We can't peek."

"Oh." She made a disappointed face and dropped her fork.

• • •

Dinner was ready at six o'clock and the table was soon crowded. Lenni, Diana, Patty, and I sat in our usual seats. Big Jim had dropped in, and he sat himself next to Lenni. Gertrude posted herself in her usual spot by the kitchen door, which made it easy for her to grab second helpings. Even Jillian deigned to sit with us.

We ate our salads and eagerly anticipated dinner as Nick ceremoniously carried in two large steaming casseroles covered in puff pastry.

"This is an old English recipe handed down from my paternal grandmother," he announced.

"I love old family recipes," Patty declared. "They almost make it worth having families!"

He set the food down in the middle of the table, then served everyone a hearty helping.

"What is this?" asked Lenni after a big mouthful. "It's really delicious."

"Steak and kidney pie."

Forks dropped all around.

"UGH!" Jillian spit a mouthful into her plate and ran from the table. "I'm not eating body parts!"

"Whose kidneys?" asked Lenni, looking at her plate with alarm.

"Veal kidneys," said Nick. **"Veal."**

"Disgusting," wailed Jillian from the bathroom, where she was vigorously brushing her teeth. "They're probably left over from a transplant or something!"

"I apologize for my daughter," Lenni said. "She's apparently lost her table manners."

"Theee only had one or two to begin with," lisped Diana.

"Aber es vunderbar!" pronounced Gertrude, slipping right into Jillian's seat and adding the contents of Jillian's plate to her own dinner. "In Churmany, vee eat dis."

"Ah yes, Churmany," I said. "Where the bot horses come from."

"Sometimes vee alzo eat der bot horses," Gertrude added.

"Well, this is good eatin'," said Big Jim, serving himself another helping. "By the way, Doc, with your name, shouldn't you have been a heart specialist?"

"Actually, I was a kidney surgeon," Nick said. Forks dropped again. He looked around with a mischievous grin. "Just kidding. And it really is veal."

"Well, I once had a urologist named Dr. Leakey," added Big Jim. "So I just naturally figured . . ."

"And I once had a gynecologist named Dr. Hyman," Lenni chimed in.

Nick nodded with the weary look of one who had heard all this before. "I once had a patient named Saint," he said. "It's all coincidence."

We started chatting about the farm and the horses.

"So, Nick, do you ride?" Lenni asked.

He hesitated. All eyes turned to him. He looked around uncomfortably.

"No," he said.

Sighs of sympathy around the table.

"Actually," he added, "I don't like horses all that much."

Gasps.

"I think horses are beautiful but just too dangerous," he continued. "Sorry."

"That's because you only see bad head injuries from people falling off them all the time," I said defensively.

He shrugged. "I rest my case."

Big Jim had to agree. "I wish Lenni would stop riding those young horses," he remarked. "I worry about her every day."

"But I've been lucky," Lenni protested. "I've only had two concussions, a broken pelvis, and a cracked jaw."

"Hardly worth mentioning," Diana said.

Patty made coffee; Nick served a pear tart for dessert, and we all pronounced dinner a resounding success.

Patty and I carried some dishes into the kitchen.

"He's a terrific guy," Patty said confidentially to me as we stacked the plates.

"But he doesn't like horses," I whispered back. "That's a red flag."

"Just one red flag isn't so bad," she pointed out. "Speed had enough red flags to open a gas station."

"No, **he** had a black one," I said, "with a skull and crossbones."

Nick came into the kitchen. "Sit down and relax," he said. "I'll clean up."

"This is more than I can stand," Patty said. "Can a man be too perfect?"

But I stayed in the kitchen to help him. TheDogRuth was right behind me. I liked the way Nick piled the scraps into her bowl and scratched her gently behind the ears as she ate. I liked the way he meticulously cleaned up the kitchen, humming happily as he worked. He didn't even flinch when Diana came into the kitchen carrying the last of the dirty dishes. He just set to work washing them, too.

"Look!" I peeled Diana's lips back like a banana and showed Nick her front teeth.

"My sister's a dentist," he said. "She can fix that, I'm sure."

He fished through his wallet and found a business card with his sister's name on it. Dr. Lorraine Hartwell. He handed the card to Diana and made her promise to make an appointment.

"I promith," said Diana. "I'll do it thoon."

They chatted a bit before she left the kitchen. I liked that he was soft-spoken and unassuming and caring, and I knew he was definitely ranking in the upper levels of the apartment approval meter.

But I was getting very tired very quickly. I yawned, then grabbed for a chair to get myself through a dizzy spell.

"I think we'd better get you to bed," Nick said, putting his arm around my waist to steady me. I hobbled into my bedroom with his help.

"Isn't this a little advanced for our first date?" I teased as he lifted me into bed.

"Not considering that you were in bed without underpants the first time I met you." He sat down next to me on the bed. "Make Diana call my sister about her teeth." He reached behind me and plumped up my pillow. "So she can stop talking like Elmer Fudd."

"It would be nice for Diana to be in a relationship," I said, burrowing down into the covers. "I know she gets lonely."

"I think they'd like each other," he added. "As long as she's not—you know—with Patty or someone."

"There's no one, and Patty's not gay," I told him. "She's a chocosexual."

"Very common orientation." He nodded. "They form intense partnerships based on frequent infusions of cocoa."

I laughed. Our eyes met.

"May I?" he asked. Then, before I could answer, he leaned over and gave me a long, sweet kiss on my lips. I put my arms around his neck and kissed him back.

"I have another name for you and your new specialty," I whispered.

"And what would that be?"

"Dr. Kisswell."

"Let's just keep that between us," he said.

Chapter Thirty-nine

Diana was holding a mirror up to her mouth and examining her front teeth. She had made the appointment with Dr. Lorraine Hartwell a week earlier and had been measured and fitted with a new bridge. And now during her first breakfast with her new teeth she was having trouble breaking them in.

"These teeth look so big," she said, "I look like Bugs Bunny."

"It's because they're new," I reassured her. "They have to settle in."

"Teeth don't settle in," said Patty. "They grow in and then they just hang out."

"At least you're not lisping anymore," Lenni said, hopping to the door while pulling on a riding boot. "I was beginning to feel like I needed a foreign-language tape." She stood up, fully booted. "When

Jillian comes out of the bathroom, tell her I left for work."

"By the time Jillian gets out of the bathroom, you'll be home for dinner," Diana said, "so you'll be able to tell her yourself."

Lenni made a face and left.

Diana took up the mirror again and turned her head from side to side. "How about the color?" she asked. "They look so plain."

"Maybe a nice set of decals," I suggested.

"Or monograms," said Patty. "Your first initial on one tooth, last name on the other. Very personalized."

The bathroom door opened and Jillian came out. "Where's my mother?" she asked.

"Already left," we answered.

"Isn't that just like her!" she snarled, "Just when I needed a lift!" She snatched up her pocketbook and stomped to the door.

"So inconsiderate of your mother to leave for work," Diana said to her, but Jillian had already slammed out of the apartment.

It was a routine morning.

Diana put the mirror down and made a

blowing sound through her lips. "That child is revolting."

"It's the purple hair," I said. "That would turn anybody off."

"No, I mean she's more rebellious than usual. She's been defying everything but the laws of gravity."

Diana was right. Jillian had been ramping up her obnoxious behavior more and more over the past few weeks and was upsetting every one in the apartment. And we knew that Lenni was trying her best. Normally, Lenni and Jillian greeted the morning with spring-loaded tempers, but Lenni had started a new psychology. She had decided to be less confrontational with her daughter, hoping Jillian would eventually mellow. She remained unruffled by Jillian's outbursts, forcing herself to stay calm, cheerful, and reasonable, which, of course, drove Jillian to heights of frustration. There is nothing worse for a teenage girl than a mother who's calm, cheerful, and reasonable. It seemed as though Jillian desired nothing more than to be thoroughly hated by her mother. And challenging though it was, Lenni still loved her. However, Jillian was resoundingly successful with the rest of us. We detested her. She spent long, languorous hours in the bathroom; left clothes, garbage, dirty laundry, and dirty dishes on every open surface; and turned her CDs up to deafening volume. Any mention of politely sharing the apartment's facilities would throw her into an argumentative rage.

"She's out of control," Patty agreed. "No social graces at all. You'd think she'd been raised in a barn."

"We just have to talk to Lenni," I said. "And we should all do it together."

"Like a lynch mob," said Diana.

"I just think it's her resentment of Big Jim," I said.

"Yeah, but before Jillian resented Big Jim, Jillian resented Lenni," said Diana. "And before Lenni, she probably resented her prenatal environment. Big Jim really has nothing to do with it."

"What do you think, Patty?" I asked.

"I wonder why he's called Big Jim," she answered. "He's only five foot seven."

We did speak to Lenni. She agreed that

her daughter had become very difficult, and so she decided to implement several suggestions given to her by Big Jim, who she thought was eminently qualified, due to the law-enforcement courses he had taken in deviant behavior.

Nothing worked.

Jillian continued to defy Lenni at every turn, even taking to disappearing from the apartment early in the evening and returning late into the night, then sulking all the next day. She made life miserable for all of us.

Finally, Big Jim himself stepped in and firmly set up rules. He wanted Jillian to treat Lenni with respect, treat the apartment with respect, come home by eleven o'clock, and cut the volume down on both her voice and her music. He was determined to become the father she'd never had.

That didn't work, either. Things came to a head after Big Jim invited Lenni and Jillian out for a weekend of fishing at his lake house. The weekend lasted until 10:30 Saturday morning, when Big Jim and Lenni returned to the farm with a raging teenager in tow.

"I hate him," Jillian shrieked as she stamped her way back to the apartment. "He can't tell me what to do! He isn't my father!"

Lenni, with Big Jim's encouragement, finally grounded Jillian.

"Great," Diana said to Patty and me. "Now we're all getting punished."

We were sitting on hay bales, eating lunch in Kat's show barn, which, though it was considerably quieter than the apartment, lacked certain amenities. Air conditioning and a bathroom, for example. We had been there since morning and were hot and dusty, although not willing to risk the apartment.

"Are you allowed to sell other people's children?" Diana asked. "Maybe we can raise enough money to get a TV for the barn."

"Maybe Big Jim is wrong about treating Jillian like a youthful offender," I said. "After all, she's only offended the three of us.

She might need a different approach. You raised a daughter, Patty. Don't you agree?"

"Does anyone know why he's called Big Jim?" Patty replied. "He's only five foot seven."

We finished our lunch and washed ourselves off with the barn hose.

"This isn't helping my concussion," I said, letting the cold water from the hose pour over my head and face.

"I am not going to rough it like this for her entire adolescence," Patty called from inside a stall where she'd gone to pee. "We're all afraid to go use our own apartment with Jillian in there. Something's got to give."

Something did. Jillian ended her own grounding by storming out of the apartment and disappearing across a pasture where fifteen horses were peacefully grazing. Unfortunately, in her fury, she left the gate to the pasture wide open.

Horses have the uncanny ability to locate any weakness in their environment. They found the open gate almost immediately. And though they spent their days roaming

over one hundred acres, carefree and unfet-
tered, fifteen horses, giddy with delight,
now made their way to even greater freedom within minutes. Galloping through
the farm, they quickly crossed the parking
lot, hung a left at the driveway, and
swarmed onto the front road.

Diana quickly had to implement a
roundup. She had every able-bodied person
saddle up a horse and ride out after the
fugitives.

She cast a look in my direction.

"I have a concussion," I said.

She leapt into the Jeep and skidded down
the driveway. She was back a few minutes
later.

"I need something to divert the front
horses," she yelled, vaulting out of the Jeep
and looking around for inspiration. "We
have to head them off at the pass."

"We have a pass?" I asked.

"Well, the highway."

Suddenly, she had an idea. She ran to the
equipment shed and returned quickly, bran-
dishing a small leaf blower.

"Get in the Jeep," she commanded me.

"I have a concussion," I reminded her. "And a bad leg."

"We're not using your head. Get in!"

I hobbled in. She thrust the leaf blower into my hands, jumped behind the wheel, screeched out the driveway, and raced down the road. In a few minutes, the herd was directly in front of us.

"When I give you the signal, turn on the leaf blower," she shouted, "and point it at the lead horse."

"We can't turn the leaf blower on in the car," I protested. "We'll roast ourselves from the back draft."

The Jeep came to an abrupt halt.

"You're right. Get on the hood."

"I have a concussion," I said. "I'm supposed to be lying down and resting."

"You **will** be lying down."

"I have a bad leg," I said.

"I'll hold it for you!" she replied, then pointed. "Now mount the car."

I got out of the Jeep and she gave me a leg up onto the hood, where I lay down on my stomach, leaf blower next to me. I tucked

my toes into the windshield-wiper channel
for support while she leaned out of the Jeep
window and grabbed my ankle.

"Hang on!" Diana yelled, gunning the
motor and easing the Jeep in among fifteen
galloping horses while tooting the horn.
They obligingly cleared a path for her as
they headed for life on the road. We reached
the front of the herd.

"Point!" she yelled.

I aimed the leaf blower toward the face of
the leader. The appliance was cumbersome,
but I held on to it as we pulled ahead of the
racing horses.

"Blower on!" Diana yelled.

I pulled the rip cord. The leaf blower
roared to life and I positioned it to give the
lead horses a blast of hot air in their faces.
They skidded to a stop and spun around.
The entire herd followed suit.

"Hang on." Diana jockeyed the Jeep into
a 180-degree turn.

"I have a concussion!" I screamed back,
digging my fingernails into the hood of the
car, the leaf blower roaring next to me as I
slid around.

We continued our pursuit. Now the horses were racing back toward Kat's farm, the leaf blower menacing them from the rear.

We managed to blow the horses down the road and up the driveway, where the mounted posse awaited to herd them all back into their field.

Diana stopped the Jeep and helped me off the hood.

"I have hood burn," I moaned.

"You did great." Diana patted me on the back. "We couldn't have gotten those horses home without you."

I proudly tucked the leaf blower under my armpit. "Just call me Ah-nold."

But that was it for Jillian. Lenni knew, even before Diana sat her down to have a serious discussion, that Jillian would have to be sent away. Lenni made a phone call.

"My mother said yes," Lenni said to us after hanging up the phone. "She thinks I turned out badly, but she's willing to take on Jillian."

"If you turned out badly, isn't that really your mother's fault?" I asked.

"But if Jillian turns out better than Lenni, then it proves that Lenni turned herself out badly," Patty said, "which lets her mother off the hook."

"Right," said Lenni. "That's why my mother agreed to take Jillian. So she can show me that not only did I turn out badly because of myself but my daughter is turning out badly because of me, too. If Jillian turns out better than I did, it will prove that my mother is totally blameless about me turning out badly."

"Your mother should be grateful you're sending Jillian. This gives her a chance at redemption of her motherhood skills," I said, "just like Patty got with The-DogRuth."

"And don't forget the retaliation factor," Patty pointed out. "If you or your mother have any leftover grudges, this is the way to even them all out."

"You would think that the strongest, most universal conflicts of all time would concern riches or kingdoms." Diana sighed. "But it's mothers and daughters."

Arrangements were made and Big Jim

and Lenni took Jillian to the airport, where Lenni had a teary good-bye and put her on the plane for Grandma's. Then Big Jim and Lenni returned to the apartment.

Lenni was glum, and Big Jim tried to cheer her up. "If you should ever marry again, I'm sure Jillian would be ready to behave and come live with you."

"If she doesn't turn out even worse from my mother," said Lenni.

"Then it's Jillian's fault," said Big Jim. "Here's a new concept: Sometimes we are responsible for our own behavior."

But Lenni continued to mope around.

"I was hoping that Jillian would grow up to be my best friend," she told Patty sadly.

Patty gave her a hug. "She will. Just give her some time."

"You think so?"

"Oh yeah." Patty smiled. "It may take awhile, but at some point the heart takes over and finds its way home."

Diana was listening to them. "You turned out pretty good, Lenni," she said. "If Jillian turns out as good as you, your mother should be proud."

"Thank you," Lenni said. "And until Jillian's heart comes home, you three will be my closest best friends."

"It's settled." Patty gave her another hug. "And look how we spared you the trouble of raising us."

Chapter Forty

Big Jim continued to bring Lenni boxes of her favorite Gummi Bears to cheer her up after Jillian was sent away.

Lenni was sharing yet another box of candy with us. "Look at all these Gummi Bears," she said. "Big Jim really has a big heart."

"So is **that** why he's called Big Jim?" asked Patty. "Because, you know, he's only five foot seven."

"That's not why." Lenni giggled. "It's because of his size."

"That makes no sense," said Diana. "Usually the title of 'Big' is to distinguish him from other, smaller Jims, but he seems like just a regular Jim to me."

"I could understand if Big Jim's father was also a Jim, then Big Jim should really be Little Jim," reasoned Patty, "unless his father is shorter than he is. Then he could still be Big Jim and his father could be Old Jim, because it would be confusing to call his father Little Jim."

"But if his father is Old Jim, they should call Big Jim, Young Jim," I pointed out. "Just to keep things parallel."

"Or Jim the Elder and Jim the Younger, like they do with Dutch painters," added Diana.

Lenni smiled. "Let's just say he deserves the name."

"Well, it can't be what I'm thinking," I said, "because his feet and nose are regulation size."

"That's right," Diana chimed in. "Otherwise, the law of metabolic conservancy would be violated."

Lenni was shocked. "Big Jim would never violate a law."

"But if he did, it really wouldn't be his fault," I said. "He would be the exception that proves the rule."

"I have to disagree," said Diana. "There is a constant symmetry that nature observes, where everything stays proportionate."

"Some things aren't always equal," said

Lenni. "Remember, Bozo the Clown had big feet."

"And most likely a very small dick," I said. "That's probably why he entered the clownhood."

Lenni continued to argue with us. "Well, all I can say is Big Jim is named Big Jim for a good reason."

"You're in love with him," said Patty. "Objects always look bigger than they really are when you're in love."

"I know what I see," Lenni called behind her as she grabbed a towel and headed for the shower.

"Seeing is believing," Patty muttered to Diana and me. "And I won't believe it unless I see it."

"Even **I** would be interested, strictly as a scientific researcher," said Diana. "Just in case he does skew biological precepts."

Big Jim came by that evening to take Lenni to dinner. Patty and Diana and I were playing a game of Scrabble and sharing a good bottle of wine.

"Big Jim was promoted to detective,"

Lenni said proudly. "We're going to celebrate with the rest of his precinct."

We wished them well and returned to our
game. They were back around eleven
o'clock, having thoroughly celebrated. Big
Jim's eyes were bloodshot, his speech was
slurred, and his walk had a wobble.

"Gonna shleep here tonight," Big Jim announced. "If you galsh don't mind."

"One of his friends drove us home."
Lenni giggled and teetered over to the sofa.

Big Jim swayed over the table and looked
at the Scrabble game.

"Who'sh winning?" he asked.

We couldn't remember. We were still on
our first game, but it was our third bottle of
wine and we had forgotten to keep score.

"Guess we'll turn in," Big Jim said.

"I'll be right there, honey," Lenni called
from the sofa.

Big Jim saluted us a good night and
headed for Lenni's bedroom, leaving the
door open for Lenni. But Lenni had put her
head back and fallen instantly asleep.

We heard Big Jim groan as he peeled off

his clothes and threw himself across the bed, immediately falling into a deep, sonorous sleep. The door was still ajar.

Lenni's snores were a soft purr as she sat on the sofa.

We continued our game of Scrabble. Patty opened another bottle. We eyed one another and the bedroom door for a few minutes. Patty poured the wine. We sipped it thoughtfully. A few more minutes slipped by.

"We'll need a plan," Patty finally said.

"We'll need a flashlight," said Diana.

"We have to be tasteful," I added. "And nothing strenuous. I have a concussion."

"If Lenni's right," Diana said, "Big Jim might even become the gold standard."

"Then he could get listed in the Naval Observatory," added Patty. "Isn't that where they list all the gold standards? Even if it's not his navel that we observe?"

"Actually, I think the Naval Observatory sets the gold standard for **time,**" I told her. "You're thinking of **Ripley's Believe It or Not!**"

The open door beckoned to us.

"Lost opportunities are never found," said Patty, downing her glass of wine.

"Duh!" I said. "Otherwise, they would be found opportunities."

"No, then they are just plain opportunities," said Diana. "That's what an opportunity is."

"Then this is an opportunity," said Patty, "if I ever saw one."

We formulated a plan, something simple, so we would all be able to remember it.

When Big Jim had reached the proper state of REM sleep, to be determined by the resonance and pitch of his snoring, one of us would slip into the bedroom and delicately slide off his covers, thus uncloaking the appendage in question. The other two would be peering discreetly from the doorway.

We sipped wine and waited almost two hours, then sneaked cautiously to the bedroom door to listen in. Big Jim was snoring loudly enough to bring the big ships in from the sea. And to make it even easier, his sheet was titillatingly askew.

"Who's going in there?" I whispered.

"Diana should," whispered Patty. "First of all, she has a Ph.D. in reproductive biology. This is right up her alley."

"It is not," Diana hissed. "My Ph.D. is in reproductive **biochemistry.** This doesn't fall under biochemical principles."

"Secondly, you're gay," Patty hissed back. "You can be more objective."

"But you're a chiropractor," Diana whispered.

"I'm not going to **adjust** anything."

"Yes you are," I whispered. "His covers."

Patty was defeated. We handed her the flashlight and she tiptoed into the bedroom and over to Big Jim's bedside. She hovered there a moment, trying to work up her nerve, then was just about to reach out, when TheDogRuth, her wolf instincts alerted, realized that a social pack had formed without her. She ran into the bedroom to bark and howl.

Big Jim stirred. TheDogRuth barked even louder.

The three of us immediately dashed from the bedroom just as Big Jim reached down and grabbed for something from the floor.

We all collided in the hallway from The-
DogRuth running underfoot. Patty toppled
over the dog and fell against a wall; Diana
and I fell atop Patty. Diana's teeth hit
my chin.

"You bit my chin," I screamed. "And I
have a concussion!"

"You chinned my teeth!" she screamed
back. "And they're new!"

Big Jim was in the hall right behind us,
wrapped in a sheet and grasping his service
revolver.

"Halt!" he commanded, accidentally
stepping into our pile of bodies. His arm
bounced into the air, firing off a shot toward the kitchen. We heard a metallic **ping,**
followed by something shattering across the
floor. "Halt right there!" he yelled.

"Don't shoot us," Patty begged from under the pile. "We were only going to peek!"

"We have a burglar!" Big Jim shouted
over her. "Don't anybody move. His flashlight was right in my eyes!"

Diana got to her feet and switched the
hall light on. Patty and I untangled ourselves and stood up.

Big Jim looked around, bewildered. "I could have sworn I saw a figure with a light standing over my bed. Shouted something, too."

"It could have been TheDogRuth," Diana said. "Sometimes she howls for no reason."

"Sometimes she even carries a flashlight," said Patty helpfully.

Big Jim checked the apartment thoroughly, then made his way to the barn below, still wrapped in his sheet. The three of us headed for the kitchen and ice packs. Lenni was still asleep on the sofa. Patty turned on the kitchen light. Lying on the floor was Edna Fern, shot through the pot, her ferns shattered. Apparently, the bullet went right through her and ended up in the refrigerator door.

"He killed the fern," said Patty. "And shot the refrigerator."

"She's just wounded," said Diana, setting the plant upright. "We can fix her in the morning."

Big Jim came back upstairs. "He got

away," he said. "But I'm buying new locks for you gals first thing in the morning."

• • •

It was a moment of divine retribution as we all sat around the breakfast table the next morning. I had a bite mark on my chin, Patty had a large black bump on her forehead, Diana had a bloody lip, and Edna Fern had been defronded.

Big Jim apologized. "Sorry for the ruckus last night, ladies." He had just showered and dressed and was pouring himself some coffee. "I was half-asleep. But damned if that guy didn't make a fast getaway!"

"I didn't hear anything," Lenni said. "I slept like a baby."

We thanked Big Jim for his concern and told him how much we appreciated his presence in the apartment. He thanked us for our faith in him and sat down to a cheery breakfast.

Then he noticed the bite mark on my chin, and Diana's swollen lip.

He shook his head. "Remind me never to

get mixed up with the three of you," he said. "You gals sure play a mean game of Scrabble."

After breakfast, he and Lenni left to buy locks.

"We can never mention this again," said Diana through her swollen lip. "It was all for nothing."

"We weren't tasteful at all," said Patty. "And how are we going to explain a bullet stuck in the refrigerator door?"

"My concussion is killing me," I groaned.

Diana passed out more ice. "We'll never know if Lenni was right. **Ripley's** will have to go on without Big Jim."

But some good came from it. Big Jim proposed to Lenni that very afternoon while buying a steel slip-bolt lock for the apartment door. He insisted they set an early wedding date, as he realized that he loved her and had an overwhelming need to protect her from crime.

"A murder brought us together," he announced to us, "and a burglar inspired me to propose."

We let it go at that.

Chapter Forty-one

The orthopedist fixed my meniscus a few days after the failed unveiling of Big Jim. I was supposed to be recuperating and I was bored and in pain. Motrin had become my comfort food and I was spending my days stationed in the armchair next to the living room window, my throbbing leg propped up on the sofa. TheDogRuth lay across my ankle to keep me company. She was the only terrier I had met without an agenda, and I actually welcomed her company while I spent my days looking out the window through a pair of binoculars.

"Very **Rear Window**," commented Patty when she saw me.

"I can't stand television anymore," I complained. "It's all soap operas, or advice from Dr. Phil. I can stand only so much southern-fried Freud."

"At least you have Nick at night," she

said. "Isn't he coming by again this evening?"

"Yep, we'll probably go somewhere for
dinner."

I knew Nick was courting me, and despite the red flag, I really liked him. He was
sweet and affectionate, calling me every day
with some new idea of things we could do
together. But I was toying with the idea of
taking things slowly.

"After the Speed thing," I told Patty and
Diana, "I need to catch my breath. I don't
want to just jump into another relationship."

Diana counted on her fingers in exasperation. "Doctor, lawyer . . . are you waiting
for an Indian chief?"

"I can't get past the red flag."

"You're not in the Indy Five Hundred,"
she replied, "I thought you were hoping
that someone like him would come along."

"I was, but I shouldn't be making decisions about love when I have a concussion."

"Does that mean we have to rename him
Dr. No?" Patty asked.

"Maybe Dr. Not Yet," I said. "Remember,

he doesn't like horses. I can't give up my horse for a man."

"It's kingdom for a horse, and you don't even **own** a horse," Patty said. "Or a kingdom, for that matter."

"Well, if I did . . ."

But Nick was persistent.

He brought chocolates and flowers. He sent funny cards. He dropped by on his lunch hour to check on my knee.

"How soon do you think I can ride?" I asked him one afternoon as he gently slid my kneecap back and forth.

"As soon as you grow a new knee," he said. "This one's shot to hell."

• • •

The next day, Diana insisted I come down to the barn to take a look at another horse that Kat had just sent from Europe. Patty came with me.

"As your surrogate mother, I'm going to keep you from harm's way," she declared as I hobbled along next to her. "I couldn't bear the strain of going to the hospital again."

Gertrude led the horse over, already

saddled. He was a deep red chestnut, with four long white stockings and a white blaze.

"Look at his markings. Lots of chrome," Diana enthused to me, "and a wonderful personality. This is the horse you should think about buying for yourself." She held out his papers. Patty intercepted them and scanned them quickly.

"According to his papers, his name is"— Patty spelled out his name—**"F u c h s"**— then pronounced it—**"Fucks?"**

"Odd name for a horse," I said. "Even one from Germany."

"Maybe that's his job description," she mused. "Is he a breeding stallion?"

"No, it probably means something be- nign," I pointed out. "Like **fahrt** means to drive."

Gertrude took the papers from Patty and read them through.

"Is that pronounced **Foox** or **Fush?**" I asked her.

"Hiss name isst Mercedes," she said, looking up from the papers with disgust. **"Fuchs** isst his color. It means schestnut."

"See? He even has a great name," Diana

turned to me. "And when your leg is better, you are going to ride him."

"No she's not," said Patty, "Not unless I know he's perfectly safe."

Diana lifted a stirrup toward Patty. "Why don't you try him out for her?"

Patty stepped back. "I don't do safe. I'm sure Judy will be able to tell when she's ready."

Secretly, I was having major reservations, too. The last horse Diana had urged me to try was Magneto.

"At least watch him go for a few minutes." Diana mounted him and trotted him around the ring. He looked like a very nice horse. Gentle, friendly, and kind. All he needed was a blue sweater and he could have passed for Mister Rogers.

Candy became very interested in the horse, too. Her own horse, Lexus, had shown increasing signs of lameness during the last two months and had finally been diagnosed with arthritis. His show career was over and he was slated to become a pasture potato for the rest of his life. But despite her irritating superiority, Candy was a timid rider, and reluctant to actually try Mercedes herself.

"What do you really think of him as a riding horse for me?" she asked Diana several times when she thought I was out of earshot.

"He's a great horse," Diana reassured her. "Rides like Magneto."

Kat called Diana from Europe later that afternoon to check up on the farm and let us know that she was coming home soon.

"Did you tell her about the stampede and how Big Jim shot the refrigerator?" Patty asked when Diana hung up.

"I just told her things are running in their usual way," Diana said. "And unfortunately, they are."

The next phone call was from Nick.

"It's my day off," he said to me. "I'm dropping by and taking you home for dinner."

"I am home."

"My home."

He was at the apartment half an hour later. Big Jim had dropped in by then, too, to take Lenni to the movies. And Diana was getting ready for a dinner date with Lorraine Hartwell.

"This is like Noah's ark," Patty complained, watching us pair up at the door. "Everyone has someone but me."

"The countess said that your true love will come from the east," I reminded her.

"Oh, right," she said, then thought for a moment. "Anyone feel like Chinese food tonight?"

We all had plans, but with a quart of shrimp and lobster sauce, a side of fried rice and two spring rolls, Patty found a temporary love match.

• • •

Nick's condo was surprisingly neat for a bachelor's. Maybe doctor bachelors are different, I thought, more studious about cleanliness, but it was probably because they never have enough time to go home. This was my first visit, and I hobbled around, taking in his taste in furniture. A few antiques, some art, soft colors. Our tastes were similar. He started dinner while I looked at the framed pictures of his family that were sitting on his desk. A picture of his parents, arms around each other, stared back at me.

"This your focus group?" I asked, gesturing to their picture. "They've been evaluating me since I got here."

"Family is important to me," he said, glancing over at the picture.

The red flag slid down a few inches. I followed him into the kitchen.

"What's for dinner?" I asked. "I hope not your kidney thing."

"No, this time it's liver and onions."

He laughed when he saw my face, then threw two steaks in a pan. Once again, I was assigned to the salad.

"Who decreed that if something's green, it's good for you?" I asked, tearing lettuce into a bowl, then slicing in cucumbers. "I don't know why we can't just shave chocolate over little marshmallows and call that a salad."

"And where did you get your degree in nutrition, Miss Truffles?" he asked. "Godiva University?"

It was a lovely dinner and he was a solicitous and caring host. He even saw to it that we had a chocolate cake for dessert.

"How did you manage something this wonderful?" I enthused.

"One of the other doctors told me about a bakery that makes the best pastries in the state."

The red flag was now dragging on the ground.

After we finished, we sat on the balcony, drank wine, and looked out over rolling green fields outlined by amethyst mountains.

"We seem to have a lot in common," he remarked softly, taking my hand.

"Yeah, long limps in the moonlight, and I can be the organ donor for your next meal."

"We like the same music, and we both read a lot," he began.

"I ride horses and you hate them," I offered.

He gave me a knowing smile. "And your concussion and torn meniscus came from where?"

"That was a crazy horse. There are good horses out there."

"You mean the ones that come with seat belts so you can't fall off?"

"I didn't fall off Magneto; he went over backward and rolled on top of me."

"Good God!" he said. "I didn't even know horses could do that. And somehow, it doesn't put all that much of a different slant on things!"

The red flag was getting resurrected.

Now the sky darkened into indigo and the mountains disappeared into it. We went inside. He took me into his arms and kissed me.

I liked it in his arms and kissed him back. We kissed for several long, sweet minutes before he stood back and took a deep breath.

"Time to get you to bed," he said softly.

"I always follow doctor's orders," I murmured, and started for his bedroom, but he grabbed his car keys from his desk and opened the front door.

"Is there something wrong with me?" I wailed to Patty after Nick had driven me home and given me a good-night peck on my cheek at the apartment door.

"Besides your concussion, your bad leg, and current ill temper?" she asked.

"He just gave me a good-night kiss on my **cheek!**"

"I thought you wanted to take things slowly," she reminded me.

"Only if **he** wasn't. It's not fair that he actually **is** taking things slowly."

"Why does it matter who wants to take things slowly?" she asked.

"I only said I wanted to take things slowly so that I could if I wanted to, not that I was really going to!"

"Well, now you'll have to take things slowly, because that's what he is obviously planning to do, and you have no control over it, unless you push him into taking things fast," Patty said.

"You're not getting it," I snapped at her, frustrated. "I wanted him to want to take things fast so I could slow it down. But I don't really want to take things slow, I just want him to **think** that I want to take things slow. Taking things slow should always be the woman's prerogative."

Patty thought about it. "How slow is he taking it?"

"Safe pecks on the cheek."

She looked at me quizzically. "Safe sex on the cheek?"

"Pecks, and it worries me."

"You think he's gay? His sister is gay. . . . Or maybe he's acting gay because—"

"Gay is not catching. Otherwise, we'd all be dating Diana."

"Or maybe he just wants you as a friend friend, not a romantic friend."

I thought of the wonderful kisses in his apartment. "But some of his kisses weren't friend-friend kisses. They were 'Let's have more' kisses."

"I guess you'll just have to wait it out and see if there **is** more."

Wait it out, I did. We went to a museum and he held my fingers. We went to the theater and he held my hand. We went to a concert and he put his arm around me. We spent an afternoon rowing on a private lake.

This would be a good place to make love, I thought, and while I contemplated how the gentle bobbing motion of the boat would enhance our sexual pleasure, he was already rowing back to the dock.

Our next date topped off my frustrations. I snapped the door behind me after yet another good-night peck, threw my pocketbook across the room, and screamed, "I know what it is!"

Lenni, Diana, and Patty were playing a game of solitaire at the kitchen table.

"Know what what is?" Diana asked, flipping a card.

"His fatal flaw!"

They all looked up.

"There's no other explanation," I added glumly. "I mean, four years studying in medical school, five years doing internship and a residency? That's about nine years of enforced celibacy. You'd think he'd be lunging at me." I sighed with tragic realization. "I think he's a eunuch."

"He's unique because he's shy," said Lenni.

"Eunuch."

"Eunuchs **are** unique," said Diana.

"Right," said Lenni. "That's what makes them shy."

"Here's a way to tell," said Patty. "When you kiss, is there anything else happening?"

"Like third waffle rising?" Diana smirked.

"No," I said sadly, heading for bed. "He won't even let me get close to the waffle iron."

I decided to outslow him. I returned only every other phone call. I declined every third date. Keeping my lips unavailable, I kissed the tips of my fingers and caressed his cheek with them when we said good night. He picked up the pace a little.

He made my favorite dinner a few nights later—burgers stuffed with bleu cheese and mushrooms.

"I would ask you to stay the night," he said softly after dinner, "but you're probably not ready."

"Yes, I am," I said. "I am ready. And willing. And able. Even if I do have a concussion."

He swept me up and carried me into his bedroom. He gently removed my clothes and lifted me onto his bed. He unbuttoned his shirt and took it off. He took off his pants. He wasn't a eunuch at all.

"You're being too quiet," he said after we made love. "What's wrong?"

"I was just wondering," I said. "You don't secretly own a navy blue robe, do you?"

Chapter Forty-two

I spent a wonderful night with Nick and got home the next morning just as Diana was informing Patty and Lenni that she had planned a little getaway with Lorraine Hartwell. They were going to leave later that afternoon.

"Just a few days away," she announced. "This farm has had almost every plague in the Bible, so try to keep a lid on things until I return."

"We haven't had locusts," I reminded her.

She started packing a little while later and I stretched myself comfortably across her bed to chat as she dug through her closet like a terrier, trying to locate her long-unused leisure clothes.

"No britches?" I noted as she tucked shorts and T-shirts into a small suitcase.

"This is civilian time," she said emphatically. "I don't even want to anyone to say 'Hey' to me."

She carried the suitcase to the front door and disappeared into the kitchen to pack some fruit for the car ride.

"Take some cookies," Patty said as she pulled a box from the cabinet.

"No thanks," Diana said, washing grapes under the kitchen faucet. "Just fruit."

"You'll get the puckers," Patty warned.

"The puckers?"

"When you've eaten too much fruit and you need something sweet." Patty wrapped the cookies and pushed them into Diana's hand. "Cookies balance the palate from all that healthy stuff. As a mother, I know this."

Diana stuffed the cookies into her handbag, picked up her suitcase, and stood in the middle of the living room, hesitating. "Well, I'm going."

"I'll take care of everything," Patty said.

"And I'll help," I said. "Even though I have a bad knee and a concussion."

"Please," Diana said, "if you see locusts

474 Judy Reene Singer

heading toward the farm, shut the gates."
She gave each of us a kiss before leaving.

I hobbled over to my window chair, sat down, and propped my leg up. Diana waved to me before getting into her car. Binoculars in hand and TheDogRuth across my ankles, I resumed my vigil at the window. It was a peaceful, quiet day.

The locusts arrived early the next morning.

There was a knock at the door and Lenni answered it. It was Anna-Sofie.

"Magneto iss avay."

"He's a what?" Lenni asked.

"Avay."

"Do you mean, 'oy vey'?" Lenni asked. "Is that like Jewish Swedish?"

"Avay. AVAY! He iss not on der farm."

It took Lenni and me a few minutes to understand what she meant.

Magneto was missing.

We yelled for Patty. I grabbed my crutches and hobbled down the steps and across the grounds to Kat's barn.

Sure enough, his stall was empty, the door ajar. Gertrude had already reconnoitered the area. She raced back to the barn when she saw us.

"I vas lookink in der mare barn to see if he makes romance," she puffed.

"Who found him missing?" Lenni asked her.

"Lenni," I said, "he wasn't **found** missing; he went missing."

"He didn't go missing," Patty corrected me. "He went and then he became missing."

"I never heard of anyone becoming missing," I retorted. "They are just missing."

"You might be right," Patty said, then turned to Gertrude. "Who found him missing?"

"Anna-Helga," said Gertrude. "She giffs him der breakfast."

"So, he ate breakfast?" I asked.

"**Nein,**" Gertrude shook her head. "He vass already missink."

"But he was here for dinner last night?"

"Ja. Aber diss morning, Anna-Helga come to me und say, 'Magneto is avay.' "

"We heard that part," I said. "Did she look for him?"

Gertrude shook her head no.

"Why not?" Patty asked.

"Because she haff to feet all horses der breakfast. Anna-Helen look for him."

"Where did she look?" I asked.

"In his shtall."

"But he was already missing from his stall," I pointed out.

"Ja! Anna-Helen say he vassn't in his shtall."

"Where else did she look?" Patty asked.

"Anna-Sofie look in his paddock. Und he vassn't deer. He isst noveer."

"He can't be **nowhere,**" I said. "That's physically impossible."

"He had to have disappeared during the night," said Patty. "Because horses don't like to miss breakfast."

"Who would want him?" Lenni asked.

"Hopefully, he went back to Germany," said Patty.

"**Nein,**" said Gertrude. "Churmany sells der bot horses. Not take dem beck."

We searched the immediate area. There were no squeals, no whinnying, no sounds of hoofbeats anywhere. There were no maimed townspeople storming the driveway with torches. Gertrude and Lenni saddled up two horses and rode out across the property. They were back about an hour later. There was nothing. Not even a hoofprint to follow.

We were all mystified and very worried.

"I'll call Big Jim," Lenni said, dialing her cell phone. After a minute or two, she reported back to us: "He's sending a squad car."

But there was nothing the police could do. They questioned the Swedish girls for the rest of the day, mostly because the girls were wearing very short cutoffs and stretchy tube tops. They took lots of notes but had no suggestions for us. They promised to file a missing horse report, listed him as AWOL, and said they would keep an eye out for any unaccompanied animals running through town.

"You do know that we have to call Diana," Patty said to me.

"It's her first vacation in years," I said.

"She'd want to know."

I dialed the number for Diana's cell phone, dreading this call.

"What do you mean, 'gone'?" Her voice was a mixture of impatience and incredulity.

"Gone," I repeated.

"Did he break out of his stall? Maybe he's running somewhere on the farm. There're three thousand acres out there."

"Unless he's disguising himself as a tree, he's not on the farm."

"Please find him before he breeds with half the state," she warned. "Jesus, my first vacation in five years, Kat's due back in two days, and her best horse is missing. What are the police doing?"

"Well, they're not sure yet if anyone actually took him, but one of them has a date with Anna-Helen, and the other one brought a pizza to share with Anna-Sofie and Anna-Helga."

"Their usual thorough work," she said. "I'll see how fast I can drive back."

We hung up.

"She's coming back," I told Patty, who was anxiously polishing off a bag of chips.

"Poor Diana," she said between crunches. "Her first vacation since I can remember."

"Well, we've got to do something. Kat's due back in two days."

But we had no leads at all.

Patty called horse friends for information but came up with nothing.

"Should we be checking the want ads?" Lenni asked.

"You think he's going to take out an ad that he wants to come home?" I asked.

"Maybe someone wants to give him back," she explained. "Maybe we should be looking around the barn for ransom notes."

But there was no sign of Magneto.

"He was definitely horsenapped," Patty declared. "The locusts have landed."

Chapter Forty-three

Evening fell.

Diana was due back late at night. We were in our pajamas; all we could do was wait for her. Lenni and Patty were curled on opposite ends of the sofa, watching television. I had dozed off over the newspaper.

Lenni finally stood up, stretching and yawning. "I think I'll get to sleep." Patty stood up, too, and flicked off both the light and the television. The room darkened and they went to bed.

But the room hadn't totally darkened. A bright beam of moonlight fell across the floor. I stared at it for a moment, then race-hobbled into Patty's bedroom. She was lying in bed with a pillow over her head. TheDog-Ruth was stretched out over the pillow.

"I bet I know where Magneto is!" I gasped. "Black stallion! The full moon!"

Patty peeked out from under her pillow. "You think Magneto's on the moon?"

"Speed!" I yelled. "Speed and those creeps have him!"

"But what can we do about it?" Patty asked, pushing the pillow aside. TheDogRuth crawled under her covers. "We're in bed."

"I know where Speed has his meetings. I'm going."

"Are you crazy?" Patty jumped out of bed, waving her arms like the robot in **Lost in Space.** "I warned you about Speed, and you didn't listen! I warned you about riding Magneto. What good is a surrogate mother if you don't listen to her?"

But I was already pulling my jeans on and heading for the kitchen. "You're right!" I called back to Patty, "I should have listened to you, but this is different! This could mean Diana's job. Or even Magneto's life. I have to go."

She stood in the kitchen doorway and thought over what I had just said. "Call the police and let them handle it."

"All I have is a hunch. If I'm wrong, we'll look like idiots."

Patty threw her hands in the air. "You think we don't already look like idiots?"

"This may even be a chance to redeem ourselves a little."

"You're not going to do anything foolish, are you?"

"Of course not." I gave her a hug. "I'll be okay. I'm a big girl now. I'll be okay by myself." Then I realized that I had been waiting a long time to say those words to somebody. "I need to do this." Patty watched as I took the flashlight out from a kitchen cabinet.

"I'll drive you," she said.

"That's okay." I turned to reassure her. "I don't expect you to come with me." But she had already gone into her bedroom.

"What kind of mother would I be to let my child face danger alone?" she said, returning to the kitchen in sweats.

"Thanks, Patty."

"We'll need supplies." She opened the refrigerator. "Get a couple of forks while I grab the pie."

We drove to the little clearing off the road. I recognized some of the cars parked there.

"Speed, Candy, Gail." I ticked off the names on my fingers. "The unholy three."

Patty turned the car lights off and shut down the engine; I directed her to a nearby spot and we rolled into it.

"I guess we can do a stakeout here," I said.

"Oh God," she said, "steak."

"Let's see if we can hear anything," I said. I lowered the window and craned my head out, but the only thing I could hear was Patty eating.

"You're making too much noise," I complained.

She handed me a fork. "We could be here for hours. Take sustenance."

We ate a few bites of blueberry pie and waited with the car windows down. Soon the sound of voices drifted through the trees, soft at first, then louder. Then I heard the whinny of a horse.

"That's got to be Magneto," I whispered, jumping out of the car. "I'm going to get to the edge of the clearing and see what's going on. Turn on your cell phone. If it's Magneto, we'll call the police."

"Take the fork with you," Patty whispered back. "Just in case. And don't do anything foolish."

"Of course not."

I left the car and limped down the path through the trees. The group was in that same spot next to the lake, just ahead of me. I sneaked closer and pulled a few branches down to see better. There were the same thirteen, in the same circle, surrounding a table that looked like it was set for afternoon tea. Speed had his arm around Candy, who, ever the good hostess, was pouring drinks. Gail was holding Magneto, who had a large sack over his head.

I wondered why they wanted Magneto incognito. Then I realized it was to keep the normally skittish horse calm. Gail was holding him by a lead line that drooped from the sack. Everyone was in a party mood.

"To the power of the black stallion," someone shouted, and they all cheered and toasted. Candy poured some more. They toasted some more. They cheered some more. One by one, they began removing their robes, then quickly began peeling off clothing and underwear. They waved their arms and danced around. Other, less flattering body parts waved around, too. The clothes were flung in the air with abandon, amid squealing and cheering. It looked like a satanic spring break. Suddenly, someone tossed a pair of boxer shorts into the air, and they landed on Magneto's rump. Something stirred in my mind as I watched the shorts cling to the horse for a moment before they slid to the ground. Underpants on a black stallion! The countess had been right after all! Then I saw the flash of a long knife. Magneto was in danger! Driven by anger and stupidity, I leapt out of the bushes.

It was time for Ceremonius Interruptus.

Dragging my bad leg, I lurched into the clearing and made a grab for Magneto's mane to pull myself onto his back. I immediately realized what a poor offense tactic this was. My mounting leg was the one harboring my bad knee and it refused to support me. I wobbled sideways against the table. It's foolhardy to crash a party where there are thirteen couture-challenged revelers dancing madly and you are too lame to do anything about it.

"Call the police!" I screamed back toward Patty.

There is nothing like yelling for police to put the dampers on a good party just heating up.

"Get that bitch," somebody screamed, "damn her!"

I knew I had to get out of there; these people were probably professionals at damning, and I couldn't take any chances. Hands grabbed at me. I forked them back and crawled up onto the table to get away from them, accidentally knocking off a large chocolate cake, and serendipitously ending up right next to Magneto. Pulling off his disguise, I flung myself onto his back. No saddle and just a lead line—it was a nightmarish replay of my lunge lessons with Diana. Magneto spun in a circle from the surprise mount. I urged him forward, but he backed up and reared before trampling through the clothing and knocking

over the table, along with a few errant servants of evil.

"Forward," I screamed at him as hands
grabbed for my leg.

Magneto stepped sideways, knocking
over the coffee urn. I could have used a
good cup of coffee earlier, but now I was
high on adrenaline. I urged him out of the
circle and we lunged toward the woods.
Suddenly, clouds slid over the moon and
the night darkened, turning the woods even
blacker. How was I to steer a black horse
into black woods on a black night?

And where to go? It was too dark to see.
I hadn't accounted for the clouds. Suddenly, two small figures appeared in front
of me—white bodies with brown spots.
They barked excitedly and spun in little circles around Magneto's heels before dashing
ahead a few feet, then doubling back. I suddenly realized that they wanted me to follow them. Like **deux terriers ex machina**,
they had come to rescue me.

"Go," I screamed again. "Forward!"

They didn't need my encouragement.
They raced ahead, yodeling furiously, and I

urged Magneto to follow. We galloped along the back trails. I had a sudden image of a huge stockpile of human bones from unsuspecting people the terriers had previously led to their deaths, but I had no choice. I had to trust them.

The path started to look familiar. The terriers were leading me back to Kat's farm! Branches caught me in the face and ripped at my hair. I thought if Ruth could see me now, she would be convinced that I had gone totally mad.

The clouds parted and I recognized the back of the farm's mare pastures. I urged Magneto on. He galloped along, his withers pressing into my crotch, giving me a frontal wedgie, possibly sacrificing my future sex life. He finally slowed to a tired trot as I leaned forward and hung on around his neck. As we passed the mare fields, the mares and foals nickered to us. Magneto raised his head with interest and neighed back.

"Shaddup," I screamed into his ears, kicking him on. "Keep your mind on business."

He obeyed and we trotted up to Kat's

barn. The terriers circled us, panting with delight.

Diana was at my side in a flash. I slid off the horse, limp as a piece of string, and handed him to her.

She grinned and gave me a hug. "So you finally learned to ride him."

"How did you know we were back here?" I gasped. "Did you hear the hoofbeats?"

"Hell no," she said, clipping a lead line onto Magneto's halter. "The dogs were yapping and you were screaming bloody murder the whole way."

I hobbled along next to her as she led him back to the barn.

"I smell chocolate," she said.

"I do, too. I think it's a sign from God that I did good."

She put him into his stall, then came over to thank me.

"Bloody scratches could be expected, I guess," she said, touching my face, "but why are your teeth bright blue?"

"Omigod!" I gasped. "Blueberry pie! And Patty is still there, eating it."

"No, I'm not," said Patty, coming into

the barn and giving me a hug. "I came home after I finished it. I had to get some milk." She sniffed the air. "Odd, but I just got the strongest whiff of chocolate."

"Judy thinks it's her guardian angel," Diana said with affection.

We started back to the apartment. I looked around for the terriers, but they had already disappeared into the darkness.

Chapter Forty-four

"Big Jim just called me," Lenni gasped, greeting us in her pajamas as we all got back to the apartment. "Are you okay?"

"Yes, I am," said Patty, sitting down in the armchair and fanning herself. "It was quite an experience, but I think I'm okay."

I kicked off my shoes and threw myself across the couch, exhausted. "Remind me never to crash one of Candy's parties again."

"How did the police get there so fast?" Diana asked Patty.

"I called the police just as soon as Judy disappeared into the woods," said Patty. "I wasn't going to sit there all alone."

"Wow," I said from the couch. "I saved Magneto even with my bad knee and a concussion." Then I fell asleep.

I awoke to Nick giving me wet, passionate kisses all across my face.

"I'm okay, darling," I reassured him. I raised my arms to embrace him but got an armful of terriers instead. My eyes flew open. The terriers were standing on my chest, licking my face and grinning from ear to ear. Diana was standing next to the couch, smiling down at me.

"Well, you can thank Octavia and Gilberto," she said.

"Who?"

"Octavia and Gilberto." She gave me an impatient look. "The terriers. They saved your ass."

That the terriers had names had never occurred to me.

"Octavia and Gilberto," I repeated several times. "Why would anyone name dogs Octavia and Gilberto?"

They stood on my chest for several minutes, sniffing my face carefully. I tried not to think where their noses had previously been.

"Thank you for your help," I said contritely.

They acknowledged my gratitude with another lick or two, then jumped down to the floor.

"How's Magneto?" I asked Diana.

"Perfectly fine," she said. "They hadn't touched him."

I stood up. The terriers were at my feet in a flash, looking up at me with expectant faces, waiting for their next assignment.

Patty brought me a cup of coffee. "Looks like you've got permanent sidekicks."

I bent over and scratched their heads. "I really am grateful to them."

Lenni walked over, Big Jim behind her.

"Good detective work," he said, reaching out to shake my hand. "How are you feeling?"

"I guess I'm okay." I touched my knee gingerly. "Did I really save Magneto?"

"Actually, no," said Big Jim. "He was only the guest of honor at their ceremony. They had a big chocolate cake in the shape of a horse and they were going to serve it with coffee."

"Chocolate cake!" Patty moaned.

Big Jim looked at her. "They were going to eat the horse in effigy."

"And I guess they never made it to Effigy," said Lenni. "So they did it at the lake."

"No," I explained to her. "Effigy is when you do something to something instead of doing something to somebody. It's very symbolic."

"It was part of their big summer power ritual," Big Jim continued. "Eat cake in the shape of a horse to give them the power of a black stallion. They were going to return Magneto in the morning."

"They should have tried eating fish in effigy," said Diana. "Maybe get some brains into that group."

"So what will happen to all of them?" I asked.

Big Jim poured himself a cup of coffee and sat down at the table. We all sat down with him. "Depends if Kat presses charges. She came back a day early from Germany and is looking over the paperwork right now. But I think last night's scare sure took the starch out of their underwear."

"No underwear," I said.

"Big Jim says they arrested the guy in charge," Lenni said proudly.

"Bravo," I said, remembering the leader in the green robe.

"Thank you," said Big Jim, smiling modestly. "Yep, he was charged with receiving stolen property. The horse alone is grand theft. Plus, we found a whole cache of electronic equipment in his garage. So it looks like we solved more than one crime."

He gulped down a last mouthful of coffee. "Well, there's a lot of paperwork involved. Thirteen idiots, thirteen pages." He gave Lenni a kiss on her cheek and left.

"I wonder what will happen to Speed," I said. "He looked pretty hot for Candy last night."

Patty gave me a plate of bacon and eggs. "Who cares!" she snorted. "I think there should be a law that men aren't given their penises until they reach the age of forty and have proved that they are responsible enough to have one."

"You make it sound like it's a special reward." I laughed.

"I think it's more a consolation prize for not being a woman," said Diana.

"Except for Big Jim," said Lenni. "If he didn't have his penis, I couldn't call him Big Jim."

"I wonder what will happen to Magneto," mused Patty. "That horse is becoming a liability."

The apartment finally emptied out, leaving me and Patty to recuperate. She was quite exhausted.

The phone rang.

It was Nick, and he sounded upset. "Diana called me. How are you?"

"I saved Magneto," I said.

"Isn't that the horse that tried to kill you? You couldn't return the favor?" His voice took on a peevish tone. "What made you do something so foolish?"

"Oh Nick," I said softly. "I can't change who I am."

"Does that mean I have to spend the rest of my life worrying about you?"

"Only if you want to spend the rest of your life with me," I said.

"Ah, Judy," he said softly, and nothing

more. We hung up.

I sat by the phone, wondering if I had just made the biggest mistake ever.

"Bad?" Patty asked, noting my stricken face.

I nodded miserably.

"Pint-of-Cherry-Garcia-for-dinner bad?"

"Two. Maybe even three."

"Ah, Judy," she said.

I excused myself to take a walk around the farm to think. I realized that I loved Nick and I loved my life of horses. The terriers walked slowly next to me as I gimped along. There was no solution.

Diana was riding Magneto in the outdoor ring. She saw me and waved. They made a magnificent partnership. Patty's words suddenly came back to me. I wondered if Magneto's future really was compromised. I found myself limping over to Kat's office, the terriers accompanying me.

I needed to talk to her.

I knocked on the door. Kat was sitting at her desk, reading through some papers from the police.

"Zhoody!"

She got up and greeted me with a hug, then kissed me on each cheek. She looked lean and fit and even more Teutonic then when she left. She sat back down at her desk.

"I want to buy Magneto," I heard myself say.

Her eyebrows shot into space.

"He ist ferry expensive," she warned me.

"How much?" I asked.

She wrote a figure down on a piece of paper and pushed it across her desk. It was a very high figure.

"Why so much?" I asked. "He has a miserable temperament, and Diana is the only one who is able to ride him."

She stared at me. The terriers closed ranks next to me and stared back at her. I appreciated their moral support.

"He ist ferry talented," she protested. "He ist Olympic kvality."

"He nearly killed me. I have a concussion."

She remained expressionless.

I scribbled an offer on the piece of paper and pushed it back across the desk.

She took the paper and read it. **"Aach, nein!"** she exclaimed, turning the paper over.

"That's about what he's worth," I said firmly. "Besides the fact that I got him back for you, who knows what the those nuts did to ruin all of Diana's training. He's probably crazier now than when he came from Germany. And you wouldn't want him to go on and hurt someone else. Think of the lawsuits."

She blinked at me, wordless.

"And did I mention that I also have a bad knee?"

She started thinking. The terriers leaned forward. I held my breath.

She made a face, turned the paper back over, and studied it for a moment. "He's yours."

I hobbled back to the apartment as fast as my knee would allow. Octavia and Gilberto ran ahead of me, yapping with excitement. "Don't ruin the surprise," I called after them.

Diana was sitting with Patty, looking over a brochure.

"I have such great news!" I gasped.

"I do, too," said Patty.

I grabbed Diana by the arms. "I just bought you a horse for the Olympics!"

She was speechless for a moment. "Is he black and crazy?"

"The very one. Just don't ever ask me to ride him again."

Chapter Forty-five

Nick didn't call for days. I picked the phone up several times to call him but then put it back down each time.

"What's the point?" I said to Diana. "He's made his choice, and I've made mine."

"Since you gave up your man for a horse, you may as well ride," she said. "Meet me down at the barn."

"But I have a bad knee and a conc—"

"Shaddup already," she said. "You only need your knee to hold your leg together for mounting."

When I got to the barn, she had Mercedes tacked up and ready for me.

I sat on his back and took up the reins. He arched his neck and waited for my command. He rode like a gentleman as I put him through some of his paces.

Diana was right. He was a wonderful

horse. I rode him again the next day, and the next. I fell in love with him.

"Why don't you buy him?" Diana said to me. "He's the kind of horse that gives you confidence and he's fancy enough to be a good show horse."

"I don't want to buy another horse right now."

"Nick?"

I nodded. It was hard to give up the man you loved for a horse; the sacrifice made loving the horse very difficult.

Diana looked disturbed. "I appreciate so much that you bought Magneto, but I feel bad that you're passing up Mercedes. He's a wonderful horse. I heard that Candy is very interested in him. She'd have to take him to her farm, of course. She's persona non grata here now—because of the Magneto thing."

"I'd hate to lose him to her," I said, "but I just don't feel good about buying a horse for myself."

She gave me a sideways glance and sighed. I didn't want to talk anymore, so I steered Mercedes for the gate, walking him outside for a long trail ride.

I reflected on what a good horse Mercedes was. Normally, I would trust a new horse on trails about as much as I would trust myself in a Godiva chocolate shop. There was just too much temptation to go wild. But he just walked along, checking out the scenery and waiting for me to cue him on where to go and at what speed. He was a **very** good horse.

But in truth, I would have liked very much to walk the trail hand in hand with Nick. I loved horses, but unless you were willing to bed down on a heap of straw every evening in the barn, they weren't going to keep you warm at night.

Birds sang and fluttered by. Rabbits hopped along near the horse's hooves. I wondered if there were birds that gave up their true love for a life of air acrobatics. Or if there were rabbits that considered going on the road as a magician's helper instead of settling down. Is that how we got the Easter Bunny? After all, he'd always been single. Or was it just humans who allowed themselves to make noble sacrifices? Was giving up Nick a noble sacrifice? Or a supremely asinine one?

I loved horses. I loved riding them, watching them, grooming them, handling them, and, with a minor success under my belt, I could even love showing them. But Nick had adamantly refused to consider a life with them. He worried too much about the consequences of horse life, like skull fractures and broken arms, cracked ribs and dislocated pelvises, broken legs and bruised kidneys. . . . Suddenly, I decided to cut my trail ride short.

Well, I thought, it's too late. I've made my choice. I knew horses were inseparable from my life. To give them up would only make me miserable. To force them on Nick would make him miserable. It was much better to end things now and make us both miserable at the same time.

I continued to ride Mercedes over the next few weeks and Diana continued to train us. She let the matter of my purchasing him drop, but she kept suggesting that I show him.

I refused.

"You seem to have forgotten my last show," I said to her. "I disgraced myself in front of the whole horse show community."

"You give yourself far too much credit," Diana replied. "You think any more than a few people were watching you? Or even cared?"

"Great. So now you want me to disgrace myself again for the few who missed me the first time."

"This horse will not make a fool of you," she replied emphatically. "He has too much dignity."

I contemplated Diana's suggestion of getting back into horses by showing Mercedes, but I was lame and out of practice, and neither shortcoming was something I wanted to display at a horse show.

Kat had the last word, as usual.

"You rite Mercedes fur me. He ist for sale und qviet. Venn pipples see how qviet he rites for you, dey vill vant to buy him. Denn I giff you perzentage."

I got her point. In other words, If I could ride him, anyone could, and that would make a good selling point. I knew it would be a good comeback for me. And I did love the horse.

"Okay," I agreed.

"Und maybe you vant to run der mare barn?" she asked. "Zince Gail iss no lonker verking here."

Gailzilla had left the morning after I rescued Magneto, and the mare barn was being covered by the Swedish Annas, who had to run it in addition to their regular work and were grumbling and complaining about it in three different languages.

"No thanks," I said, "but I bet Lenni would take you up on that offer. She is getting tired of saddle-breaking the babies."

"**Vunderbar!** I talk to her. Und denn you go to horse show dis veekent."

The matter was apparently settled.

I left her office and headed to the apartment for lunch. Patty was sitting at the table and reading a brochure.

"I have good news," she said.

The phone rang and I excused myself. It was Ruth.

"Judy, I have good news. Guess what?"

"You're pregnant!"

"How did you know?"

"You're finished decorating, what else is left?"

"You're right, darling."

"So, life is perfect!"

She paused, then drew in a breath. "Well, no. Oh, Judy, I think Henry might be cheating on me."

"Didn't you tell me once that they all fuck around?"

"But this is me and Henry."

"Suck it up, Ruth."

Her voice took on a quaver. "Oh, Judy, I wish I were brave like you. The way you just packed up and left. Ran off to someplace no one's ever heard of and began another life, just like that. I admire you so much."

"You do?" I whispered. "Wow, Ruth you never told me! So does that make me the smart one?"

She hedged. "Well, definitely the brave one."

"And the pretty one, too?"

"Okay, the brave and the pretty." Then I thought I heard her sniffle.

"Listen," I said, "you can come down here and visit anytime you want. I'll teach little Ruth or Henry junior how to ride. I'll be the crazy aunt. I'll always be here for you, because I know how much it sucks to have this happen."

"You're the best," she said. "I love you."

"Gosh, I get to be the brave one and the pretty one and the best one all on the same day."

She gave a tentative laugh.

"And," I added brightly, "at least you'll have two to shop for."

"Will you help me decorate the baby's room?"

"As long as it's not mauve and hunter green or peach and navy."

"Teal and ivory."

"It's a promise."

After I hung up, it occurred to me that I hadn't told her about Magneto or Nick or my next horse show. But it didn't matter. I didn't need her approval anymore. Or Mother's. In fact, it made me feel good that she had actually looked up to me for once.

"Whoa!" I said out loud. "Whoa!"

• • •

The sun shone brilliantly on the morning of the horse show. Mercedes and Magneto popped into the trailer as easily as putting a piece of bread in the toaster. Some road music by Willie and we were on our way.

I was shocked to see Nick waiting for me at the show. I didn't want him there. It was enough to embarrass myself in front of one lover at a horse show, but to make it a serial event just didn't appeal to me.

"Diana told my sister you were showing," he said, pointing to his sister, who was chatting with Diana.

"Oh Nick," I said.

He gave me a lopsided half smile.

"I had to see my rival," he said with a touch of sadness, nodding his head toward Mercedes. The sun glinted across his face and his blue-gray eyes touched my soul. What was wrong with me? My heart spoke. I loved this man.

I ran into his arms.

"You have no rivals." I hugged him. He

wrapped me in his arms and kissed me gently on the forehead.

"Hey! Let's go," said Diana, tapping me on the back. Mercedes stood patiently beside her. She held the reins out to me. "It's time to rock and roll."

• • •

Mercedes rode like his namesake. Speed was on the rail with Candy, giving me hostile stares as I performed my test. I didn't give them a second glance. Nick stood by the gate with his arms folded, watching me intently. I rode like a queen.

Diana rode Magneto and they made a magnificent pair. It wasn't long before the announcer was ready with the results. Diana won her class.

And I won mine. My first blue ribbon! The ecstasy was overwhelming, and my heart spoke again. I couldn't deny it. I loved that horse and had to buy him. Maybe I could promise Nick I would never get hurt. Maybe I could wrap myself in pillows when I rode, but I knew what I had to do. I found

Kat by her trailer, getting ready to ride Merkury.

"I want to buy Mercedes," I said firmly. "I've fallen in love with him."

She wouldn't look me in the eye. "He ist already solt," she said.

I looked at her in shock. My heart fell into my boots. It was one thing to give up your man for a horse, but quite another to have to give up the horse, too.

"But he wasn't sold before I went into the class," I protested.

"He vass solt vile you rite him. I get offer. I take offer."

I could only look at her, speechless. My heart had no more advice for me. I walked back to the trailer. So Mercedes was moving to Candyland after all.

Nick was at the trailer. He took me in his arms and gave me a kiss.

"Congratulations on your blue ribbon," he said.

I couldn't hold back the tears.

He raised my face with his fingers. "You sure do get choked up over a piece of fabric."

"Kat sold the horse I was riding."

"So? Doesn't she sell a lot of horses?"

I couldn't answer him. Tears were pouring from my eyes.

Nick held me tightly. "I have something I want to ask you," he whispered.

"What?" I sobbed.

"Will you marry me?"

I sobbed louder. "Yes!"

"I didn't get you a ring, but I do have something else," he said. He pulled away from me and waved to Diana. She led Mercedes over. I stared, uncomprehending.

"Will a horse do as an engagement ring?" Nick asked. "I beat out some skinny blonde who was right behind me in line to buy him."

I screamed. "Horses make the best engagement rings!"

Nick smiled. "I figured that if you had your heart and soul set on horses, you might as well have a doctor at your side. God knows, you need one."

I threw my arms around him and covered his face with kisses.

It had been the best day. We got back to

the farm exhausted and happy. I led Nick up to the apartment, where Patty was sitting with a book. She jumped up when I walked in.

"I have good news," she said.

"I do, too!" I gasped. "I got a blue ribbon! And I'm engaged! My ring is down in his stall."

She gave me a hug. Diana came in, followed by Lenni and Big Jim and Gertrude, the Swedish Annas, and Lorraine Hartwell. The apartment was soon crowded with well-wishers.

I suddenly remembered. "Patty, what was your good news?"

She took a deep breath. "Well, I've been thinking things over and it seems to me that since I'm not in mourning anymore, it's time to move on." She smiled and held up the brochure. "So I bought a house." She flattened a prospectus on the table for all of us to look at. It was a lovely Victorian set back on a lush green lawn.

Lenni blinked. "You're leaving?"

"First, I think I'll travel a bit through Europe," Patty said, "then move my furniture into the new house and see how things go from there. But I'll still keep Sam here and come and ride him."

"Well, I'll be staying on," said Diana. "Running the farm and training with Kat. If I'm lucky, maybe I will qualify Magneto for the Olympics."

They all looked at me. "I have Nick and Mercedes and I am going to write," I said. "Maybe even about us."

"What's there to write about?" asked Lenni.

"A book would be fun," said Patty. "And maybe one of us can write the foreword."

"Ja," said Anna-Helen, "iss alvays gut to rite forvahrtz."

"Write the foreword," I said, correcting her.

"Rite forwahrds," she repeated.

"You **go** forward," said Patty; "you don't write forward."

"Who cares?" said Lenni. "As long as we go forward, onward."

"Actually, it's onward, upward," said Diana.

"I thought it was 'Up yours,' " said Lenni.

"It doesn't matter what it's called," I said, "as long as we do it."

And for once, we were all correct. Forvahrtz is the only place to go.